I0712580

ETERNITY'S RISING

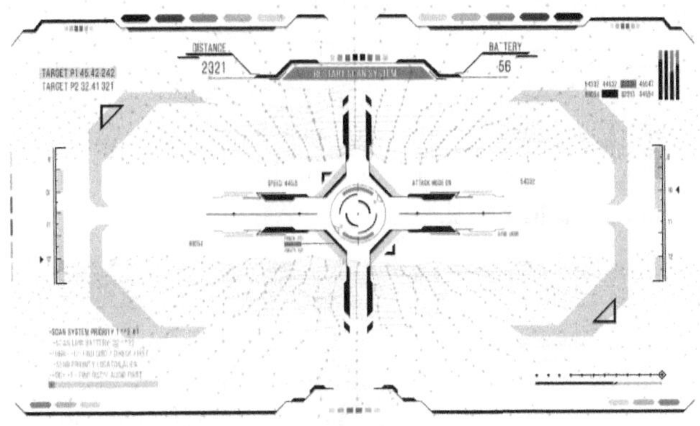

ETERNITY'S RISING

A KARL LARK STORY

ERIK LANGE

This book is dedicated to Barbara Herzog.
A truly awesome teacher.

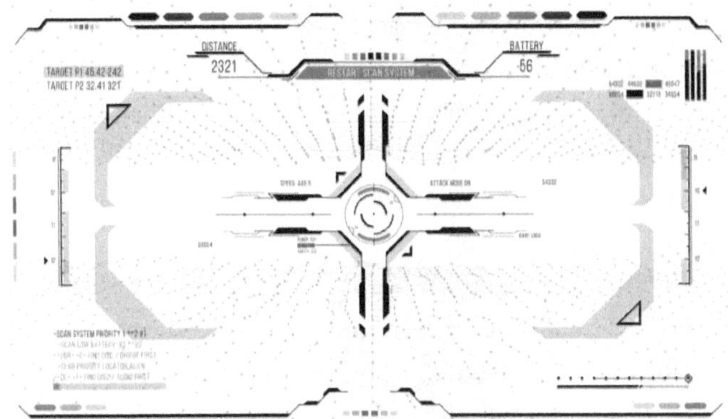

PROLOGUE

In the future . . .

Phillip Held endured the blandness of the room from his hospital bed. Dull throbs alternated with sharp stabs of pain from the terminal lymphatic cancer that was keeping sleep from him. There was a button to push and drugs would pump into his blood to decrease the pain. Each press of the button reduced his ability to think and remember. The stark choice: awareness or lessened pain. Mostly, he chose pain over oblivion. Closing his eyes, he focused; all he had left then was the ability to remember.

No treatment options.

Nothing to do but wait for the end.

The flat-screen TV on the wall was off. Somebody once told him that television is bubble gum for the eyes, a waste of time. He hurt too much to read. The food served in this place was awful, and the nurses wouldn't let him order anything from outside.

For as much as this private hospital cost, you would think they'd have a chef on staff.

Wincing as he took a deep breath, he steeled himself to make it through the next minute, just as he'd done for the previous minute. And the one before that. He intimately understood that boredom, exhaustion, and pain were an awful combination.

The door to the room opened, and light from the hall outside fell across the bed. Phillip reflexively turned his head to look. It was probably the nurse coming to check on him. She was pretty, and he looked forward to her visits. Her name was Susan. For an instant, the faintest smile appeared.

What if only I were forty years younger?

Unfortunately, it was a male form backlit in the doorway. Even contrasted by the light from behind, he was able to make out details. Average height and wearing a dark suit and tie. The face was familiar, but the hair was darker than he remembered . . .

Squinting against the light, Phillip felt an instant of almost nostalgic familiarity. *Who is the shadow figure? How do I know this man?*

Phillip's eyes settled on the man's fancy walking stick with a large brass sphere handle in his hand. Its overt eccentricity was striking.

Who carries a cane like that?

Instincts rooted in combat experience triggered. Curiosity and wonder twisted into something cold. Phillip knew something was wrong.

The man in the doorway smiled—a wide, toothy Cheshire cat grin.

Phillip's eyes widened.

With the suddenness of the gears of an old rusty clock breaking loose, catching, and then moving again, the terrifying recollection flared. That first realization drove up his heart rate on the monitor.

Oh, God! He's back after all this time?

The figure of the silhouetted shadow spoke, "Hello, Phillip."

The cold claws of anxiety and fear clutched his heart. At that point in his life, Phillip considered himself a man beyond fear of anything. He could not hurt any worse. Any threat of imprisonment was meaningless, as he was already trapped in that bed until the end. An offer to put him out of his misery would have been a gift.

But the man in the doorway could do things.

Phillip fought back the urge to reach for the nurse call button, knowing it wouldn't make a difference.

He whispered, "You've never called me Phillip before." The effort to speak added to his discomfort. The man had always called him by his last name, like those in the military often do.

The figure's head tilted just slightly, "How long has it been, Phillip?"

Phillip remembered. *Lark.* His name was Karl Lark. And the last time he'd seen him was twenty years ago, give or take.

But why is he here?

Mr. Lark walked into the room, closing the door behind him. The bright light from the hall was suddenly cut off. Taking a few steps to the foot of the bed, he looked at Phillip. Close enough for old eyes to better see him.

Philip swallowed painfully, his brain struggling to process what he was seeing.

Younger? Why does he look younger?

The last time Phillip was in Mr. Lark's presence, the man at the foot of the bed had completely white hair. He and his companions had called him "the old man" because he looked older—white hair and wrinkles. Never knowing for sure by how much, they had guessed perhaps twenty-five or more years.

Except this version of Karl Lark looked decades younger than the last time he had seen him. The wrinkles were gone, and the white hair was replaced by distinguished black with grey highlights. The smiling man looking at him then could pass for early forties.

"You look terrible," Mr. Lark said, still grinning.

Phillip's thoughts began to race. He knew Mr. Lark was not there to pay his respects or say goodbye. Nor would Mr. Lark take the time to end his suffering by killing him. Such things required empathy or common humanity. Mr. Lark had neither.

Philip knew from past experience the old man had come for something–for his own self-interests.

Mr. Lark turned his head from side to side, looking around the hospital room. "This is a bleak place to spend the remainder of your life."

Karl Lark always had an odd formality to his speech, much like an out-of-place aristocrat.

"I hope you enjoyed your time off, Phillip."

Karl's gaze returned to Phillip, the smile gone, he continued, "I am in need of your services again, Mr. Held."

Phillip laughed, unable to stop even though it hurts. What came out was a pathetic choking sound. He was in no condition to do anything, and Mr. Lark knew it.

Mr. Lark's head tilted down, and he looked Phillip straight in the eye. The old man's expression, his eyes and the curl of his lips, betrayed a hint of mischief: "This private hospital proved a convenience. I arranged for your time of death to be recorded as having occurred five minutes ago. Unfortunately, there will be a mistake in the next-of-kin notification. They won't learn of your demise for two more days. An unfortunate error compounded by your body being cremated in violation of your written last wishes."

Philip gave the smallest of nods. That was the Mr. Lark he remembered. Learning after the fact you were now caught up in something horrible without knowing where it all leads.

Mr. Lark relaxed his gaze, looked about the room again, and took a deep breath. His eyes then locked with Phillips: "They will receive a box of ashes."

"I can't even walk," Phillip mumbled. He thought to himself, *So, I am now dead. At least on paper. What could he want with a crippled, terminally ill old man? My uselessness makes whatever my former employer wants me for a laughable request. But is he still my former employer, or has that just changed?*

"A short-term inconvenience, I assure you," said Mr. Lark, reaching into his tailored suit coat. He pulled out a small metal box about the size of a pack of cigarettes.

Phillip's heart skipped a beat at the sight of his former employer producing an unknown gadget. *This can't be good.*

Mr. Lark walked around the bed to stand by Phillip's wrinkled, emaciated left hand. The grin was back. Phillip learned a long time ago what that grin meant. Mr. Lark wasn't going to kill him. He was a man with a plan, and that plan now included Phillip, whether he liked it or not. Whatever came next, he was not going to like it.

Karl Lark said, "I hope you have used the time since our last parting constructively. As for myself, there has been no end of things begging my attention. Now there is a current state of pressing tasks desperate for my consideration. As in the past, my solitary existence must be altered. Your service is required."

Philip was not surprised by Mr. Lark's uninspiring explanation. The old man was never a good salesman.

Mr. Lark reached across the bed to pull the hospital gown away from above Phillip's heart, exposing the age-spotted skin beneath. He pushed something on the metal box in his hand. With an audible *click* from the broad, flat face of the box facing Phillip appeared an unpleasant-looking collection of needles. Without hesitation, the box, needles first, was forcefully pressed to his chest.

The cutting tear of needles punctured his skin, followed by the sensation of metal sliding into his geriatric flesh until the cold, flat metal of the box was pressed flush to his chest. It hurt, but the pain competed in his mind with wonder at the box's purpose. Through the added discomfort, Phillip agonized: *What fresh hell is this?*

The procedure was complete, and Mr. Lark was no longer smiling. "You are not well, and your body's current condition will not serve my interests. This little box is going to cure your cancer and then regenerate your body back to something useful to me."

Mr. Lark shifted the hospital gown back to cover Phillip's chest.

"This process would usually take two years if allowed to progress normally. Your age, the cancer, and the overall poor condition of your body are all factors."

Returning to the foot of the bed, Mr. Lark turned to face Phillip, and continued, "I do not have the patience for a two-year convalescence. Those two years will be compressed into three months. Do you remember growing pains from when you were a child? This experience will be similar, but the pain far greater."

Philip made a choking noise in place of a laugh.

Really, there is an eleven setting on pain?

The cold metal of the box on Phillip's chest grew warmer from his body heat. He looked down at it and could only wonder, *What does this thing do?*

Mr. Lark moved away from the bed, drifting towards the door. "I am having you moved to a more secure location for your recovery."

Phillip mustered the effort to ask, "The others?"

Mr. Lark nodded. "Thomas will be joining us. Now that you are sorted, I shall be visiting him."

Mr. Lark looked right at Phillip. "You were done. You know that. I am taking nothing away from you."

"Like the last time," Phillip croaked.

"Yes, Mr. Held, like the last time," Mr. Lark grinned again, opened the door, and walked out into the light.

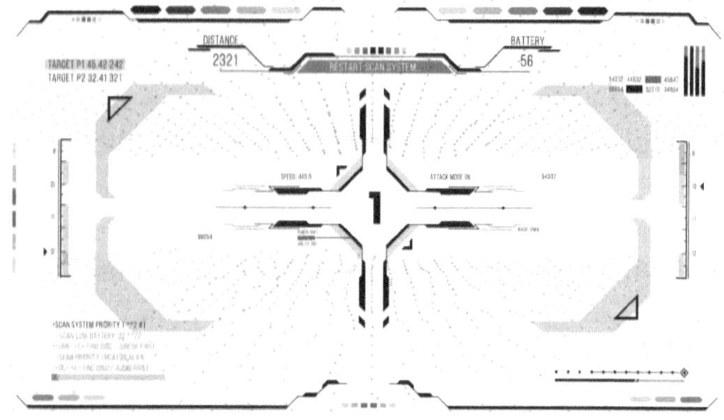

CHAPTER ONE

Karl Lark stood in the middle of his living room, trying to remember what he was there for.

It is because I am getting old that I can't remember.

Now that he was in his sixties, he could not recall things like he used to. Used to be everything he wanted to remember came back to him instantly.

He knew it would come to him shortly. While he waited for his memory to catch up with his body, he looked around his living room. The house was old—he was born there in 1944. He had inherited it from his parents when they passed. Now it was the residence of a confirmed bachelor. Lacking a woman's touch, there were no decorations, nothing hung on the walls. No distractions, he liked it austere. And no television; it was bubble gum for the eyes.

Still waiting, his eyes shifted to the only color in the room, the fireplace mantle. Here were the only effects in the house. His college diploma in applied physics—yellowed with age. A faded black-and-white photo of his parents. A decades-old color photo of two young boys standing in a wooden pavilion in a park.

That was from before my brother was a failure.

Centered on the mantle, larger than the others and in a fancy silver frame, was a recent professional glossy photo of a woman wearing college graduation robes.

Now he remembered: *The kitchen, I was going to the kitchen.*

Once there, he was surrounded by garish colors, everything dated to the '60s and early '70s. The last thing his parents did to the house before they were gone was have the kitchen modernized.

On the table was what he had come in here for: today's newspaper, *October 27th 2007, Saturday*. Next to it was his letter of termination. Forty years of dedicated service, long days, working weekends, ended like this. It hadn't been optional, even though they called it retirement. Telling them he had two years until he was sixty-five had not helped.

They wanted to be rid of him. His supervisor had told him to be more diplomatic. Learn to play the game, they said.

The negative votes finally outweighed the positive, and here he was, standing in a museum dedicated to the worst in American kitchen design.

Unemployed and adrift, he was a man without a plan.

He read the letter again to double-check the numbers and confirm his understanding. It was a good severance package, and he was financially set for retirement. Even the health insurance was fully funded.

Grim understanding of a situation unique in all his life experience. He had all the time in the world, but what he did not have was a purpose. He needed a purpose.

Putting the letter down, his eyes shifted to the newspaper. The headline story was about an Army Green Beret with a Russian-sounding name convicted of murder. While stationed in Afghanistan, there had been an altercation with a child-molesting Afghan officer. The officer had died. The man's appeal had failed, and the life sentence was upheld.

On page four was a story about a man who'd found a giant emerald at a flea market in Arizona. It had been mixed in with other valueless rocks. He'd bought it for close to nothing and sold it for a princely sum. The rest of the paper was mundane and sundry, nothing else holding his attention.

Turning, he walked the few steps to the door leading down to the basement. Built after the First World War – but before the Second – it was typical of construction before there were building inspectors and spec homes: the ceilings low, the doors narrow, and the steps down to the basement tight enough to make one claustrophobic. They creaked and groaned with each step down.

Whereas the rest of the house was almost exactly as it was when his parents were alive, this part had been updated.

This was his sanctum sanctorum. Quiet and calming. When he was home, this was where he could be found.

The low-ceilinged space with its exposed floor joists above, and cool walls made from concrete mixed with fieldstone, felt good. He was where he should be.

Shelves and bench space lined the walls. All were populated with complex-looking technical gadgets and devices. Walls festooned with hanging cables covering what little vertical space remained. Born out of a lifetime of exploration and experimentation, he had an exceptional collection of technical paraphernalia.

The basement walls were set inside the first-floor footprint. The result was a tiny basement that would be uncomfortably small to some. From the stairs to the workbench was a short path through stacked boxes and old, abandoned experiments. Only four strides to the focus of the space: a solid oak workbench covered with a riot of wires, control panels, and devices of inexplicable nature. This was Karl's destination.

Taking a seat on a worn stool, he looked at the creation on the workbench. It was ready. Months of his spare time and no small amount of money. A true technical achievement inspired by a single photo. That one photo had jumpstarted a lifelong pursuit of similar images of the unexplainable.

Looking up, he reviewed the series of photos sitting on the edge of the bench, leaned back against the rough foundation wall. These were the original inspiration for what he had created.

Each photo was a mundane picture of normal life—a picture of a little girl in a field, another of children at a birthday party. The unique part of these photos was that they each had something out of place in their image, resembling a double exposure. Ghostly images superimposed. One showed a man in a spacesuit standing in the distance behind the girl in the field. They called it *The Solway Firth Spaceman*.

Picking it up off the bench, he considered the photo of the little girl with a man in a white spacesuit in the background. The angle of the picture made it look like the suited figure was perched on her shoulder like a parrot.

Why or how? How do these things exist?

Once he started looking, he found these types of photos were far more common than made sense. Each one in turn analyzed for double exposure or some other trickery. Each subsequently confirmed as true.

Returning the *Solway* photo to its long-held place on his workbench, he then picked up a photo of a much older daguerreotype with a ghostly screaming face in the background.

He had been collecting these photos of unexplained phenomena for decades. Each one helped to reveal another piece of the puzzle. This one photo was the first, however, and the inspiration for what followed.

His parents had taken him to a county fair, and among the vendors selling sugary treats and cheap knockoffs was the only kiosk that had managed to capture his attention. A short, tanned carnie in eccentric leather clothes selling photos.

His parents had left him for a moment, as his brother had run off. This one photo caught his attention. The man behind the display never spoke but pushed the photo on the young Karl. Taking it up, he went looking for his parents to ask for money to pay for it.

After he found them and his brother, they went back to the vendor. Except he was gone, along with his kiosk. His father had been quite stern, concerned that his son was stealing. They gave up after an hour of looking. His parents finally decided he could keep the photo.

That was over fifty years ago.

Returning the faded photo to its place among the others, he looked down at the contraption on the bench. Its purpose was to finally prove what had happened in those photos.

During his years with his employer, his many assignments required him to sign confidentiality agreements. They called them *special projects*. Karl considered them pieces of the puzzle. With the last piece now falling into place, it was time to test it out. His termination, in many ways, was a convenience, as he could now focus on this one project.

This day had been a long time coming. It would have taken longer. Unemployment changed that.

Karl picked up a leather suitcase from the floor. Worn, faded, and cracked in several places, he hefted it on to the bench and began packing all the gadgets and the riot of wiring into the aged container.

He needed to be careful. This was a prototype. Not much more than a collection of bits barely connected. It would not travel well. With a close of the cover and a snap of the latch, it was time to go.

A trip up the creaky stairs, case in hand, and out the kitchen door to the garage saw him carefully placing the suitcase in the trunk of a grey Toyota sedan. Reliable transportation, and Karl liked reliable. Getting in, he started up the car. It was a cool fall day, and he adjusted the heat up as he drove away from his home.

The neighborhood was in a post-WW2 boom area that had never gentrified. Cookie-cutter homes evenly spaced with old-growth oak and maple trees towering overhead. A bubble of peaceful, orderly Americana. Looking around his yard, he added to that thought: *Except the leaves. Raking the leaves in the fall is a chore. So much clutter.*

The freeway was only minutes from his home, and he was soon turning onto the onramp. With the engine buzzing, he accelerated into traffic. Thumbing the cruise control, he settled in for the trip. His eyes landed on a billboard with a movie advertisement. A well-endowed woman in a tight-fitting uniform covering very little skin was the centerpiece. Karl's eyes narrowed, not seeing the appeal. It looked to be an action-adventure story, and her clothes looked tight-fitting and restrictive. And the story appeared to take place in a cold climate. No protection, impractical, and cold. *Why dress like that?*

His focus returned to the task at hand, he realized the drive to his chosen destination would take more than an hour. This appealed to him. Driving was also time for uninterrupted thought.

Looking out the driver's side window, he noted the housing density decreasing. The leaves on the trees were just starting to change color. Fall was here, and winter was coming.

His destination—the place to perform the test—had been chosen specifically for its likely lack of people. Interruptions and questions—he appreciated neither. A state park far from urban development. A patch of wilderness several miles across in all directions, only accessible through a single dead-end road. This testing at a remote location was critical. If anything went wrong, it wouldn't be his home burning down.

A highway exit delivered him onto a rural blacktop road. The park was close now. Having memorized the map, he estimated less than fifteen minutes.

There was no sign at the highway exit indicating a state park located nearby. Karl found a similar situation at the park entrance – there was a sign, but it was small and inconveniently located behind poorly trimmed foliage. For a moment, the difficulty in finding the entrance made him question his memorized directions. A gust of wind moving a tree branch revealed the park sign, just in time to keep him from missing his turn.

As he maneuvered onto the gravel road into the park, he wondered why the sign was so far back from the road.

Karl winced as the car jounced over the potholes and ruts. The car's tires threw up rocks, which he could hear bouncing off the body of the car. The roughness forced him to drive slowly. His memory confirmed a parking area close to the center of the park.

Slowing below twenty-five miles per hour, he mused about how the park service did not take care of this place: *Who would come here with a drive-in experience like this?*

He found the parking area, a rough circle of patchy gravel. Off to one side was a bent and twisted billboard, the paint faded and chipped. Above was an equally dilapidated awning—its cedar shingles weather-beaten and curled from the sun and age—pronouncing the park's name.

Townshend Park.

To one side was a dented mesh-metal trashcan half-filled with petrified garbage.

He was pleased with his apparent good fortune. This appeared to be the perfect place to conduct his tests uninterrupted. This was truly the park that time forgot.

Exiting the vehicle, he retrieved the suitcase from the trunk, opening it to check how it survived the bouncing drive in. Thankfully, everything appeared to be in order. Closing the cover, he straightened up. Turning, he considered his surroundings. Now, where to do this? Looking around for a place to setup, he spied a waist-high rock under a nearby tree a few feet off to one side of the parking lot.

Leaving the car trunk open, he walked over and hefted the case onto the rock, the yellow and red leaves above providing shade. He crouched down and opened the leather lid. With a flip of a switch, his creation came to life.

Picking a copper-colored sphere from its nest in the mass of wires, he lifted it free. It fit comfortably in his right hand. With his left hand, he untangled the braid of wiring connecting it to the display in the case.

Karl felt a sensation, perhaps pride or satisfaction. This was the moment where all his work paid off. Or failed. This was not his first complex undertaking, and past successes gave him confidence.

Switching hands, he held up the sphere with his left hand. His right hand worked the controls in the case. Images appeared on the display.

Karl stared at the colors on the display, alive and flowing. None of it made any sense. The riot of colors was as if modern art and a paint factory explosion made a baby.

This was expected. Everything around him was being layered over everything else. The result was the chaos on the screen in front of him. Filter adjustments were needed. Karl twisted knobs, pushed buttons, and flipped switches. Each action stripped away a layer or added focus.

The outline of the nearby trees appeared. By rotating the sphere and adjusting the controls, each one was isolated in turn. Their leaves glowed with a golden hue. The light of the sun. From each leaf flowed a single delicate strand of silver. Each leaf strand combined with others at the small branches. The small branches joined each other as major branches, forming a narrow stream of silver. The branches joined the tree trunk, and a river of brilliantly-pulsing silver flowed to the roots. Understanding that he was seeing the flow of energy from the leaves to the roots of the tree exhilarated him.

Shifting the focus, he angled the brass sphere to look further out. Through a nearby rise of earth, on the other side of the hill, there was another tree, and it was glowing gold and silver.

Looking in the direction of this tree, he realized there was a mound of earth in between it and his position, preventing him from seeing it directly. He smiled and nodded with the realization that his invention could see through things. A sort of X-ray vision.

Changing the settings, he shifted the focus to his car. Could it be limited to only show metals?

In moments, the disembodied profile of the car materialized on the screen. A constellation of small dots could be seen below and to the sides of the vehicle. Another shift in direction, more focus, and the nails holding the park billboard together appeared. The display showed them suspended in space.

That was what the dots were. Smaller bits of metal. That would be a useful feature; he was sure of it.

His new invention was outperforming his expectations. The possibilities of such a device filled his thoughts. The potential was almost unlimited.

What about range? How far could this see?

Turning the sphere out towards open forest, he adjusted the focus ever outwards. Setting the sensitivity to register heat. The thermal image of the heat of the sun on the trees and the forest floor where it shined through, brilliant reds and yellows mimicked the colors of autumn leaves. A more artistically minded person might have found this stimulating.

A passing rabbit glowed warmly against the background of the cooler forest floor. Its paw prints leaving bright patches that slowly faded away.

Glancing at the settings, he realized the images were from more than two miles away.

It was difficult to estimate the device's maximum range prior to testing. What he was seeing was better than expected or even dreamed of.

A silhouette entered the viewscreen. A ghostly image, really, almost invisible. Its body heat only a fraction greater than the surrounding environment.

Vertical, two arms, two legs, and a head. Somebody was out there in the forest, not more than two miles from him. A hiker?

He paused while his mind worked through the possibilities. The immediate questions that came to mind: *Where was its body heat? Was he viewing a corpse?*

The realization that the silhouette was standing upright dispelled the notion he was looking at a dead body.

It moved. Taking a few steps, its gait was less than elegant.

Looking at the settings, he mentally calculated an estimate of the ghost image's height to be approximately four feet. He was confident in the number. His math was rarely incorrect.

Karl frowned and looked closer at the display. Was he seeing a child? Short adult? Foreshortened person? *Why was its body heat missing?*

More focus, a filter shift, and the outline of the figure was clarified.

Its legs and arms were emaciated and thin. Its posture slouched. A too-large—more oval than round—head sat atop a square body. A child, and not a healthy one? Perhaps lost in the park?

He would be obligated to assist a lost child. Then he would need to locate the authorities. Unlike everyone else these days, Karl refused to own the government tracking devices that were cellular phones.

Letting out a sigh, Karl Lark resigned himself to a day of testing now ruined by the inconvenience of the presence of other human beings.

Shifting his thoughts to this new and unwanted task, he wondered, *Which way to the child?* He looked from the display in the suitcase to the brass sphere, and then his eyes tracked to the woods beyond.

Having determined the direction he needed to travel, he moved to close the case. Just as he was reaching for the switch to power down, his eyes settled on the figure one last time before shutting down the device. The silhouette on the screen had stopped moving, and its head was rotating. The movement ended with the figure's face looking in Karl's direction.

Now the body of the figure rotated in the same direction the head was looking.

It took a few steps in Karl Lark's direction. Paused. And then it strode straight towards him.

Karl blinked and pulled back from the display for a moment. He considered how unlikely and odd such a coincidence was.

There are two miles of densely overgrown forest between us.

The ghostly image's pace was blistering. Karl watched it effortlessly negotiate the forest floor obstacles. Dodging between trees and stepping over rocks and forest floor detritus. Coming to a stream, it leapt across a distance that would have made an Olympic long jumper proud.

Something was not right. No body heat, unnatural appearance. A glance at the distance on the display confirmed that whatever was running towards him would traverse the remaining intervening distance in minutes.

He felt a compulsion to leave. Whatever that thing was, Karl was unsure whether meeting it in person, alone in the middle of nowhere, was prudent. As a matter of fact, he was sure it was not.

Without powering the device down, he shoved the sphere into the case, wincing as he slammed the cover shut. That thing was moments away and coming fast. He could worry about breakage later.

Years of sedentary living prevented him from running to the car. More of a bouncing, shuffling, fast walk that carried his old body the distance. The suitcase was tossed unceremoniously into the open trunk with one hand while the other slammed it shut.

Seconds later, he was sitting in the driver's seat with the doors closed and locked. Protected by a locked door provided an instant feeling of improved security. A turn of the key, and the car started.

Having parked nose-in, he needed to turn around. Shifting into reverse, he pushed the accelerator hard. The velocity of backing up exceeded the ability of the vehicle's suspension to compensate, and the car jounced over potholes and the roughness of the parking lot. Looking forward out the windshield, he saw the drive out and away from this place. Shifting into drive, he paused.

His head turned involuntarily to look to his left, to the tree he had been standing under just a minute ago. On the other side of the tree was a rise of earth, almost a hill, or maybe more of a berm. The view only partially blocked by the tree.

Atop the grassy mound stood . . . *What was that?*

Whatever it was, the silhouette was the height of a pre-teen child with spindly arms and legs and a head distinctly oval in shape, more broad than high, with overly large, solid, black eyes. This disturbing image included a steam-shovel-like mouth hinged open, showing numerous crooked, needle-like teeth.

The thing's appearance was made all the more disturbing by its green skin.

Even from this distance, he saw the creature's eyes were its dominant feature—much too big for the head they were set in, and solid black.

Clothed in an ill-fitting jumper made up of red and brown-colored patches of crude, rough cloth stitched together in no discernible pattern. No shoes, just long, narrow, crooked feet. It looked like a raggedy doll someone's dog chewed on.

The creature's eyes were locked onto the car. Its right hand raised with a long, crooked finger extended towards Karl Lark.

The unnaturalness of it repelled and frightened him. He had never expected to find anything like that.

Something…*alive?*

For a brief moment, he wondered what it was and if it was properly alive.

Breaking free from his moment of consideration, Karl pushed on the accelerator, and the car lunged forward. The creature's face rotated to follow the car. After several car lengths of forward motion, Karl was able to break his stare and confirm the forward trajectory onto the road ahead. Glancing up in his rearview mirror, he saw the mound of dirt receding behind him, and the thing was gone.

The drive out punished the suspension on his vehicle. His sixty-three-year-old body repeatedly slammed into the seat belt with a force that had him seeing stars, but he did not dare slow down. The Toyota flew out onto the paved county road in a shower of gravel and dust. With a howl of tires on blacktop, the car flirted with the ditch. White-knuckled hands barely able to compensate before catastrophe.

Free of the park and the immediate threat of whatever that thing was, and with the car stable on dry pavement, the reasoning part of his mind resumed control. *What had he just seen?* Was it even a real threat? What if it was a practical joke?

Karl shook his head—it was real all right. But it registered no body heat. He did not care how good a practical joke it could have been. It would have generated heat.

At the on-ramp to the highway, he pulled off to the side of the road in a shower of gravel, kicking up a cloud of dust. His heart still pounding, he shut off the car.

It was like something out of a fairy tale. A goblin?

One part of the whole experience gelled in his thoughts: a run-down, poorly accessible park nobody visits, populated with a fairy-tale creature. What if those details were all on purpose? *Now that was an interesting thought.*

Starting up the car, he drove out onto the on-ramp towards the freeway.

Retirement was more interesting than he'd expected it to be.

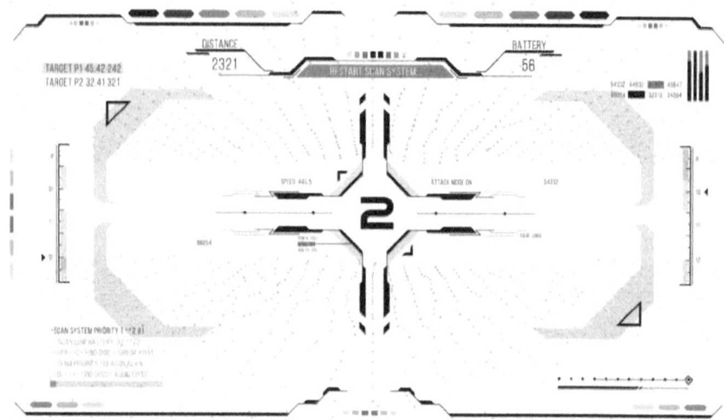

CHAPTER TWO

Traffic on the freeway was light. Not that it mattered. Karl kept to the right lane and obeyed the speed limit. A glance at the fuel gauge inserted a task into his immediate future.

At the next exit, he stopped at a gas station and filled the Toyota's tank. His thoughts on the park experience reached critical mass.

The thing's appearance resembled a mythical faerie creature, a goblin. It crossed over two miles of dense forest on foot in less than five minutes. Saying it was fast would be an understatement. No human could outrun that thing.

The gas pump whirred along, much like his mind. He wondered if Townshend Park had a history. He could not be the only one who had seen that thing. Anxiety gripped him as he finished refueling his vehicle. His mind raced with the need to be home before nightfall. There was no discernible reason for the sudden urge, but he was now driven by it.

The remainder of his drive to his home was rushed. He was even willing to exceed the speed limit by five miles per hour, in spite of it making him feel like a lawbreaker.

The sun was setting behind gold and red leaves as he pulled into his driveway.

Parking the car, he gathered up the suitcase and hurried inside. After double-checking that all the doors and windows were closed and locked, he went upstairs. Not to his bedroom, unchanged since his childhood. Instead, he entered the room that belonged to his parents. The bed was long gone, but his parents' dresser was still there, covered in a thick layer of dust.

He flipped the light switch, and the harsh glare of an ancient, unshielded incandescent bulb lit up the room. Squinting in the bright light, he was momentarily startled by the stark shadows, dark and sharp, his own body cast upon the wall.

Hurriedly, he opened one of the top drawers. What he was looking for was in here, as this was the last place it was left.

Right on top was a triangular, soft leather case. He snatched it up and pulled open the zipper on its side. Sliding his hand inside, he felt cold metal. Gripping it tightly, he removed a black revolver. Thirty-eight caliber. Father kept it as a memento for reasons never explained.

Opening the cylinder revealed six empty spaces for bullets. Next to where the case sat in the drawer was a crumpled box of .38 caliber cartridges. The print on the cardboard, faded from age, read *Ace Ammo*.

Opening the box, he found only eight cartridges: brass cases black with age, bullet lead white with oxide. He fumbled six rounds of the antique ammunition into the cylinder and snapped it closed.

Gun in hand, he walked to his bedroom. Leaving the light on and without even taking off his shoes, he curled up on the bed.

Normally, attempting to fall asleep with the light on would be an unacceptable irritation. Not tonight—now it brought comfort.

Gripping the revolver with both hands, he drifted off to sleep.

●　　●　　●　　●　　●

Karl's eyes opened to a lit room. His eyes came to rest on the revolver lying on the bed next to him. The business end pointed right at his face. Still wondering why the room light was on and why there was a gun in his bed, he added the question of why he was fully clothed to the list.

His eyes widened as the recollection of the previous day's events rushed in.

Yesterday had been quite stimulating. His experiment worked better than he had hoped. And then there was that other thing.

It really happened.

If anything in his life could make him question his memory, it was what he had seen yesterday. But no, the images in his mind had not faded. That thing was real.

He needed answers, and answers would require research. *The library.* He would be going to the library today. Yes, a Sunday visit to the library was in order.

Returning to his parents' room, he unloaded the revolver, returning the pistol and cartridges to their place in the drawer. After closing the drawer, he shook his head at his behavior after returning home last night. Silly over-reaction. Clutching a revolver like it was a teddy bear.

Midway through preparing to leave for the library, he realized it was early and it would be hours until it opened.

That left him some time to get a few things done.

After stopping in the kitchen for a robust bacon and egg breakfast, Karl, suitcase in hand, navigated the creaky stairs into the basement.

An inspection of the suitcase's contents confirmed his suspicions. The contraption inside had not survived the rush to escape the park. Karl sighed and pieced it back together. Once reassembled, he powered it up to find the device was again fully operational.

The last image the device had observed was still on the screen—a silhouette of the creature midleap in its race through the forest towards him. Yes, indeed, it really did happen.

The reason for yesterday's test in the park was to mitigate something going wrong. Aspects of his creation could have unintended side effects. It would have been unfortunate if disaster was inadvertently delivered to his home. His very being recoiled at the thought of firefighters or police rifling through his lab.

So, Mr. Lark, what were you doing? Do you have a permit for this kind of work? Perhaps it would be best for everyone if this were confiscated while the misunderstanding is worked out.

His calculations had, however, not taken into account the improbable. It turned out the worst thing that could happen was seeing things that should not exist.

With the device restored to working condition and time remaining until the library opened, he activated the controls. Curiosity took over.

I wonder what can I find in my own neighborhood?

Turning the brass sphere to focus on his next-door neighbors, he found empty homes. It was Sunday morning, and they were elderly. Perhaps church?

Across the street he found there were people home. Adjusting the focus, he zoomed in.

Close proximity, repetitive motion. *What were they doing?* Realization dawned, and Karl Lark quickly shifted his attention to the next nearest home.

This was the home of that one fellow—the one with the red beard. Karl had seen every house in the neighborhood change ownership during his long residence. This house was the most recent to bring a new owner to the neighborhood. Karl had never met the man, and he had only seen him outside on a few occasions.

Tall, pale, husky, thinning gray hair contrasted with an unkempt red beard. *Unsavory* was the word that came to mind as how he would describe him.

The display soon revealed Red Beard and his car were gone.

Karl was becoming more dexterous with the device's controls, and he was able to navigate Red Beard's home interior in short order. Its layout not all that different than his own residence.

The fact that he was violating his neighbor's privacy began to weigh on him, and he decided this would be the last house for today.

The scan finished up in the basement. Karl was surprised to find Red Beard had a guest. And thankfully, they had body heat. Whoever they were, they were not terribly tall. Perhaps a teenager or a woman?

After what he had just witnessed with his across-the-street neighbors, he avoided inspecting closer. Having successfully tested his reassembled creation, he judged the device fully operational. There was no further need to spy on the locals. And the library was opening soon.

Closing the case, he paused, his eyes remaining focused on the aged leather. This thing needed a name; calling his creation "The Device" was incongruous. He could steal from popular science fiction and call it a tricorder. Or maybe more Flash Gordon, like the *Viewtron 5000*? The military liked three-letter acronyms. RVD for Remote Viewing Device?

Karl Lark sighed. Too presumptuous, too contrived—none of these ideas were appealing. To be honest, naming things was not one of his skill sets.

It had to be something simple. He nodded to himself, the *Oculus*. Not sure where that came from, but it worked.

Lifting the case from the bench, Karl carried his invention up the stairs to leave for the library.

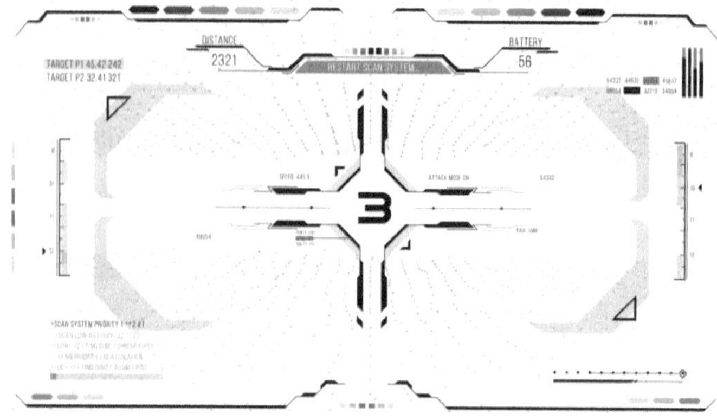

CHAPTER THREE

During the return drive home, Karl reviewed the day's activities at the library. It had been a productive day's work, and he was pleased with how much he was able to find.

He'd started with a review of Townshend Park in the local newspaper. There was a history even before the land was donated to the state and became a park. It went all the way back to the thirteen colonies days, pre-1800s.

The park had once been part of the holdings of the Townshend family, which settled this area in the early 1700s. The recognizable name of the family was still found on public structures. The land had been turned over to the state to be made into a park. This happened when Teddy Roosevelt was president.

A hunter had disappeared there in 1919. That was the only article associated with a disappearance that mentioned Townshend Park by name. The adjacent areas showed irregular missing person incidences spaced out over decades. The information had been hard to find, but Karl had long ago developed a skill for locating the nearly impossible.

Nothing he read could be classified as a distinct pattern, but when he looked at the complete record over more than two centuries, he could not help but come to the conclusion that Townshend Park was not safe. After what he had seen there, Karl was fairly confident he knew why.

Computer-searchable, digitized newspapers. It was all very convenient. The grandson of the missing hunter, also a Townshend, had written a book on his grandfather's disappearance. Karl was not able to locate a copy, but the author was still alive—now retired and moved south.

What about other parks? Was there a pattern? Were there other secrets out there waiting to be discovered?

The library had a big book of federal and state parks, including maps. A fair number demonstrated common characteristics. The interesting part was how many were the circle or block shape, as if something were in the center, and the park was a protective wrapper keeping people away.

The more underdeveloped ones interested him most. Few roads in, minimal visitor traffic. After sifting through the many choices, he found an almost ideal candidate. One of the largest parks in his home state. It checked all the boxes: square-shaped, remote, and limited road access.

His theory intrigued him.

Was something hidden in some or all of these parks?

The hours of searching and studying still left him time to read a book by author David Paulides, *Missing 411*. Karl concluded the author was onto something after what he saw at Townshend Park. *If something was there, the oculus would find it.*

Arriving home, he noticed Red Beard doing yard work and wondered where his housemate was. He had never seen both of them at the same time. Or, for that matter, he had never seen the other one. Never.

Shrugging, he continued inside to a dinner consisting of a peanut butter sandwich. While chewing, he considered the next day's activities.

Instead of looking for faerie creatures in a state park, I could just sell the oculus *technology and buy an island to retire to.*

During his career at his previous employer's, he had seen fantastic developments never make it to market. There had never been an official explanation, but he always suspected they were suppressed.

At my stage of life, what would I do with all that money? What I have planned for tomorrow will be much more interesting.

●   ●   ●   ●   ●

Following a good night's sleep, Karl packed the *oculus* into the car and drove to what his research showed as the most intriguing of the state parks. Located in a rural area, the nearby roads were paved, but there were no public roads into the park proper. This was a hiking-only park and undeveloped, with only minimal dirt fire road access. And that name, *Abyssal Park*. Where had that come from?

Driving the perimeter of the park, he stopped every few miles to observe with the *oculus*. Karl did not find any faerie creatures. Only now, in person, viewing through his invention, did he realize how large this park really was. Scanning was a time-consuming, manual process. Undaunted, he continued his search.

Pulling into an observational site on the far north side of the park, overlooking a shallow valley, he operated the *oculus* without leaving his vehicle.

Still nothing.

Karl was beginning to doubt his faerie encounter at Townshend Park. Today had been a lot of work with little to show for it. His hands continued to cycle the *oculus* controls. Lightning could strike twice. Not one to believe his success would be delivered by luck or coincidence, he remained focused on the center of the park.

Bingo!

A structure of some sort buried halfway into a hill. Concentric circles, one inside the other, at odd angles to each other. It was big—the size of your average home.

Through five miles of overgrown forest. No trails. Almost dead center in the park.

Predictable.

The settings needed on the *oculus* to reveal what he sought were peculiar to begin with, and the structure was different than anything around it. It appeared to be transparent. How was what he was seeing on the display even possible?

Karl raised his eyes, looked across the valley to the rough terrain beyond, and sighed. He wanted to get close to the structure, but hiking through miles of rough terrain would not be kind to his 63-year-old body.

Not willing to give up, he prepared himself. Setting the direction of his destination by a distant tree-covered hilltop, he locked up the car. With the *oculus* case handle held tightly by his right hand, he hiked out.

The woods started out fairly reasonable. The forest floor was clear, if somewhat uneven.

This was not too bad.

Then, like crossing from day into night, the forest changed. Dead wood covered the uneven forest floor. The trees were older, thicker, and closer together. The dense leaf canopy blocked out the light. Continuing through the wooded twilight, Karl took care. Breaking a leg here, with no chance of rescue, would be bad.

Hours of hiking, mixed with numerous rest stops, found him closing in on his intended destination. The terrain changed yet again. The tree cover was even denser than he would have thought possible. Light dimmed to almost twilight levels. Steep, sharp, washboard ridges forced Karl to climb up and down. He was soon puffing and out of breath.

The physical exertion was uncomfortable and had him wondering if this was really so important.

On the other side of the last ridge, he found himself looking down into a pit surrounded on all sides by sharp ridges like the one Karl was standing at the top of. The spherical structure shown by the *oculus* was, of course, not visible to the human eye. But the *oculus* showed it was there, half buried in the side of the pit.

The overlook where he had parked his car had been alive with chirping birds and insect noises. Not here—this place was as dark and silent as a tomb.

Karl consulted the *oculus*, and its bright display contrasted with the gloom, making aged eyes—already adjusted to the dark—squint.

The sphere had layers to it and rings embedded around. One of the *oculus'* settings showed rod-like shapes mounted to the rings, standing straight out from them. They almost resembled handles to grab onto.

Walking up to the sphere, or at least where the image on the *oculus* screen told him it was, he reached out to where one of the rods was. As his hand touched it, the rod and the ring it was attached to moved.

His head tilted to one side while he considered what had just happened. This was interesting. *He wondered . . .*

He did it again. It moved. He watched how the ring moved in relation to the other rings.

It was a puzzle. Like a Rubik's cube.

He reached for different rods, manipulating the positions of the rings in relation to each other. Some required climbing up the ridge a bit. Accessing one had him digging into the ground to reach it. Sequenced one by one, the rings aligned. As the last one settled in place, they meshed and merged. The image on the *oculus* screen shifted. *A portal?*

Karl considered the situation. He was far from other people and any hope of rescue. If anything inside was hazardous or he was injured, the outcome would not be constructive.

Looking at whatever the doorway represented, he took a step closer.

He nodded and smirked. *Who would miss one old man?*

Without further thought, he took two quick strides and entered the portal.

•   •   •   •   •

Everything was black, and for a moment, Karl wondered if he had been blinded.

His eyes adjusted to the dark, and he shivered. Wherever this was, it was about twenty degrees cooler than the forest he just hiked through.

Slowly, the dim space around him revealed itself. Looking down, he saw that his feet were planted on an even, solid surface. Around him, points of light materialized like unmoving fireflies in the distance. Some were relatively close, and others were far enough away to be tiny pinpoints.

Karl took a breath. The cold air smelled stale with a metallic tang to it. Consulting the *oculus* showed the makeup of what he was breathing. It was the appropriate mixture of oxygen and nitrogen. And the air was really dry. Single-digit humidity dry. *Cold and desert dry.*

Pulling a flashlight from his pocket, he switched it on and swept his immediate surroundings. Looking behind, he did not see how he has just entered. There was no door. It was like magic. He had walked into the portal and just appeared here in this dark and cold place.

Anxiety gripped him, and he worked the controls on the *oculus*. He soon found himself standing inside another invisible portal structure. This was the way back to the park woods. He wouldn't know for sure until he tried, but this was not likely a one-way trip.

The *oculus* showed him standing on a circular platform similar in size to a helipad. Along the perimeter of the circle were black stone pillars the approximate height and width of a man. Each was evenly spaced from the other, completely around the circle. Looking back and forth between several of the pillars, a thought occurred to him: *They look almost like a miniature Stonehenge.*

After a quick count: twelve pillars, like a clock.

The *oculus* told him he was in a large, oval-shaped chamber with the Stonehenge platform he was standing on being at one end.

Switching back to the flashlight, he shined it around, and just outside the stone circle was a wall of reddish, granite-looking stone that smoothly arched upwards. The flashlight was not strong enough to see how far up above the ceiling was.

Illuminating the floor under his feet, he bent down to look closer. Its smooth, flat surface had the finest layer of grayish-silver dust upon it. The only footprints were the few he had made since arriving.

He had no absolute proof, but Karl speculated that he was the only visitor to this place in a long time, possibly a very long time considering the portal's location in the park and the impossibility of finding it without something like an *oculus*.

On the side of the platform facing the open area of the chamber was a ramp downward. At the bottom of the ramp, off to the side, was one of the firefly lights. Karl slowly walked down the ramp to inspect the light.

It looked like a cylindrical metallic candle. Except instead of a flame, the top had a plasma glow. Stepping within perhaps ten feet of the candle, the plasma glow suddenly expanded vertically, lighting up the surrounding area.

Startled, Karl took a step back, and the glow receded. Stepping closer, it expanded again. Karl looked out into the surrounding darkness and did a quick count. There were, perhaps a dozen of these lights irregularly scattered around.

What is this place? Where am I? He had questions, but precious little to answer them with.

Holding the *oculus* case with both hands, Karl consulted the display. The *oculus* displayed what the flashlight could not reach. Apparently, walking into the portal had deposited him in a cave of some sort. Strangely, the *oculus* could only penetrate a few meters into the walls. There was no seeing anything outside the cave.

Shaking his head, he found this odd. The *oculus* should be able to see through a mile of solid stone. It was like there was no world outside the walls of that chamber.

There was an exit opening from that space on the opposite side of the chamber from the circular platform. The long axis of the chamber was almost a mile in length and one-quarter as wide, almost like a gallery. From where he arrived to the opposite exit, there was a straight path. The *oculus* showed physical features like raised platforms on each side of the path. They were different sizes, and each had a ramp up from the path.

Shrugging his shoulders, Karl began walking towards the opposite exit. As he walked, he shined the flashlight around. The luminescent beam revealed empty platforms and ramps around him. Karl also kept checking the dust on the floor for evidence anyone other than he had walked here recently.

About two-thirds of the way on his walk to the opposite exit opening, the flashlight revealed a platform with something on it. Centered on it was a huge mass of amber-like material with a size and shape comparable to a locomotive. One of the glow candles was at the base of the ramp leading up to the amber construct, and another one was up on the platform. They flared into brilliance as he drew close.

Walking up the ramp to look at the amber shape, he held the flashlight up to inspect the object of his curiosity. The surface had cracks in it, and some fist-sized pieces of the amber-like material had broken off and were lying about the platform.

Putting the flashlight right up to the translucent amber made the whole thing glow. There was something inside—something suspended and filling up more than half its volume. The amber was too opaque to make out any details, though.

Karl shrugged his shoulders, walked back down the ramp, and continued his journey to the exit. The flashlight revealed a pipe-like tube leaving the chamber. Without hesitation, he strode into it. This level and straight hallway was also made from the same reddish granite.

Karl's flashlight revealed scratches, gouging, and dents on the walls, floor, and ceiling.

Many of the gouges and scratches were perpendicular to the length of the tube. They did not come from something being dragged through there. Random clusters of scratches? Perhaps claws? He speculated that whatever made those scratches was likely as big or bigger than a grizzly bear.

The tube opened onto a ledge made from a pitch-black material. Looking back through the tube, he could still see a few pinpricks of light from the plasma candles in the gallery he just came from. Turning back again, he was looking into black nothingness.

The platform continued both left and right.

Consulting the *oculus* revealed something difficult to believe. The platform he was standing on ran the inside equator of a massive sphere of open space just over a half-mile in diameter. A giant empty orb of black nothingness. Whatever was in front of him was not just empty; it did not properly register with the *oculus*. The huge chamber contained *nothing*.

What is this place?

Somehow the air was breathable, but one step past the edge of the platform was nothing but a profound eldritch void.

On the opposite side of his current position—adjacent the sphere of nothingness—was an alcove of sorts. Walking the equator ledge would bring him there.

Karl took a moment to consider the situation. This was dangerous. The black material the ledge was made from was only barely distinguishable from the void. A misstep would find one falling into the void sphere. Karl's solution was to hold the flashlight and *oculus* case handle with his left hand and put his right hand against the wall.

He had come this far. It was only logical to see it through. One foot in front of the other. Nothing ventured, nothing gained.

It was slow going, and he stopped midway to finish the only bottle of water he brought. The dry air was sucking the moisture out of him. It would be prudent to leave and come back better prepared. Karl dismissed the idea almost instantly. He needed to know what was in that alcove.

His destination turned out to be a depression in the side of the sphere's outer wall that looked like it had been created by scooping it out with a melon baller. Its surface was covered in raised hexagons, like oversized buttons on a control panel.

The *oculus* showed each hexagon interconnected to the other. Perhaps another Rubik's cube?

For a long time, Karl stared at what the *oculus* was showing him. He knew he could not leave without figuring that out. His focus and need to solve the puzzle were growing by the minute.

There was a reason for this. It existed to be discovered and solved. This place. The void sphere. The challenge displayed in front of him.

He began with the first sequence. A half-hour later, feeling increasingly tired, Karl completed it.

His breathing became more labored. His arms felt heavier. By the time the second pattern was complete, he was sweating.

Why was this so hard? Pushing buttons was not commonly considered an arduous challenge.

He could not deny the need to begin the third sequence. Soon he was sweating profusely, and his arm and shoulder muscles were starting to burn. Completing the third sequence, he staggered back to catch his breath. Then he caught himself.

Careful of the edge. That is a long way down.

While standing there pondering the fourth sequence, Karl felt something running down his upper lip. He swiped at it with his hand and shifted the light to see what it was. His hand was covered in blood. Both of Karl's nostrils were bleeding.

A thought entered his mind that he should stop. Quiet and tenuous, it was drowned out by the need to continue. He couldn't stop. He must finish.

He started the fourth sequence. Finishing the last movement to complete it, he dropped to his knees, and the darkness around him was lit by a brilliant white light. Turning his head, he saw the center of the spherical chamber filled with light.

The light is so white, so pure.

So beautiful that it penetrated and flowed through his being.

A loud voice said, **"You must continue!"**

The words shocked Karl. He could not tell if he heard them or if they were in his head.

You must continue!

Karl nodded and stood up on shaky legs. Falling to his knees had been painful, and they throbbed now. He turned and considered the fifth sequence. Each movement was a struggle, and his burning muscles were beginning to shake. His hands no longer had the strength to hold the *oculus*, and he was forced to place it on the floor, angled up, so he could look down at the viewer while manipulating hexagons. With one final push, he completed the sequence and collapsed to the floor. Curling up in the fetal position, he just wanted to close his eyes and sleep.

Something warm and wet was flowing on both sides of his head. He brushed at it and looked at his hand illuminated in the clear white light. He was bleeding from his ears now. He rubbed his cheeks and found blood coming from his eyes. A faint voice in his head told him this was not good.

It must be done!

Karl felt the words and the compulsion to continue, but his body was no longer responding. His vision dimmed.

Is this what it is like to die?

There was a touch. Perhaps more inside him than on him. Exactly where was impossible to discern, but something touched him nonetheless. He saw and felt the age of the being. It was impossibly old. Scenes from the depths of time played out in his mind.

A realization, like a slap in the face, jolted his mind. The glowing figure had been trapped here. This place was a prison. It needed to escape, and Karl was going to help.

Yes, I am willing to help. The mind is willing, but the flesh is weak.

Something was happening. The being was changing him. Making him different.

You will continue!

Karl felt like *more*. His thoughts clarified and expanded. The pain he felt everywhere receded. He felt strong. Not normal strong. Different strong, *more strong*. Connected to his body in ways he had never felt before. In an instant, he was on his feet.

Looking at the white light, he saw it for what it was. Not an effect of nature or a thing. It was a being of incomprehensible beauty. Beautiful, majestic, and wise— words insufficient for what he was witnessing.

Finish!

Karl turned to the alcove and began the sixth sequence. His muscles no longer hurt, and his movements demonstrated a dexterity he never had before. Not even in his long-ago youth could he move like that. The last three sequences were completed in less time than the first six. His labors totaled nine patterns. With a feeling of triumph, he backed away and turned to face the light.

The spherical chamber reverberated with the sound of trumpeting horns.

It is done!

Karl's eyes could barely stay open viewing the being of light. Gradually, the brilliance began to diminish. The shape of a man of perfect dimensions began to form in the center of the sphere and drifted towards Karl. By the time it drew close to the alcove, a tall man in white robes stood before him.

The voice of power was in his head again.

I am reduced!

It was necessary!

It cannot be undone!

The angelic form towered over Karl, regarding him with pure white eyes.

Go forth, man!

The white figure disappeared, and Karl was alone in the dark. The abrupt loss of light and the magnificent presence of the being left an empty feeling.

It is gone. What was that? What just happened? What have I done?

Pausing for some time, he realized something had changed. He felt different.

Checking his eyes, ears, and nose, he found that the bleeding had stopped. His mind was sharp and clear. The ache in his shoulders had almost disappeared.

Gathering up the *oculus* and flashlight, he further inspected the alcove. The interconnectedness between the hexagonal stones was no longer detectable. His device showed them as inert.

Looking down at the floor, he was surprised by the still-drying blood. He should not feel this good after leaving a pool that size on the floor.

A little voice in his head told him it was time to go. Perhaps more a feeling than a voice. Regardless, he knew it was time to leave.

The walk out was far different from his original cautious, anxiety-filled push into the darkness. Confident strides traversed the distance to the exit. He did not even need to put a hand on the wall. He could see the edge of the ledge in a way he did not on the way in.

He continued on through the interconnecting tunnel. Without pause, he strode the length of the gallery and its platforms. Upon reaching the exit with its invisible portal rings, he paused to look out over the chamber and its pinpoint lights.

Why was this place built? And what did I just release?

When he arrived back in the park, would everything be on fire? Did he just unleash some ancient creature, and an apocalypse was now raging? For an instant, he had connected mentally with the being, and he was fairly certain its release was a good thing.

He reached out to the spot the *oculus* had shown him and began aligning the rings, activating the exit portal. One step later, he was gone.

Nothing was on fire, and the woods near the portal were as he left them. There was less light, making the woods even more spooky. Karl realized the sun was lower and it was now late afternoon or early evening.

The walk back to the car took less time than the walk in. Karl acknowledged to himself that he was feeling pretty spry considering all that happened today.

Not even the drive home gave him enough time to process what just happened. The epic nature of all that had just transpired and the feeling that all outcomes were beyond his full understanding.

●　　●　　●　　●　　●

Arriving home late, he put everything away, ate a light dinner, and headed to his room, intending and expecting to get a solid night's rest. The physical nature of his park outing and his age guaranteed a deep night's sleep.

It was not to be. He laid awake half the night.

Cursing his insomnia, he got up, dressed, and returned to his lab.

He was not looking forward to a foggy day. The expected typical outcome of an incomplete night's rest and his advanced age.

Instead, he was full of energy. Not just through the night. All the next day as well. He did not even need a nap.

The next night was the same. He expected a night of sleep, only to not need it.

The next day, he checked himself with the *oculus*. Karl was not a doctor, but he was beginning to suspect his encounter with the angelic being had changed him in a profound and, as yet, poorly understood way. Only two days as data points might be considered anecdotal, but it appeared to be a fact. He no longer needed to sleep. Karl Lark smiled.

This changes everything.

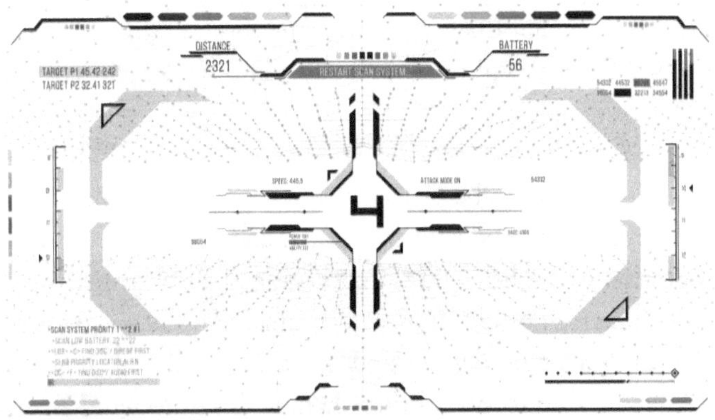

CHAPTER FOUR

The Super Duty Ford F-250 was a big truck. He needed a big truck for a remote desert destination in the great state of Arizona. Washed-out, rutted dirt roads were the only way in. His car was unable to navigate such conditions. He tried and quickly determined a more robust form of transportation was in order. After a visit to a car rental place, he was now driving the right tool for the job.

The plan called for purchasing a low-cost piece of land where his finding something of value would not be disputed. It also had to be in the middle of nowhere, where no one could see what he was doing. After some research into where something valuable could possibly be found – finding something of extreme value in a small, Midwestern town for example, would draw unwanted attention – what followed was a fairly straightforward affair. This accomplished Part One of the plan.

Plausible deniability was key.

It also had to be a place where he would be able to find something of value with the *oculus*...and then move it to the location where he could "discover" it and claim ownership.

The fruit of his effort landed him in this place. A parcel of undeveloped desert land in the middle of nowhere Arizona. And it had cost less than he had expected. Mineral rights were a different story, but with enough searching, he had found land that contained nothing anybody wanted, above or below ground. A long-ago-mined-out, remote patch of desiccated desert earth not far from the Superstition Mountains.

He recalled a saying from his childhood. *Out where Christ lost his shoes.*

Getting there proved to be a much more challenging experience. There were no road signs or civilization of any kind, and GPS was a requirement. Paved roads were left far behind as he traveled to his destination. Just dust and sand, heat, and the bright sun that blazed down from overhead.

Even with GPS, it had been impossible to find that first entry road in. It was not on the navigation or on the paper maps he had for backup reference. Fortunately, he chanced upon some fellow travelers on a dirt road near a parked pickup truck. Stopping and asking them for directions got him back on track.

The GPS announced his arrival at his property's coordinates. Karl stopped and parked on a flat section of the largely bland brown and tan terrain. Stepping down, he debarked from the truck. The bright sun and penetrating heat reminded him how inhospitable this place was.

Sweat broke out thickly while he looked upon his newly acquired domain. A featureless expanse of sun-baked, hard-packed sand and dirt, populated by sparse and lifeless brown bushes faded to the heat shimmer in the distance.

Being there and viewing his newly acquired holdings, he nodded in realization that this was the place. *This will do perfectly. There is literally nothing here.*

Climbing back into the truck, he was glad for the air conditioning and shade. Reaching over to the passenger seat, he picked up and activated the *oculus*. He had not been idle the last few weeks since the angel incident in Abyssal Park. The delicate contraption in a suitcase was gone. Now it was a box and display mounted ergonomically on a pistol grip, more closely resembling an industrial tool.

Forty acres of nothing. Hours passed as the *oculus* confirmed this. Sand, dirt, rocks, and the occasional bit of trash—his property was the poster child of worthlessness.

Time for Part Two of the plan.

Karl climbed back out of the truck and grabbed a shovel from the truck bed. Walking over to a nearby washed-out rut adjacent to a small hill, he began digging.

Never one for manual labor, he was surprised by his strength and endurance. In spite of the scorching heat and beating sun, he dug with gusto. Shovel after shovel of material flung onto a growing pile as the hole developed into a proper pit.

This had been one of the changes from the angel incident. He would not find himself tired, or even sore, by the time the hole was complete.

Karl stopped for a moment and gauged his progress. As he paused, he also considered another outcome from releasing...whatever that thing was. A side effect he was having trouble understanding was the slow subsidence of the normal aches and pains that came with age. Ever since the incident in that other place, his health and well-being had continued to improve in unexpected ways.

Returning to his work, a steady rhythm of shovel after shovel of earth followed. An hour of work in the blazing sun produced an empty pit. It had to be deep enough to be believable. That was an important part of the plan. *Plausible deniability.*

Eventually achieving what he deemed a credible-enough-sized hole, he climbed back out. He may not be tired or sore like a regular mortal, but he still sweated like one.

Returning the shovel to the bed of the truck, he resumed the driver position in the cab and cranked up the air conditioning. A bottle of water later, and he was ready.

Time for Part Three of the plan.

Piloting the truck out of the wilderness and back to blacktopped roads, he gave a wave to the men who had provided directions. They nodded in return.

He exhaustively researched his next destination before making his land purchase: public lands in a region with a large number of played-out gold mines, with geology supporting the likelihood of the high-value yellow metal being present. Past mining and its low density of occurrence prevented large-scale mining from being successful. But hobby prospectors still made valuable finds. And that was what he needed. A valuable find.

His objective was to find enough gold to pay for his next research effort. Somewhere out there was what he needed.

Arriving at his destination, he sat in the truck, scanning with the *oculus*. Its twenty-kilometer range covered a lot of territory.

Karl considered all the prospectors who spent years scratching at the earth trying to find a fortune, and here he was using the *oculus* to look for gold for miles in every direction. It almost felt like cheating.

Hours passed, with him finding only small nuggets. The sun set, and he continued in the dark of the night.

There it was!

Well into the night, he found what he was looking for. And it was close to the surface.

He was not an experienced geologist, but it was obvious this gold find did not fit the terrain. *Maybe someone had stashed it? Planning for a return that never happened?* The deposit's location was not near any road or trail. He would have to drive over the desert terrain to get the truck close enough.

The terrain was not cooperative, and the best he could do was get within a mile. Grabbing the shovel, he hiked out through the chill, night-desert air. Quiet and cold, the overhead night sky filled with stars. Briefly, Karl considered the stark difference to the urban settings he'd grown up in. Wide-open spaces did not sit well with him. Being alone was comfortable. Being alone in the wide-open wilderness in the middle of the night was unsettling.

Part way there, he checked the *oculus* and made a slight course correction. Arriving at the dead end of a shallow box canyon, his goal was under a ledge and behind several feet of dirt and sand. A stash of raw gold ore.

A near repeat of the dig on his land followed. An old man, alone in the dead of the night, digging a hole in the ground.

This whole adventure was not his idea of a constructive use of his time. *An undignified activity to endure just to acquire funding.*

Since the angel incident, he had upgraded the *oculus* and worked on a number of other projects. In a *Eureka!* moment, an idea began forming. An obscure concept blossomed into a theory. That theory begat something eminently practical but also likely impossible. It would be even more of an achievement than the *oculus*. With laser focus, he began his great work.

And immediately hit a financial wall. What he was developing was expensive, and Karl Lark was not a moneyed individual. This work was going to require a level of resources that would need to be supported by proper wealth.

The frustration was unbearable, and with the knowledge he could never include an investor, Karl bent his intellect to the challenge. Arriving at a solution, he had immediately put his plan into action, resulting in his current situation – digging holes in the Arizona desert for gold.

Scraping earth from his goal, he used a high-powered flashlight to illuminate the stash. From how the ore was piled up, it was obvious this was not a natural formation. Equally plain to see, it had been there for a very long time. Karl shrugged, as he cared not how the largesse had arrived. He only cared that the *oculus* was telling him there were several hundred pounds of gold ore in nuggets, some half the size of a person's head. The purity of the precious metal promised that what was there would provide his needed funding.

The gold ore was removable in manageable-sized chunks. By the time he had lifted and carried each oddly-shaped rough aggregate the mile back to his truck, the bed creaked under the weight. During the process, he came to understand an omission in his plan. He had not brought gloves, and the raw ore cut his hands as he carried it. This had not changed. Other things had changed since his encounter with the angel Being. Improved health and physical abilities. Lack of need to sleep. Better mental acuity and processing.

Karl thought: *But I still bleed.*

The good news was he recovered much faster from injury now.

While walking back and forth with his new wealth, he wondered if he should have just gone with using the *oculus* to find something valuable nearer to his home and stealing it. With the *oculus*, theft would be child's play. He dismissed the thought just as he had when it first came to him. Nothing he accomplished would be built on criminal activity.

Hundreds of pounds of high-grade gold ore now half-filled the truck bed. A perfunctory filling in of the stash hole, and he was back in the truck, driving through the night back to his land.

And now for Part Four of the plan.

The sun broke the horizon, evaporating the desert's night chill just as he arrived back on his land. Parking the truck as close to the hole as possible, he exited and started moving the ore from the truck to the pit he had just dug.

Removing each chunk of ore, he knocked as much superfluous dirt and sand free as possible. This left just the fundamental ore itself. The nuggets were then tossed in the pit, rolled in the dirt and sand, and then partially buried.

A thankless, monotonous task that continued until the whole find was re-buried. An important part of the plan was having it look like he found the ore on his land while amateur prospecting. Plausible deniability must be observed.

To help with the story, a newly purchased metal detector was in the cab of the truck. An expensive, German made model. Anyone asking would look at that and know he was serious.

The physical effort and mid-morning heat had him sweating and thirsty. Returning to the truck for water, he sipped from a bottle while running the plan through his mind. His mid-morning musings were interrupted by a rumbling sound that was coming closer.

Karl sat up straight in the driver's seat. *A vehicle approaching?*

Someone was close by in a car or truck with a muffler in poor condition. This being the literal middle of nowhere and also his private property for as far as the eye could see, begged the question: Who were they, and why were they here?

My private property. No one should be here.

Thinking how the timing could not be worse, he reached over onto the passenger seat to grab the *oculus*. With his other hand, he pulled his father's loaded .38 from a small duffel bag.

Better part of valor. He could not think of why anyone would be out here. Perhaps they are as lost as he had been when looking for this place.

Moving quickly, he exited the truck and walked to the east. Navigating around a mound of earth, he settled into an erosion cut on the slope opposite his vehicle. The hot morning sun reminded him of the harshness of where he was.

Activating the *oculus*, he observed an approaching pickup truck and its three occupants.

The arriving truck parked next to his F-250, and the three men exited.

A familiar male voice carried through the hot desert air. "Where's the old man?"

Karl recognized the voice. It was the man who had given him directions for the road in. Were they checking up on him?

A second voice rang out, "He's not in the truck."

After a short pause, Second Voice spoke again, "Doors are locked."

First Voice said, "Looks like he was walking back and forth to somewhere over there."

Karl shook his head and frowned. They were going to find the pit he had just dug.

Setting the *oculus* to look down on the situation, he followed his visitor's movements. With some fancy control work, he was also able to identify what they carried. One had a military-looking rifle with a curved magazine. Another had a pump shotgun. The third had a hunting rifle, with the *oculus* able to even show its scope.

That was a lot of firepower to just be checking up on him. And all he had was an ancient .38 revolver. With only eight bullets. Scratch that. Only six were in the pistol. The other two were in the truck in a bag.

A shootout with bandits had never been part of the plan. The revolver was for rattlesnakes or maybe coyotes. In this situation, none of the scenarios playing out in his mind had outcomes that favored him.

But what if they were just here to check up on me?

They had not done anything nefarious yet. This could just be neighborly concern.

First Voice, fainter than before, "That's a big hole!"

After a pause, First Voice spoke again, "Phil, go get a shovel. John, walk around and see if the old man's nearby. He either went for a walk or he heard our truck and is hiding."

On the *oculus*, the man with the shotgun traveled to the pickup for the shovel, and the one with the hunting rifle walked a short distance away from the vehicles and then stopped to look around.

Phil carried the shovel back to the hole. Apparently, First Voice was in charge because he just stood there while Phil jumped in the hole and started digging. The sounds of a shovel rhythmically stabbing into the earth banished the desert silence.

John was wandering about. He walked back to the vehicles and then circled them. He did this twice. Like the hands on a clock, with the trucks in the center, John stopped in alignment with the berm Karl was hiding behind.

After taking a few steps, stopping, then taking a few steps more, John figured it out. The direction Karl had taken from his truck. The figure on the *oculus* display began walking purposefully straight towards Karl's hiding place.

Footprints—he had to be following my footprints.

Karl looked down at his own feet. It became obvious. The virgin ground clearly showed each footfall.

I left a trail of breadcrumbs.

There were two possible outcomes that immediately came to mind. Either capturing them or shooting it out. Neither was likely to be successful. He did not see any possible scenario where he survived a confrontation.

Another option would be to take advantage of his visitors inspecting the pit and trying to escape. Walk away and avoid any confrontation. The problem with that possibility was that the place where he was standing was at least forty miles from anywhere or anyone. He was not confident that even his newly enhanced physique would get him out of the desert alive.

Looking out into the desert away from the vehicles did not provide comfort. Flat and featureless, with no cover to break up a line of sight. Running away was not an option.

Perhaps there was another way.

Karl picked up a rock while pushing himself back into the crevasse and watched on the *oculus* as John approached his hiding place. When it was mere seconds away from John locating him, Karl threw the rock almost straight up and high over John's head. It landed behind the approaching man with a distinctive whump.

John whirled around to the sound.

Karl shifted out of the crevasse and pointed the revolver at John's back, with perhaps only ten feet separating them.

Karl barked, "Drop it."

John spun about again and exclaimed, "What the hell?!"

Seeing the revolver, he began shifting the business end of the rifle towards the old man who just popped out of the ground and was now pointing a gun at him.

Karl pulled the trigger. The hammer dropping made a loud click, followed by nothing.

The sudden movement of Karl's arm and the revolver click startled John, whose own arm jerked reflexively. The sound of the rifle firing was deafening. John had not completed aiming, and his shot did not find its target. The shock wave of the discharge and its heat washed over Karl.

Karl did the only thing left to him. He jerked the trigger again and double-actioned the next round. The revolver kicked, and the sound of another firearm discharge echoed across the desert landscape.

John dropped to one knee, his face registering shock. The rifle slowly shifted to the ground. He fell backward and lay there, gently rolling from side to side.

Karl's hearing returned in a rush. First Voice called out, "John, what are you doing?"

John was apparently in no condition to reply. His initial low moans were now progressing towards more of a gurgle.

Karl saw the path forward in this situation. Striding the few feet separating him from the hunting rifle, he snatched it up from the ground. Then he spun and returned to the berm.

Settling back into the crevasse, he took in his predicament displayed on the *oculus*. The two remaining men had left the pit and were walking toward Karl. Splitting up as they closed in, they circled the berm from opposite sides.

Karl only now realized his dash for the rifle had been out in the open, and the two men coming for him had seen the whole thing. They knew he had John's rifle. They could also see their companion lying on the ground.

Peeking out from his hiding place, Karl could see John was no longer moving.

Moving his eyes back to the *oculus*, it showed him a quickly deteriorating situation. The one with the shotgun – *Phil* – was almost running around the berm. There were only a few more seconds until another armed confrontation ensued. He looked at the hunting rifle in his hands.

This was called a bolt action, I believe. Never seen one up close before.

Recalling the operation from the movies, he grasped the metal rod sticking out the side. It rotated upwards with a metallic clack.

Now pull it back.

Karl was startled as a spent brass cartridge ejected right into his too-close face. It was hot and stung his cheek. Looking down into the open bolt, he saw there were more cartridges.

Convenient.

Being mechanically inclined helped the situation. With one quick motion, he pushed the bolt forward, watching as a single cartridge was fed into the rifle. Snapping the bolt rod down, he concluded another round could be fired. Consulting the *oculus*, he realized Phil would be in view momentarily. His companion, First Voice, was moving much more cautiously though. Karl would not need to face both of them simultaneously.

I can deal with them one at a time.

Their knowledge of his general location precluded a second try of the rock trick. Instead, he considered the angle of the crevasse and a recess in the dirt to give him a view of Phil's approach without giving his opponent much of a view of him.

This would be about probabilities, and he understood probabilities. *We would see each other almost simultaneously, but we would present unequal targets to each other.*

His adversary stepped into view. Another of the men he had asked directions from, Phil had his pump shotgun shouldered and aimed. The two men locked eyes from much too short of a distance for long guns.

The shotgun's barrel bore was cavernous from Karl's viewpoint. Phil was quick, and the roar of his shotgun firing blotted out Karl's hearing for the second time that day. He witnessed a jet of flame from the shotgun's barrel, and the terrain around his head resounded with the impacts of numerous pellets.

His target was so close that he ignored the scope and just eyeballed it up the barrel. The rifle barked in response to his trigger pull. For the briefest instant, he saw the bullet strike Phil mid-chest. Then the rifle butt slammed into his right shoulder. Simultaneously, the bottom edge of the scope impacted Karl's brow, cutting deep.

Phil crumpled to the ground. In spite of the scope cut and a shoulder beginning to pulse in agony, Karl's right hand actuated the bolt. Another spent brass cartridge whirled through the air. Even with ears still recovering from the shotgun and rifle firing, he heard the satisfying *click* of the bolt locking into place.

Another weapon started firing. A glance at the *oculus* told Karl that First Voice was coming up on the crevasse. The rounds fired were evenly spaced. The figure on the display took a step, fired a shot, took another step, and fired another shot.

First Voice knew Karl was close.

But he doesn't know my exact position...

Karl placed the rifle on the edge of the crevasse while remaining wedged deep inside. Holding the rifle with one hand, he worked the controls on the *oculus* with the other.

He focused in on the rifle barrel, changing the viewpoint to place First Voice's approaching image on the other side.

Angling the rifle on the *oculus*, he was able to look straight down the barrel as if it were a riflescope.

When the angle of the bore of the barrel aligned in the middle of his target's chest, Karl pulled the trigger. Without a shoulder to push against, the recoil thrusted the rifle back violently, and he almost lost his grip on it.

First Voice crumpled to the ground in a similar fashion to his companions.

Karl's hearing returned, and he switched the *oculus* back and forth between the prone forms of the men he had just shot. Phil had stopped moving, and the thermal image showed he had passed.

First Voice was still alive, though. Karl cycled the bolt on the rifle, stepped clear of the crevasse, and approached. The man on the ground was struggling to breathe, his hands clutched at his chest as blood flowed out onto the ground. The man's eyes locked with Karl's. The panic and questioning required no words.

The whole situation unfolded so fast. Karl had never considered the consequences. *Should he attempt to save the man's life?*

Karl approached the wounded man. First Voice was still looking at him. Gasping one last gurgling breath, his body shifted to relaxed lifelessness. The last of the highwaymen was dead.

The effects of the adrenaline caught up with his sexagenarian body. He found himself kneeling with the hunting rifle on the ground in front of him.

The heat of the sun and blood running down his face from the scope cut returned his focus. His right shoulder throbbed from the rifle butt strike.

Why does my left shoulder hurt?

Looking at the location of the offending pain, he saw a neat little hole in what passed for the meaty outside of an old man's shoulder.

One of the shotgun pellets? I think they are called buckshot.

It was not bleeding much, but it was painful, and there was no exit hole. The bullet remained inside.

What a mess.

None of this was part of the plan. He was wounded. There was the carnage of three dead bodies on his property. His gold was still in the pit.

Walking back to his truck, he climbed in and cranked up the air conditioning. Not to sleep, but to think and rest—drinking water and thinking.

What to do?

Somewhat refreshed, and with the effects of painkillers he kept in his bag kicking in, a new plan gelled in his mind. Climbing back out of the truck, he got to work.

After a cursory review of the highwaymen's truck, he noted a jerry can. Opening it, the smell of gasoline told him what he needed to know.

That would help.

Karl picked up the highwaymen's weapons and shovel and tossed them into the truck bed. Each body was, in turn, dragged close to their truck.

The goal was to place them in the back, but lifting the corpse of a grown man was not within Karl's physical abilities, before or after the recent changes. He did find he could make platforms or steps from rocks and, in three shorter, easier lifts, move each body into the back of their truck.

More hard work in the afternoon hot desert sun. It continued until the sun was low on the horizon.

Dusk settled in, and the desert was cooling. Grabbing the bag with his reloaded revolver and other sundry supplies, he started up the old pickup with its deceased cargo and drove out into the open desert.

Navigating slowly, he found the terrain impassable in places. The *oculus* did not always register every subtle detail, and several times he had to back up and look for another route.

The *oculus* eventually found what he was looking for: a pit close to ten miles from his property. Parking the highwaymen's truck pointing into the depression on a downward slope, he emptied gasoline from the jerry can onto the corpses and their gear in the truck bed. Releasing the parking brake, he stepped away to watch as gravity did the work, and the pickup rolled into the pit nose first.

One sputtering road flare later, and everything burned.

It was the dead of the night, and he now had a ten-mile hike through the cold, dark desert ahead of him. The starry night provided enough illumination as he trudged over the dusty terrain towards his land.

As he walked, the events of the last hours played out in his mind. Were the three men just checking up on an old man who wandered out into the desert alone? They never did anything hostile prior to his confronting John with a gun. Their carrying firearms into the wilderness could be considered prudent planning and not necessarily an indication of violent intent.

Was it possible the carnage that had just played out and resulted in three deaths was all just a horrible misunderstanding?

By the time he arrived back at his own vehicle, he understood that operating alone had critical disadvantages. Also, he would likely never know if the shooting deaths were justified or not.

Grabbing the shovel from the back of his truck, he trudged to the pit. Time to get his gold and leave this place.

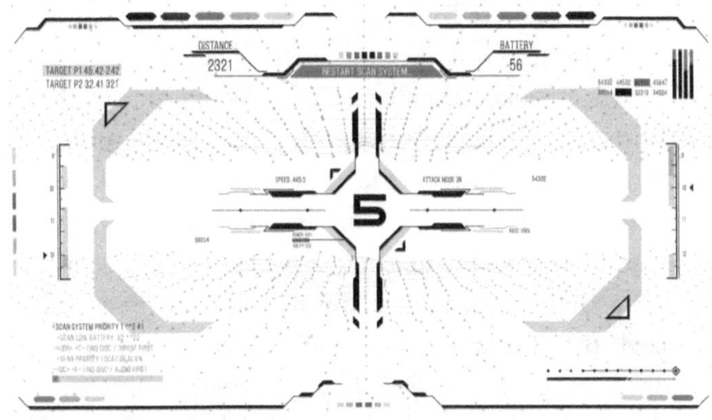

CHAPTER FIVE

The sun broke the horizon as Karl returned to the land of blacktop roads.

His clothes were filthy, both shoulders ached, and the cut on his brow had scabbed over. Whenever he squinted from the sun, though, it pulled and bled.

The next step in the plan—a visit to the assayer's office to cash in the gold—would have to wait. It was early morning and they would not open for several hours. The pause did give him time to visit his motel room. A hot shower and a change of clothes. The emptiness in his stomach reminded him he had not eaten in a full day. Food was in order but it would have to wait.

Parking in front of his motel room, he paused to consider the pile of gold ore lying unguarded in the open bed of the truck. He dismissed his security concerns. To casual observers, it looked like a bunch of rocks someone might use in landscaping, not a fortune in shiny treasure. Regardless, he kept the *oculus* close by and focused on the truck bed. If someone started paying an inappropriate amount of attention, he would be able to intervene.

Standing in front of a mirror told him how bad he looked. Blood from the scope cut had left a reddish-brown vertical stripe on his shirt. His left shoulder had an ugly bruise around the entry hole from the shotgun pellet. This was matched by an equally ugly yellow-black bruise on his right shoulder from the rifle recoil.

None of this was part of the plan.

Feeling around the edges of the bullet hole, he found the hard, round outline of an embedded pellet. He was not a doctor, but he knew the lead projectile must be removed. Fortunately, it was not deep.

Retrieving tweezers from his toiletry kit, he attempted to remove it. Going in through the entry hole and probing for the bullet was eye-wateringly painful. After several failed attempts, he gritted his teeth and made a final push. Dropping the dripping red pellet in the sink, he tried to staunch the freely bleeding wound. His final solution was a woefully inadequate Band-Aid placed over the hole, followed by duct tape to make the whole thing leakproof.

The cut in his brow probably needed stitches. There would be a scar after it healed. Karl did not feel even remotely inclined towards a hospital visit or answering the questions that would inevitably follow.

Not willing to endure what would no doubt be a painful shower with hot water on open wounds, he opted instead for a standing sponge bath. Freshly bathed and wearing clean clothes, his mood improved.

Looking about the disaster that was his motel room bathroom, he was struck by the mess. Blood, dirt, and filthy towels covered much of the sink and floor. He decided that leaving a twenty on the dresser for housekeeping was prudent.

With aching shoulders, he prepared to leave by packing everything into the truck. He would not be returning to the motel. After cashing in the gold and returning the truck to the rental place, he would drive the Camry home.

With everything in the truck and his room key returned, he climbed in and just sat quietly for a few minutes. His improved health and ability to deal with physical challenges were being tested. The last twenty-four hours would have put him in the hospital if not for the change. Breathing deep, he started the truck.

Let's get this done.

Making do with drive-thru food on the way, Karl arrived at the assayer office just as it was scheduled to open. No other businesses were close by. Just off the main road, it was a lone building with an empty parking lot. He tried the main entry and found it locked. Confirming the opening time on the hours sign, he shrugged his shoulders and immediately regretted the act, feeling pain on both sides. He returned to the truck to wait.

A quarter hour later, an SUV with faded gold paint pulled into the lot and parked next to the building. A balding, pale, paunchy man got out and walked to the main entry, unlocked it, and entered.

Karl debarked his aching body from his truck and followed. Inside was a waiting room that took up the front of the building. The rest of the building was a caged-in open space where the assayer worked. This was no chicken wire or cyclone fence barrier designed to keep out children. The bars were thick with welded bracing. Whatever went in there was not coming out without the assayer's permission. His eyes settled on the scale, equally accessible from the waiting room as from inside the caged area.

Considering the size of some of the gold ore in the bed of the truck, a larger scale would probably be needed.

A nameplate sat on the edge of the cage's countertop: *Ernie Goldblatt, Assayer*. Karl read the nameplate twice and decided not to comment.

Karl waited patiently while Ernie worked through his ritual of getting the place ready to start a new day. The windows provided a clear view of the parking lot, and Karl kept an eye on the gold-laden truck.

The assayer, now ready for the day, slid onto a tall stool next to the countertop on the inside of the cage and announced with a joyless, flat expression, "Today's a holiday, and I'm not actually open. Came in to do some paperwork. Saw you in the parking lot and figured if you have something to sell, I'm already here. You do have something to sell, yes? This isn't a waste of my time?"

Karl thought for a moment before asking, "Today is a holiday? Which one?"

Ernie looked at Karl with a raised eyebrow and replied, "Thanksgiving."

Karl signed the form indicating the change of ownership in exchange for a tidy sum.

"Excuse me for a minute. I have to call for this to be picked up. Can't have this much gold in-house." The man shuffled away, showing the strain of the last several hours' physical labor.

With the murmurs of Ernie calling for an armored truck in the background, Karl thought about the government forms he had just filled out. Name, social security number, address of residence—these were all expected. One-quarter of the money for the gold was taken out in taxes ahead of time. The forms also required information on where and how the gold was found. He was not fond of nosy government people minding other people's business.

Ernie returned to the counter ledge, "Everything is in order. You have your receipt copies. The truck is coming, and the government forms are filled out. A cashier's check will be here when we open tomorrow morning. You can stop by any time after to pick it up."

Karl gave the obligatory *thank you,* and with a handful of paper, walked out to the truck. Driving away, he headed to the car rental place to return the F-250. Too bad, really. Driving had always been a purely functional activity, but he found the large truck appealing.

He would have to check back into the motel. One more night, and then he could go back home. The plan had worked. The money from the gold exceeded his requirements. Upon his return, he'd order the needed materials.

In spite of the muscle aches, cuts, and holes in his body, Karl felt satisfaction. The shootout in the desert had been an unfortunate distraction. But in the end, it all worked out.

Night was a strange experience. Being away from his lab and without the ability to sleep, the hours through the dead of the night were long. Karl reviewed his planned work and read a book. It was slow going until the reading pulled him in. His concentration was broken only by the morning light gleaming in through a space in the drapes, prompting a flurry of activity as he prepared to leave.

One final stretch before checking out, and he realized the aches and pains had significantly receded. Not like before the change. Before, the soreness would have lasted for days.

He returned to the assayer an hour after the beginning of business hours. Parking the Camry increased the number of cars in the parking lot to three. One of which was Ernie's.

Looks like another customer first thing.

Halfway to the door, Karl saw the government plates on the third car. Official visit? Probably the government keeping an eye on the place. Who knew what kind of shady practices would happen otherwise?

Entering the waiting area from outside, Karl paused while his eyes adjusted from the bright Arizona sun to the aged fluorescent lighting inside. Ernie was sitting in the cage, reading a paperback book. Sitting in one of the plastic chairs was a man in a gray suit. The man watched as Karl walked over to the cage.

Ernie looked up from his book: "Karl Lark, I have your check, but you have a visitor first." The pale assayer nodded towards the now-standing man in the suit.

Karl turned to face the man who closed the short distance between them and extended his right hand.

"Special Agent Donaldson. I'm with the FBI. Mr. Lark, hopefully you don't mind if I ask some questions regarding your considerable find?"

Karl looked at the agent. This was an unexpected turn of events. "Please proceed."

Agent Donaldson pulled out a notebook and began writing. "Where did you find the gold?"

Karl replied, "On my property while prospecting."

Agent Donaldson nodded. "Where on your property? Could you be more specific?"

Karl frowned and took a breath. "In the ground?"

What a strange question.

Agent Donaldson stopped writing and looked up at Karl. "How long have you been prospecting at this particular location?"

Karl said, "This is my first experience prospecting, so just a few days."

Agent Donaldson kept writing while nodding. "Uh-huh. Mr. Lark, records show you purchased that land a few weeks ago. You are not a resident of Arizona. Is this correct?"

Karl was intrigued now. This FBI agent had been busy doing his research. "That is correct."

The special agent looked up from his notebook again and straight into Karl's eyes. "What inspired you to purchase land here in Arizona and take up prospecting?"

Karl did not even pause after the question. He had figured out his cover story back when the plan was just being formed. "I am recently retired, and read a newspaper article about someone finding a large emerald at a flea market. Seemed like a productive hobby to start."

Agent Donaldson smirked, "For you, it has been productive. What are your plans now?"

Karl was hoping this tedious interview was almost over. "I am returning to my home out of state, and everything is packed in my car."

Agent Donaldson paused for a few moments of awkward silence and then continued, "Mr. Lark, I am going to share my understanding of the situation, and you tell me if I have everything correct. You arrive from out of state. The first thing you do is purchase a piece of inexpensive, remote desert property. Days later, you find millions of dollars in gold on said property. Now, after cashing in the gold, you are packing up and heading back home out of state." Agent Donaldson finished his statement while looking at Karl with a cocked eyebrow.

One of the benefits of experience—or being just old, for that matter—was the understanding that less was more. Karl replied, "Correct."

With a pronounced shrug and a questioning look, Agent Donaldson asked, "Why stop now? If it was so easy to find this gold, who knows how much more is out there?"

Karl deadpanned, "Agent Donaldson, I came here on a whim. I am retired and thought it would be fun to try prospecting for gold. I did it, and I won the lottery. At my age, a few million dollars goes a long way. That, and the desert was hotter than I expected."

Agent Donaldson stated, "Are you aware it is illegal to lie to a federal agent? Is there any part of your story you would like to change?"

Karl shook his head while wondering if it was illegal for a federal agent to lie to an American citizen. "My answers are correct."

"Good. I will be making a report about what we have discussed. Just in case." Agent Donaldson turned to leave.

Karl wondered about that last part of the departing agent's words and asked, "Just in case *what?*"

One faint word could be heard: "Exactly." The door then closed behind the exiting agent.

Karl watched through the glass while Agent Donaldson got in his vehicle and drove away.

That was unexpected.

Ernie broke the silence: "You know, hearing it laid out like that does make it sound fishy. None of my business, though. Here's your cashier's check." The assayer slid an envelope across the counter ledge.

Karl confirmed the contents: "Why was the FBI here?"

Ernie rolled his eyes and replied, "Computers. Someone bringing in that much gold in triggers a visit. Anything over a thousand-dollar payout and an FBI agent shows up. Once I entered your find information into the computer, the FBI was notified."

Karl thanked the man and left.

The meeting with the FBI agent occupied Karl's thoughts during a good part of the long trip home. While driving through the day and following night, he wondered if he had pulled off his moneymaking scheme as scot-free as he had intended.

Regardless, Karl now had more than enough funds to move forward with his plans.

He knew his encounter with the angelic Being changed him physically and mentally. Karl thought about how he had shot those men—and how he had lied to the FBI agent without a second thought—and wondered if the changes included the psychological.

The experience in the desert had also taught him that he needed better security. One man by himself was vulnerable. It would help to have someone, a bodyguard, to protect him. *Where could he find someone truly dedicated to his personal security, and who would keep his secrets?*

Karl had plenty of time during his long drive home to consider all these compelling questions. Some of his conclusions would prove to be just as interesting.

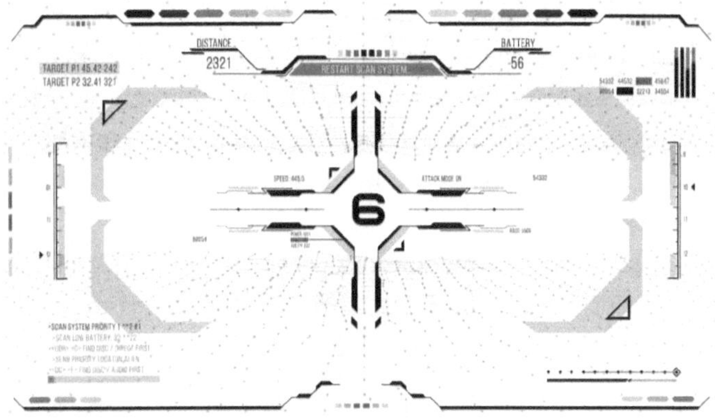

CHAPTER SIX

His return drive home was uneventful. Expected empty silence greeted him after he unlocked the door to his home and entered. The next day, Karl visited his bank to cash the check from his gold find. The bank teller called for a manager when he presented the seven-figure cashier's check for deposit. Karl filled out the required form on the origin of the check and funds. The scrutiny was as exhausting as it was unexpected. Of course, he had never had this kind of money before. The whole point of the plan was to be able to purchase expensive components for his experiments. Karl never would have figured so many people would be interested in where his money originated.

The funds would not be available immediately— he would have to wait several days, possibly even two weeks. Frustrated by the bureaucratic nonsense, he prepared his orders. Many of the items were custom and expensive. Most required a significant deposit. The good news was that the costs for this project were less than the available funds. He had extra money.

The next two weeks were a whirlwind of phone calls and preparing orders, climaxing when the bank called to say the check funds were now available to use.

●　　●　　●　　●　　●

Walking out his front door to place several envelopes in the mailbox before the mailman arrived, Karl witnessed a domestic black sedan pull up to the curb in front of his house. Two men in suits exited and walked towards him. One of them was none other than Agent Donaldson.

Karl waited on his front porch, the two men eyeing him nonchalantly as they approached. Both men had neutral expressions. He wondered if this was perhaps an FBI thing.

Do they practice this?

Agent Donaldson broke the silence: "Good morning, Mr. Lark."

Standing on his porch, Karl was a good two feet higher than the two men. From his superior elevation, he returned the greeting, "Agent Donaldson."

There was a pause while the men regarded each other. Then Agent Donaldson asked, "How have you been enjoying your new-found wealth?"

Karl frowned, "We are over a thousand miles from where we last met. Do you typically travel that kind of distance to inquire about a person's spending habits?"

The second man, whom Karl suspected was also FBI, impatiently shifted on his feet while looking around.

Agent Donaldson smiled and said, "No, Mr. Lark, the agency does not send special agents halfway across the country to check on people's spending habits. I have news about your property. Honestly, I am surprised you returned home after such a large return on your investment. Why not stay and look further? There could be more high-value finds waiting just below the surface."

Karl's frown transitioned to include a furrowed brow. "As I shared previously, Agent Donaldson, as a retiree, I now have enough money for anything I could desire."

Agent Donaldson nodded in acknowledgment and, after a long pause, asked, "Mr. Lark, would it interest you to know that a truck with three bodies all burned almost beyond identification was found only a few miles from your land? Forensics put their deaths and the torching of the vehicle as the same day you cashed in your find."

Both men were now looking at Karl intently.

Karl took a deep breath and said, "You traveled all the way here from Arizona to tell me you found dead bodies near my land?"

Agent Donaldson continued, "Murdered dead bodies, Mr. Lark. They had been shot and then burned. While you were making the biggest gold find in Arizona in more than a decade, not more than a handful of miles away, three men were shot to death and then cremated in their own vehicle."

The second agent spoke now: "Mr. Lark, did you see or interact with any other people on or near your property?"

Karl looked directly at the second presumed agent and replied, "There was no one on my land. There were three men in a pickup truck who gave me directions when I was trying to find the dirt road to my property. Is it possible they could be the men you found?"

Both agents pulled out notebooks. Agent Donaldson continued, "Three men? Could you describe them?"

Karl shared his observations of the men and their vehicle. The agents wrote it all down as he talked.

When he finished, Agent Donaldson asked, "Mr. Lark, would you be willing to come down to our offices for a statement? It could be important in helping to find the killers."

Karl shook his head. "Agent Donaldson, I am more than willing to answer your questions right here. And please feel free to return in the future with more questions. However, I have no interest in sitting in an FBI interrogation room and answering the same questions over and over again."

The agents put away their notebooks. "Mr. Lark, you can be compelled to provide a statement."

Karl responded, "Quite true, and then I would then be compelled to bring a lawyer along."

Agent Donaldson waited in silence for a good long pause and then stated, "We spoke to the cleaning lady who serviced your motel room after you left. What do you think she told us?"

Karl's patience was growing thin; he could feel it. "I left a twenty-dollar tip because of the mess I left. Digging up gold is dirty, and I cut my hands. Most likely, it was quite filthy. I don't recollect the details, as I was focused on getting my gold to the assayer. Does that align with the cleaning person's observations?"

Agent Donaldson smirked, "The housekeeper's assessment of the amount of blood is from more than a few cuts. But who knows?

After a pause, he continued, "I see that cut above your eye has healed nicely. Not even a scar really. Coincidentally, two of the men were shot with a high-powered rifle. That kind of rifle often mounts a scope."

Karl waited patiently while the three men all watched each other in silence.

Agent Donaldson finally nodded and spoke, "Mr. Lark, thank you for your time. If there are more questions, we will contact you." The two men turned to leave.

Karl called after them, "Agent Donaldson, is it possible my not returning to my land prevented me from ending up like those men?"

Agent Donaldson stopped and half-looked back over his shoulder, "Possibly."

Karl stayed on his porch, watching as the men returned to their vehicle and drove away.

●　　●　　●　　●　　●

Frustrated, Karl paused his work for a singular familial responsibility that fell on the same day every year. And today was the day—the week before Christmas. If there was ever a time in the last twenty-plus years he would have consider skipping, it would be today.

However, after an unbroken sequence of so many visits, he was loath to break faith now. Committed, he started up the Camry and mentally prepared for a four-hour drive. Not only did he have to pause for a family responsibility, but he also had to endure an interminably long drive.

Mid-afternoon saw him arriving at the agreed meeting place, a coffee shop. Karl took comfort knowing that at this point, from a time commitment perspective, his obligation was half over. Now for the hard part. Talking to someone.

Walking in, the smell of coffee was strong. He recognized the person he was looking for almost instantly. A man not ten years younger than Karl—with salt-and-pepper hair, and wearing a sports jacket—was thin, and looked like a college professor. Steve Mersen blended in more than stood out.

He was sitting at one of those tiny, wobbly tables. Karl walked towards him, and Steve stood. They shook hands and sat down across from each other.

"Good to see you, Karl. You look well." Steve was smiling.

Karl nodded. "You as well."

Steve continued, "Thank you for making the drive. What is this now? We've been doing this for twenty-two years? Yes, Danielle is twenty-six now. We adopted her not long after her fourth birthday."

Karl agreed, "Correct Steve, you adopted my grandniece twenty-two years ago. And if I may ask, how is Danielle?"

Steve smiled. "You have always been right to the point. Ok. Danielle is doing well. After graduate school, she landed at the FBI. But you already knew that.

"She finished her training six months ago and is working in the FBI's Chicago office as an analyst. Of course, she can't tell us what her work is. But what little she shares sounds interesting.

"Changing subjects real quick: Did you receive that photo of her graduation you asked for last time we met?"

Karl nodded. "Yes, thank you."

Steve tilted his head just slightly. "Your request surprised me. You have never asked for anything before."

Karl said, "Danielle's achievements are notable. The photo is a reminder of that."

The two men sat quietly for a few moments, with Karl then breaking the pause to ask, "Is there a need for money for Danielle's education?"

Steve shook his head in dissent. "Karl, there was never any need for the money. Megan and I are quite comfortable. We only agreed to your so-called scholarship fund as a consideration to you. Danielle's education is paid for.

"I do have a question, though. With Danielle a grown woman embarking on her career, how long will these meetings continue?"

Karl's expression darkened for an instant. "Steve, the agreement to meet annually is written into the adoption papers. It has no sunset clause. Perhaps if she marries and has children, we may alter our agreement. Regardless, for the foreseeable future, we will continue to meet once per year. You still have my phone number for emergencies?"

Steve replied, "Yes, Karl, I still have your phone number. You know, Danielle is an adult now. We could arrange for her to meet her estranged great-uncle. It made sense when she was four and had no family other than you, a confirmed bachelor in his forties. Instead of meeting me once per year, you could just meet with Danielle."

Karl took a breath and exhaled, "Thank you for the offer, but that will be unnecessary, Steve. I must be going now."

Steve paused while looking closely at Karl. "Have you been exercising? You appear healthier. Your color is good. Maybe getting more sun?"

Karl disliked personal questions but endured this one. "Retirement finally arrived. No stress from work, and I have been outside more."

Steve nodded, accepting the plausible explanation.

Karl mused to himself. He couldn't just tell the man he had released…*something* from what appeared to have been an ancient prison, and that whatever it was had changed him into something *more*. While Steve's reaction to such cataclysmic news might have been amusing, it would not be appropriate.

Once the social niceties had been observed, it was time to leave. Karl stood and extended his hand. Steve rose, and they shook hands. Turning, Karl walked out of the coffee shop while Steve watched him leave.

On the drive home, he considered whether a meeting with Danielle would be more efficient than the annual meetings with Steve. From the accounts shared at their meetings over the years, he had learned his grandniece was quite competent. He was happy with this.

Something to think about for the future.

●　　●　　●　　●　　●

Paying for expedited delivery was an added cost, but he did have extra money after all. Packages began arriving daily. Work in his basement continued around the clock. He lost track of time, with daytime and night blurring together. He was finally forced to set an alarm clock to remind him of meals.

While calibrating part of his soon-to-be completed creation, the doorbell in his living room above him chimed. Mentally disconnecting from the task at hand, his eyes came to rest on the clock. It was five minutes to midnight.

Who could be ringing the bell at this time of night?

Breathing deeply, he stood and navigated to the upstairs.

The chime echoed again through the house as he opened the basement door to the kitchen.

There were no lights illuminating the first floor. None were needed as a full moon outside shone a silver glow through the curtained windows. The moonlight and his improved eyesight negated the need to flip a switch. Karl walked confidently through his home to the front door. Before opening the door, he looked out into the night on his front porch.

There was no one there.

His eyes looked lower.

There was a child at the door. Perhaps ten or twelve years old? Karl couldn't be sure. He had no experience with children.

Opening the door, he looked down at the child. He could immediately tell something was wrong. Its clothes were unkempt, piecework creations. Overly long, pale feet without socks or shoes shined to the point of almost luminescing in the moonlight.

The face was that of a boy, or perhaps more boy-like than girl-like. Its angular features lacked symmetry. Karl was finding it difficult to focus on the child's visage, its alienness repellant.

Then there were the eyes.

Perhaps twice the size they should be, and solid black. The boy's face betrayed no emotion or thought. Revulsion roiled Karl'w mind. Something was not right about whatever this thing was.

"Please, sir, may I come in?"

It was a young boy's voice, very high-pitched. At least Karl thought it was a boy's voice. The sound was slippery in his mind. Difficult to tell if he had heard the sound or felt it

Karl's thoughts paused and then restarted. He should not allow this child into his home.

"Please, sir, may I come in?"

Karl closed his eyes and then re-opened them. "Where are you from, child?"

"Please, sir, it is cold." A true statement, as the late-night air was quite chill.

He almost said yes. His uncanny valley reaction was the only thing preventing his compliance with whatever this thing was requesting. Pushing himself to stop, he instead asked, "Where are your parents?"

He looked past the boy's head. There, gleaming in the moonlight, was a black car parked in front of his house.

The tone in the boy's voice changed: "You will not let me in." It was more a statement than a question.

The boy turned and walked away down the porch steps. His gait was uneven and painful to watch.

The black car's passenger door opened, perhaps pushed open from the inside. The boy figure drew close and *shifted* into the car. The door closed, and the car silently drove away. Perhaps an electric car? They might have those now.

Fool forgot to turn on his headlights.

The effects of the encounter rapidly wore off, and Karl closed his front door.

That was odd.

●　　●　　●　　●　　●

The day of Karl's creation's completion arrived. The final pieces were assembled on his basement workbench. It had taken months of planning, no small amount of scheming, and, quite frankly, operating far outside his comfort zone. Acquiring the money alone had been a herculean task.

The device—a contraption of inexplicable and sublime complexity—existed as a concept inspired by the portals he found in Abyssal Park. The changes from that experience had opened his mind to new ideas, and those manifested into reality as the device in front of him. He had tried to write it down. Keeping notes on a project was important. But the words would not come. Finding the language to describe what *it* was had not been possible. The nature and physics of it defied explanation. This was truly an enigma made real.

Karl created his own reference for it, unsure even where the name came from. It was the *ouiblet*. Nothing he had ever done before compared to this singular achievement.

How do I start? What first shall I do?

His reverie was interrupted by the chime of the doorbell. Not an unfamiliar sound these days. The cadence of the regular deliveries of the *ouiblet's* components had been an ongoing source of distraction that he was not going to miss.

Resigning himself to waiting a short while longer to try his creation out, Karl trudged up the stairs to the front door.

He opened it to find his across-the-street neighbor, Red Beard, standing at his door. In the pale man's hands was a brown cardboard box. The midday sun did nothing positive for his visitor's pale pallor.

The man's expression was one of annoyance. "This was delivered to me by accident." He pushes the package toward Karl.

Karl accepted the package and responded, "Thank you."

"Whatever." Red Beard turned and left.

Karl's thoughts coalesced around his neighbor as he watched the heavy-set man amble across his yard.

Just walk on the sidewalk. Really? Some people.

There was something about this man. Something familiar. What was it? The way he carried himself. His attitude. So close, like placing a familiar smell.

Aha! The men in the pickup truck. Red Beard reminded him of his brief encounter with the three men in the pickup truck. Something *different*.

Karl returned to the basement, picked up the *oculus*, and turned it toward Red Beard's house. Scanning the house from top to bottom, he found that one person in the same basement room, exactly as they were the last time. The smaller stature indicated a woman or child. He looked closer, reviewing the room's furnishings. No windows, a closed door, bed, sink, and toilet.

He came to the conclusion that this person might not be a voluntary resident.

In this neighborhood? Why not? Who would come looking here?

If there was something nefarious going on in Red Beard's basement, it was not Karl's problem. However, criminal activity in such close proximity was an existential threat.

What kind of people was his neighbor bringing around?

Karl's internal discussion concluded with the understanding that if something untoward was being conducted by Red Beard, it should be ended. This would remove the uncertainty of his own activities being disturbed.

However, making an anonymous tip without real proof would be malicious and unproductive. Proof was required before any action should be taken.

Karl smiled. What a perfect first test of the just-completed *ouiblet*! Short distance and in familiar territory. He would need a Polaroid camera for photographic proof. Perform the test in the dead of the night. If the person in the room was genuinely trapped there, they would probably be sleeping.

Further scans of Red Beard's residence revealed a Polaroid camera on the ground floor.

Convenient.

The approach appealed to Karl. He would use the *ouiblet* to remove the camera. That was what his new creation did. Or at least what he intended for it to do. Objects, or even people, would leave one place, move instantly somewhere else, and then re-emerge at the intended destination. *Translating*, so to speak, from origination to destination. If it worked as it should, it would be a much more convenient way to move about.

For the test tonight, he would use it to take the camera, and then again to enter the basement room and take a photo. A fraction of a second later, he would return to his basement. It would take only moments. Even if the person was awake, all they would see was a sudden flash from the camera. Then he would be gone.

Preparation for the night's test kept him focused. The *oculus* showed where everything was. The *ouiblet* required a defined origination point and destination point. All locations were relative to the *ouiblet* itself. Transportation was essentially instantaneous.

Then—*poof*—movement from point A to point B.

Karl Lark told himself this was not teleportation. Teleportation deconstructed the object in one place and reconstructed it in another. In the case of human beings, it killed them and then reassembled an exact replica. Whether the golem created was the same person was a theoretical discussion, as teleportation had not been invented yet.

The *ouiblet* shifted things out to somewhere else, moved them some distance elsewhere, and then shifted them back in at the destination. They were *translated* from place to place.

Yes, this would be a truly efficient and elegant way to travel.

A feature Karl found eminently convenient was the lack of energy use. At least in the traditional sense.

Theoretically, there was no limit to the distance of translation. Size was only limited by the device itself. This one could translate cars and probably elephants, but not houses. At least not yet. With modification, bigger objects could be addressed.

Karl felt something. Excitement? A youthful anticipation of what was to come. The brief emotion surprised him. Regardless, he had several hours to wait.

Karl's focus on preparation almost made him miss the midnight deadline for his plan. Realization of the late hour spurred action, and he activated the Polaroid camera coordinates.

The abrupt and silent appearance of the camera on his workbench was of such an instantaneous nature that Karl jerked away and almost fell off his stool.

That was unnatural to the point of being unnerving.

Karl had been expecting something. He knew something was coming. In spite of that, he was still surprised. For the uninitiated, such an experience would be most disturbing. He filed this bit of information away for future use.

Holding the camera with a gloved hand while the other held the control for the *ouiblet*, he was ready. A press of a button would send him to the basement room. Another press of the button would bring him back.

One last look at the *oculus* on the workbench. Red Beard was in bed upstairs. The diminutive figure was in bed in the basement.

Click.

The space just inside the door to his destination was the most open, and that was where Karl appeared. A nightlight plugged into a wall socket provided a faint glow. A sparsely decorated cell, for lack of a better word, greeted his arrival. It was not filthy, per se. It was not clean either. This impression was further reinforced by an unpleasant odor.

Karl aimed the camera at the sleeping figure on the bed. A bright flash lit up the room.

Click.

Karl was standing next to his bench in the basement again.

The camera whirred through its picture-making cycle. The still-developing square popped out and landed on the workbench.

A wave of nausea washed over Karl as the photo came to rest. It passed after almost a minute.

A side effect of the translation?

The image that materialized in the photo conveyed that Red Beard was indeed up to something nefarious.

With proof in hand, he wrote his neighbor's address in black marker on the back of the photo. The nearest police station was within the range of the *oculus*. While sitting in his basement and looking at the *oculus* display, he explored the police station. He found an office with someone in it, presumably a police officer, and waited. Perhaps twenty minutes later, the person got up to leave.

The *ouiblet* translated the photo into the air just above the desk. The *oculus* screen showed it floating down the bit of space to land in the middle of the surface.

While waiting for the office resident to return, he translated the Polaroid camera back to its spot in Red Beard's home.

Karl continued watching on the *oculus*. The wait was short, and the figure returned to the office and sat in the chair at the desk. The body language change was noticeable, even on the monochromatic, two-dimensional *oculus* display. The photo was picked up by the figure, who then stood and briskly walked from the room.

Karl nodded to himself. His work was done here.

Having eliminated Red Beard from his list of things to be concerned about, Karl shut down the *oculus* and moved his attention to his next task.

Perhaps an hour later, his concentration was broken by flickers of light. The narrow windows high up on the basement walls had been painted opaque black a long time ago. Regardless, pinholes and tiny scratches in the paint let in enough light for him to know whether it was night or day. Now, in the dead of night, they let him know there were flashing blue and red lights outside.

A trip to his living room revealed the scene on the road in front of his house. Numerous police cars, an ambulance, and a fire truck were parked in Red Beard's driveway and in both lanes of the street. Strobe lights turned the night into a pulsing multicolor version of the day.

A figure, presumably the person from the basement, was on a gurney being rolled from the house to an ambulance. There was no sign of Red Beard. Perhaps the authorities had already removed him? Neighbors, some of whom Karl had not seen in years, were out in the chilly night air in various states of sleepwear. He had no time for gawking and returned to the basement, hoping the disruption to the neighborhood would end soon.

Karl continued working through the night. The breaking of dawn's light washed away the strobe lights. Glad to be free of the distraction, he resumed his total focus on his work.

The doorbell ringing broke his reverie. He looked up from his work.

Karl wondered: *Time, what was the time?*

It was noon.

Taking a deep breath, he paused. These doorbell interruptions were beyond the pale. Perhaps disconnecting the button was in order. Regardless, he stood up and began the trek to the front door.

Looking through the front door window, he saw a uniformed police officer and a second man in a sports jacket. Guessing the sports jacket man was a police detective like in the movies, Karl opened the door.

He asked, "May I help you?"

Sports jacket spoke, "Good morning, sir. I am Detective Johannson, and this is Officer Belar. I am sure you are aware of the disturbance in your neighborhood last night. One of your neighbors was taken into custody."

Karl could see the detective was as much observing him as sharing details about last night's events.

Karl decided to play along. "Why was he taken into custody?"

Detective Johannson frowned. "I can't get into specifics until he's formally charged."

The detective continued, "We're going door to door in your neighborhood to raise awareness and ask a few questions. Anything you can tell us about Chester Bogart?"

Karl blinked. "Chester who?"

The detective clarified, "From across the street. Red-bearded fellow."

Karl said, "Oh, I only met him once. A few days ago, a package I was expecting was delivered to him by mistake. He brought it over."

Detective Johannson was now taking notes. "He didn't talk to you about anything?"

Karl shook his head, "No, he seemed more annoyed than anything else."

Looking up from his notebook, the detective asked, "Have you ever seen regular visitors to your neighbor? A particular vehicle showing up more than once?"

This question made Karl think for a moment before responding, "Visitors? No, I have not. The only thing I know about him is that he is the newest resident in the neighborhood."

Detective Johannson, nodded. "If you think of anything else, please call. Here's my card. Thank you for your time."

Karl took the card and watched the two police officers turn to leave.

Karl said, "What prompted the arrest?"

The detective kept walking while half-turning his head to reply, "Anonymous tip."

When the pair got to the sidewalk, they turned right, apparently going to the next house.

Closing the door, Karl was pleased that the potential problem of such a criminal in the neighborhood was now solved.

The rest of the day was spent testing a new use for his inventions. The *oculus* could be set to take an image after being translated somewhere by the *ouiblet*. And then returned. The process was almost instantaneous. After creating a second, spherical *oculus*, Karl found he could translate it to a location for an instant, where it then took a snapshot scanning 360 degrees. The tiniest fraction of a second later, it was translated back. The captured image uploaded automatically to the *oculus* display.

On a whim, he calculated the *ouiblet* settings and materialized the *oculus* for an instant at an altitude of one thousand feet above Fort Knox. The image told him something he had suspected for a long time: the nation's gold depository was empty.

His inventions, in combination, were the perfect tools to find answers to so many questions.

The ringing doorbell broke his concentration.

Really? What now?

A quick glance confirmed that night had fallen. What was the time? Was it night already?

Walking to the front door, Karl didn't bother looking out the window before unlocking and opening it. He'd had enough visitors and interruptions for one day. Whoever they were, they would have to come back another time.

Standing on the porch was a tall, pale-skinned man dressed in a void-black suit. The visitor wore a black fedora and black gloves. The effect made it appear that the man's pale face was floating like a detached orb in the dark of the night.

Black suit, black fedora, black gloves, and pale skin.

What was he…or it?

Karl experienced a jolt of apprehension and stared. The man was just not *natural*.

The man stared back at him from underneath the hat and in a calm, slow monotone said, "Mr. Lark, may I come in?"

"Come in." The words came out in a monotone response. Without Karl even considering if it was what he wanted. Compulsion and feelings of anxiety pushed him.

The man stepped in past Karl, almost pushing his way in. Walking into the living room, the dark visitor picked a spot on the sofa and sat down.

Karl closed the door and took a seat in a comfortable chair opposite his unplanned and unwanted guest. The realization that he was unarmed did not help the situation.

His face expressionless, the man spoke, "Mr. Lark, I have come to ask you questions."

This was the second time the man had spoken his name. He was sure he never said his name to the dark figure on his couch. Actually, he was certain he had not shared his name.

"Questions?" asked Karl.

There was a long pause. Karl started to feel annoyed and decided to wait the man out with silence.

"Where was the original source of the gold you claimed you found on your newly purchased property? Where did the gold come from?" asked the man.

Waves of anxiety washed over Karl. He felt a compulsion to give the stranger what he wanted. It was stronger than when the man asked to enter his home.

Just like in the place where he freed the glowing white Being. He was being pushed and compelled. Except this time, he did not want to do what was being asked.

This knowledge helped him win the internal struggle, and he countered, "You know my name. Please tell me yours."

The man in black stared at Karl.

The man repeated himself, "The source of the gold?"

The compulsion pressure increased in strength. Karl closed his eyes and opened them to find himself hugging his arms around his chest. Silence ensued while he fought to control the raging anxiety.

The pressure subsided.

The man in black asked, "Your recent purchase of exotic materials. Your sale of the gold financed the purchases. Where did the gold come from?" The man's tone of voice was stronger, more forceful.

Karl decided he had no intention of giving this man anything. Sitting quietly, he waited out the situation.

The man said, "We know who you are."

The spell, or whatever this compulsion was, broke. Karl snarled, "That is a statement of the obvious."

Another long, uncomfortable pause followed.

The same monotone voice, "You will be questioned again."

Karl got the hint. They were asking nicely now. The next time would not be as nice.

Karl nodded. "I will cross that bridge when I come to it."

The visitor stood and walked to the door. He stopped and waited for Karl to open it for him. The man walked out the door and down the stairs to a waiting black car, not unlike the one from the strange child with the solid black eyes from a few days ago.

Watching the car drive away, he came to the realization that others knew who he was and that he was up to something. This had never occurred to him—someone caring about his activities. The pale man in black's visit made it pretty obvious *someone* was paying attention.

And they were likely coming back soon.

The visit left him feeling vulnerable in his own home. Returning to the basement, he consulted the *oculus*. There was nothing nearby out of the ordinary. No box trucks filled with assault-rifle-wielding government agents ready to charge in and take his inventions.

Regardless, he needed to improve his current level of security. And he had an idea of how to start. *Oculus* in hand, he scanned at its limit and found what he was looking for: an underground formation of granite. The *ouiblet* scooped out a perfect sphere of rock and dropped it over five hundred miles away into the Atlantic Ocean.

The *ouiblet* translated itself inside that spherical void, deep underground, with hundreds of feet of solid rock in every direction.

It is safe now.

The control in his hand, in combination with the *oculus*, was all that was needed.

It is time to leave.

The thought formed in his mind, and Karl knew it was true. He couldn't stay in his home anymore. He had to disappear.

Karl grabbed a backpack he used for library visits and light shopping. Moving through his house in a whirlwind of activity, he stuffed everything of immediate use into it: his father's revolver, clothes, and all the cash in the house.

In the basement, he used the *ouiblet* to disappear his tools, notebooks, and equipment to the *ouiblet* void for safekeeping.

The sensation of impending doom was increasing. Faster, faster—he needed to leave soon.

Standing in his living room, he reviewed his work. Everything had either been moved to the void or placed into the backpack he was currently carrying. Confident that he had achieved his goal and could leave, his eyes landed on the photos on the mantel. The backpack was crammed full, almost to bursting. Regardless, he took the silver-framed photo of the college graduate Danielle and crammed it in.

He had everything now and was ready to leave. Karl had never been sentimental, but this house had been his home for over sixty years. Where was he to go?

Standing in the middle of his living room, he considered the photo of his brother and himself in the pavilion at a park not far from where he was standing—a pause that almost cost Karl Lark everything.

The lights in the room flickered, dimmed, and then went out.

Someone or something was coming right now.

Karl slung his bag over his shoulder in the darkness. His right hand went to his pocket for the *ouiblet* control.

Something felt wrong. The connection between his mind and his body was slowing, leaving him feeling disconnected. It took more mental effort to get his hand to pull the *ouiblet* control from his pocket.

Everything was slow now. Even in the darkness, he perceived his vision going gray around the edges.

He grasped the control while his legs folded up under him. With one last effort, he fumbled while activating the *ouiblet* as his backside contacted the floor. The last image in his mind was the pavilion in the photo his parents took him to as a child. So long ago.

Click.

Everything was black. Karl endured the weird sensation of consciousness returning, combined with the translation nausea. Having not truly slept in months amplified the sensation. Unconsciousness had been a stranger for a long time now. He opened his eyes to see the rafters on the underside of the pavilion's roof. The freezing hardwood floor was ice cold on his back. The translation must have just triggered as he slipped into unconsciousness.

Whatever had knocked out the lights in his basement had also rendered him paralyzed and then unconscious.

What a diabolical tool for taking someone captive.

By the time the victim knew what was happening, it would be too late. Perhaps the augmentation from the angelic encounter gave him just enough resistance to escape? He might never know for certain.

Karl filed away in his mind the need to figure out what just happened. The ability to disable someone in such a stealthy way would be eminently useful.

The *ouiblet* control was in one hand, and the backpack was next to him. As far as escapes went, this one would not be in the record books. Technically, he was less than a mile from home. A home he could now never return to.

Standing, he consulted the *oculus* and adjusted the *ouiblet* controls.

Time to find a new home. Considering the unique circumstances of his relocation, calling it a lair might be in order. Perhaps a volcano? Or a mountain peak? The Paris catacombs? *So many choices.*

None of these were secure enough. He needed real security for his work. There had to be another of those portals like the angelic Being had been in. One that was unoccupied and more hospitable.

Time for a new plan. Establish his lair.

And then get a bodyguard.

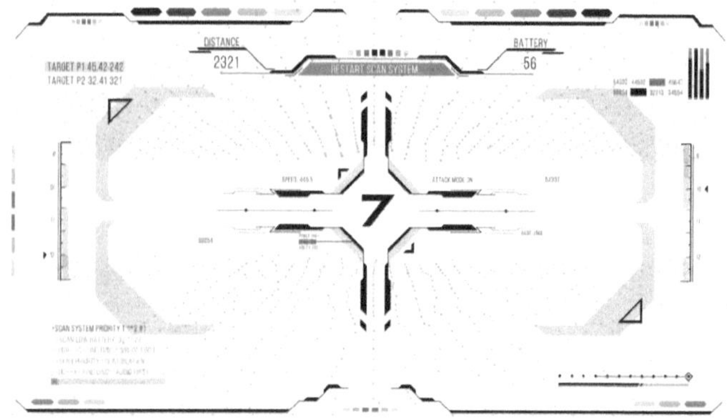

CHAPTER SEVEN

Karl Lark sat on a newly acquired stool next to a tabletop workbench. On it was the pistol grip *oculus*. It occurred to him that he was staring into space. There was no clock on the wall in this place, and he had no idea how long he had been this way.

The last twenty-four hours had been a bit much. Sitting there, he took stock of his life and the events leading to that moment. Frankly, it had been a lot of chaos. He had lost his job of almost forty years. His invention of the *oculus* had been a resounding success. With it, he had discovered some sort of creature and those peculiar portal hideaways.

That led to an encounter with another alien being and its effects on him personally. Then there was the Arizona adventure and the creation of the *ouiblet*. Using the *oculus* and *ouiblet*, he had ended his neighbor's abuse of another human being.

Apparently, his efforts had drawn the attention of someone or something else. Hence the child with the black eyes and the man in black. Then came the attempt to take him prisoner, which he barely managed to escape.

Taking a deep breath, he realized it has all been a bit much. This was not at all what he had expected in retirement.

Which brought him to today. Shrugging, he decided not to dwell on the past. There were new plans to make, and there was more out there to see and do.

Involuntary homelessness prompted the need to locate a new residence. A task completed in short order with the *oculus* and *ouiblet*. Finding another portal and its associated extra-dimensional chamber was child's play now. He was starting to believe these things were not rare but perhaps, instead, relatively common. The first one he located was just an empty shell. Taking advantage of his good fortune, Karl promptly moved in.

A simple chamber, uncomplicated, completely secret, and inaccessible. Looking about his new demesne, he catalogued the equipment he had brought here from the chamber where the *ouiblet* was stored. Everything important to continuing his work had been saved from his home and was now present.

After finding his new hiding place, he had scanned a thrift store with the *oculus*. Its warehouse had everything he needed without any workers or cameras to witness the disappearance of inventory. He'd put more than enough money in an envelope and wrote "donation" on it. One quick translation later, and this consideration was waiting in the thrift store's mail box. He might be taking things without permission, but he refused to outright steal anything.

With a bit of work, his new furniture items had been arranged in his new lab. Feeling more complete having his laboratory reassembled, Karl identified a problem. There was no power. The extra-dimensional secret space he now resided in did not have outlets.

Powering everything would be complicated. Running a generator was out of the question in such an enclosed space. It would have to be batteries. Charge them elsewhere and use the *ouiblet* to swap them in and out. With the right equipment, this challenge could be solved in short order. For now, he made do with flashlights.

All of these activities ended with Karl where he was now. In an extra-dimensional room illuminated by a battery-powered LED camping light, he sat on a stool, considering his recent past and planning his future.

Mentally, he shifted to the next task at hand—the acquisition of a bodyguard. And not just finding one, but the care and upkeep of one too. He had never even owned a pet, much less the responsibility of another person's needs. This was one of the reasons he had given his grandniece up for adoption.

He realized that if he engaged a bodyguard, they would need to sleep. Whoever he found to be responsible for his personal safety would be a normal human being. With normal human sleep patterns.

The sleeping part would be a challenge. For starters, one of the things missing from his new lair was a bed. Karl guessed that the bodyguard would most likely be a male, and he would need one. *Perhaps this person should select their own bed?* This was the downside to working with other people: the injection of the mundane into everyday life.

Karl shifted on the stool and could feel how it was different. Having spent so many hours in his basement lab, his place for sitting at the workbench was familiar. This new stool was not the same. It struck him as odd that he would be attached to something so trivial as the thing he sat upon.

This led him to consider another option: translating many of his possessions from his abandoned home was possible. He quickly dismissed the thought. The unknowns of who had tried to render him unconscious, combined with having no understanding of how it was done, ended this line of reasoning. His long-time residence was off-limits for now. There were simply too many undefined variables.

Karl returned to the bodyguard question. The logic behind selecting a bodyguard was as relentless as it was ruthless. Recent experiences dictated the requirement. However, simply hiring someone was not the correct approach. He needed someone dedicated and not just collecting a paycheck.

Having no living relations, other than his grandniece, eliminated the family option so popular in certain circles. The few acquaintances he had from his former employer provided no acceptable candidates. No part of his life experience included any bodyguard types.

Time passed as Karl put a great deal of thought into this. In a moment of insight, the solution revealed itself. *What about someone in prison?* Not your typical thug criminal, but someone who probably should not be in prison. Use the *ouiblet* to rescue them on the condition they be his bodyguard. For the right person, under the right circumstances, it might work. They could not run away because being caught as an escaped prisoner would send them back to prison. The arrangement would be mutually beneficial. He would get protection, they would get freedom. Maybe not *total* freedom, but something considerably better than they'd had in prison.

If the prisoner stayed with Karl, both of them being transported by *ouiblet*, they would never risk being caught. Should his prisoner bodyguard decide to pursue other interests, life would be very difficult without the anonymity of translation. And if they were ever taken into custody again, the authorities would never believe a story about traveling with an old man by disappearing in one place and reappearing in another. His secrets would remain his. At least, that was the theory.

Perhaps it would be important that this person be someone the authorities were motivated to keep incarcerated, perhaps more so than the average common criminal.

He decided connecting to the World Wide Web was in order. More information was needed to make a decision. Never a fan of the Internet, but he did find it useful at times.

Standing up, he gathered the *oculus* and *ouiblet* control. Less than an hour later, he was booting up a laptop in a cash-only motel room.

Searches of people in prison did not improve his opinion of humanity. Finding someone who met his requirements was proving difficult. The candidate had to be sufficiently intelligent enough to fully understand the situation. Karl suspected anyone accompanying him on his adventures might find the experience mentally taxing at times.

Then came the second epiphany: shifting his search to Ft. Leavenworth, the federal prison for the US military. Karl found many very bad people there. A large population that took more time to review than he would have liked.

All that effort only to find none of them met his criteria.

Except one. There was this one—Illych Popovich.

Why was that name familiar?

A Green Beret serving a twenty-year sentence. While on tour in Afghanistan, Popovich had killed an Afghan army officer who had a thing for boys. The officer's perverse attentions had eventually led to the death of one of the boys. The man had laughed about the situation while in Popovich's presence. This led to an altercation. Words were said, and Popovich's personal moral code had driven his unfortunate next actions. One quick movement later, and the Afghani officer was dead.

The situation had exploded into a diplomatic and political nightmare for the United States. A swift court martial followed. Popovich had been quickly convicted and sentenced to twenty years in Leavenworth.

Popovich's rank had been Master Sergeant prior to the court martial. To date, he had already served two years of his sentence.

His skill set and experience made him a likely candidate. His moral convictions and willingness to take action and suffer the consequences indicated his word was likely good. As long as he did not inject his impulsive do-gooderism into Karl's efforts. That would be unacceptable.

All of the above—combined with the fact that the sergeant was still looking at eighteen more years in prison and would be considered a high-profile escapee—made Illych Popovich almost ideal for what Karl was considering.

The *ouiblet* and *oculus* made short work of locating Mr. Popovich. Karl repeatedly translated the *oculus* near the prison. Taking a snapshot, like a single picture, and then translating it back for review.

Having located Popovich's cell, Karl settled in for a period of observation. He found his bodyguard candidate being held in isolation, apparently only being allowed outside for one hour of exercise per day.

Locked in a single room with no camera. Convenient.

He considered translating a letter into Popovich's cell detailing the offer. The possibility of leaving physical evidence of his intentions quickly ended that line of reasoning.

It should be in person. Face-to-face. Both parties must meet.

Karl decided on first contact at midnight.

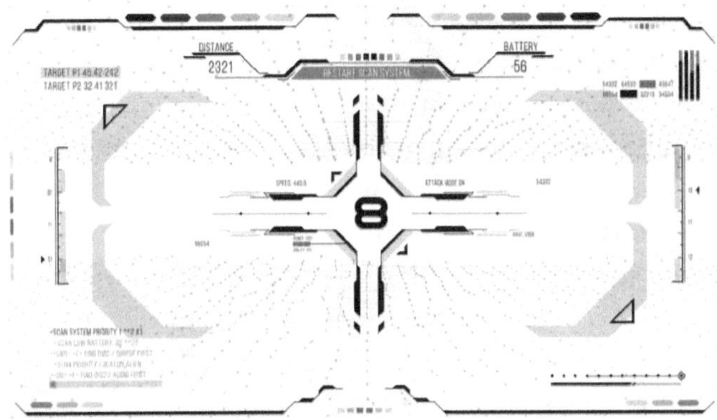

CHAPTER EIGHT

Karl translated into a corner of the cell near the door. His right hand held the *ouiblet* control to translate him out of the cell in an instant if needed.

The cell was the size of a small bedroom. There was only a single window, too small to escape through, barred and set high on one wall. The room was lit by a faint light shining in from the prison's yard lights. There was a small window in the solid iron cell door, covered from outside. This place was a concrete and steel box from which there could be no escape.

Karl observed Popovich's horizontal sleeping form.

Unsure how to start the discussion, he did not think going over and shaking the man's arm was a good idea. How do you wake up such a man, alone in a prison cell?

In the end, Karl did not need to do anything.

"How'd you get in here without waking me?" Popovich's body had shown no sign of alertness prior to his speaking.

Karl considered he should have contrived an opening statement beforehand. How should one start this conversation?

"How long have you been standing there?" inquired Popovich.

Karl replied, "I just arrived."

Popovich swung his feet off the bed and, in one swift motion, stood up. He was tall. Over six feet and towered over Karl.

Looking down on the much smaller Karl Lark, he asked, "Well?"

Somewhat taken aback by the Green Beret's impressive physical presence, he paused briefly before answering, "I am here to propose an opportunity for employment."

Popovich looked Karl up and down before shaking his head. "You don't look like one of the prison staff."

Karl said, "I am most assuredly not a prison employee."

Popovich talked while stretching, "CIA then? Here to offer me employment outside the prison? I was wondering when they'd get around to me."

Karl took a breath before replying, "You misunderstand. I am not here in any official or unofficial government capacity. This is a private party offer."

Popovich started to pace back and forth by his bed. "Private party, huh? How much did it cost you to get in here? That had to be expensive."

Karl continued, "Nobody in the prison is aware of my presence."

Popovich stopped and looked directly at Karl. "So, you're just some old guy who broke into a federal maximum security prison to offer little ole me a job?"

Karl nodded. "Precisely. To reiterate, I have a job opportunity that is likely a good fit for your unique skill set. Are you interested?"

Popovich chuckled and replied "You're going to have to get me out of this place first. Maybe you snuck in somehow, but I'm guessing the two of us aren't just going to walk out of here."

Karl flatly responded, "Removing you from this place is a mere formality."

Popovich's tone took on a comical edge: "Really? This is a fortress, and I'm in isolation. There are at least six locked doors between me and the outside."

Karl said, "*How* is not your concern. What I am in need of is someone to provide personal security for me during my endeavors. There was a recent incident demonstrating this as a pressing requirement."

Popovich yawned. The situation was so surreal that he was beginning to wonder if he was dreaming. "A bodyguard? Not really one of my skill sets."

After a pause, he continued, "Why me? Security can be hired."

Karl replied, "Anything can be purchased except a genuine desire to look out for my safety. I have the idea that removing eighteen years of living in this cage may have value to you."

Popovich nodded and exhaled, "I'd give just about anything to get out of here."

"The motivation that caused your incarceration shows you to be a moral man. A man who is unlikely to double-cross me as soon as my back is turned," continued Karl.

Popovich did not reply immediately. Instead, he smirked at Karl and said, "At least you hope so."

"I am offering to break you out of prison, not get you a pardon. In exchange for your freedom, you will provide me with private security as needed." Karl paused for questions. Popovich still did not respond and stood there quietly.

"You will stay out of trouble and maintain a low profile, and we both get what we want."

"What about friends and family?" asked Popovich.

Karl frowned. "What do you think? The only way this will work is if you disappear from this cell forever and no one knows what happened. Contact anyone, and you will probably end up back here. As soon as you disappear, everyone suspected of knowing you will fall under surveillance. One wrong phone call, and they will find you."

Another long pause followed. Popovich was obviously working through the scenario Karl had presented.

"Time is pressing, Illych Popovich, and I have things to do. I will need your decision now."

"Will any part of this working for you at least be interesting?" asked Popovich.

"We are going to do some very interesting things together, Mr. Popovich. Very interesting things indeed," Karl said, smiling now. A big, toothy, ear-to-ear, Cheshire cat grin.

The Green Beret found the grin a bit creepy, but what should he expect from some old guy who had appeared as if by magic in his cell in the dead of the night? "Never call me Mr. Popovich. Call me Illych."

Karl nodded while Illych continued, "I won't hurt people for fun, sell heroin to children, or anything like that."

Karl's voice went up an octave: "We will not be doing anything of the sort. Based on my experience, if you end up committing violence, it will be for reasons most would approve of."

The two men stood staring at each other in the deathly quiet cell.

Karl asked, "Your answer?"

Illych nodded in the affirmative. "I'm all yours."

And then there was only an empty cell.

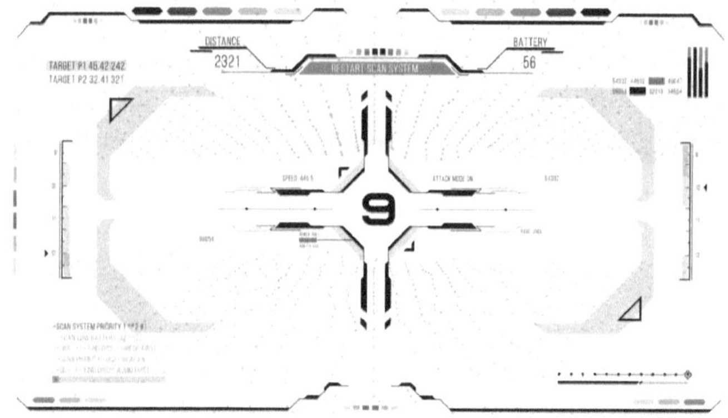

CHAPTER NINE

Instantaneously arriving back at the lair, Illych and Karl stood arms-length apart and were able to look at each other for the first time in a well-lit environment.

Illych saw a white-haired old man five-feet-nine inches or less in height. Slight of build and neatly, if unimaginatively, dressed. Not all that different from a college professor nearing retirement. Above Karl Lark's right eye was the half-moon scar of a riflescope cut. Illych smirked; he would recognize that mark anywhere. After two years in a military prison, he acknowledged that the person he was looking at was not the kind of person he was used to spending time with.

Karl was looking at a dark-haired, athletic man over six-feet tall with an imposing physical presence. Maybe six-two? Dark eyes bright with intelligence and dressed in an orange prison jumpsuit.

Clothes. He would need clothes in addition to a bed. What else would be needed?

Illych went down on one knee. "I don't feel right."

Karl watched with fascination and stated, "That is the translation nausea. It will pass in a moment."

In a shaky voice, Illych asked, "*Translation*? Is that how we just appeared here? What is that? I think I'm going to be sick." The former Green Beret shifted from one knee to all fours.

"The nausea will pass. Though, to be honest, it appears to affect you worse than it does me." Karl had never considered what translation would do to someone . . . normal.

Illych's suffering ended abruptly in less than a minute. Standing up, he asked, "Do you do this translation thing often? Because that'll take some getting used to."

Karl did not answer while continuing to observe his new . . . *colleague?*

Illych turned his head from side to side, taking in his surroundings. "Is this your basement?"

Karl said, "No, it is not. We are in an extra-dimensional space I use as a safe house. I call it the *lair*."

Illych observed the neatly organized equipment on the workbench: "The *lair*, huh? That's very supervillain-sounding."

The two men went back to looking at each other.

Illych spoke first: "Who are you?"

Karl replied, "My name is Karl Lark. I created a machine that moves people and things instantly, anywhere. Someone tried to capture me, and I was forced to leave my home. Now I am living here."

Illych nodded. "This is where your need for a bodyguard comes from? Someone tried to take you prisoner?"

Nodding in the affirmative, Karl said, "There have been some close calls. I have come to realize that working alone has disadvantages."

Illych looked around the chamber that was the lair again. "You live here?"

Karl nodded and replied, "Yes."

Illych took a breath and exhaled, "Look, Karl, I can see you are an eccentric guy, and I'm on board with the bodyguard thing. It gets me out of that cage." He pointed to the floor with his right hand. "But I'm not living here in this cave with you.

"And I'll need clothes. Bodyguards have weapons. Do you have any firearms in this lair of yours?"

Karl responded, "There are aspects of involving another person I had not considered. Perhaps as our first activity together, we should acquire more funding. Do you have suggestions as to how we do that?"

Illych blinked and said, "You have a machine that can move anything anywhere, and you aren't sure how to get money? My suggestion is to take it from a bank."

Karl shook his head. "I am not comfortable stealing. We must either sell something, find the funds, or earn them. Since neither of us has a legitimate identity, publicly selling things is not an option."

Illych ran his hands through his hair. "You're not comfortable stealing? You just broke me out of federal prison." He was starting to wonder if the old guy was all right in the head.

Karl asked, "What about drug dealers or criminals? We could take their money. I am not averse to taking from ill-gotten gains, as it were."

Illych decided *eccentric* was the right word choice. *Who says* ill-gotten?

Growing more comfortable with the surreal nature of the discussion, Illych said, "You want to take money from people who are criminals instead of just lifting it from a bank? Karl, one of those options is largely risk-free, and the other is more dangerous. Also, finding a bank full of money is easy. There will be a large sign out front that says "*Bank*." How do we find drug dealers and their cash?"

Karl sort of smiled and replied, "I have another device I call the *oculus*. It's like an x-ray machine. If we go to a place where drug dealers can be found, it can scan for money. Then the translation machine will remove it."

Illych smiled at this. "We're going looking for drug dealers to rob. Criminals, who are likely armed while we're not. What could go wrong?"

Karl frowned. "There is no need for sarcasm. You are not even an hour out of prison. Let's focus on achieving goals instead."

Illych looked around and found a wooden stool. Walking over, he took a seat. "Could this translation thing be used to steal guns *and* money?"

Karl's head tilted almost imperceptibly, "Of course."

Illych smiled and clapped his hands together. "Then I suggest we steal both. Where should we begin our criminal enterprise?"

Karl blinked from the sudden handclap but continued, "From what I have read in the newspaper, there is a significant amount of criminal activity on the south side of Chicago. We can start there."

Illych shrugged. "Go big or go home?"

Karl now looked confused. "I do not understand."

Illych replied, "Chicago is a big organized crime town. We're starting at the top, so to speak."

Karl walked to a workbench and pointed to a basketball-sized, spherical metallic device. "This is the version of the *oculus* I translate to a place so I can observe without having to go there myself. It shifts into the location, takes a picture of what it has been set for, and then it returns. What it records while there can then be viewed on the handheld version of the *oculus*.

"Modern money has what are essentially radio markers woven into it. The *oculus* is set to locate them." Karl worked the controls on the hand-held *oculus*. "Done."

"And then we send it out."

The spherical *oculus* on the workbench flickered like a light bulb in an electrical storm.

Illych said, "That's it? Did it do it?"

"Yes, the process only takes a fraction of a second."

Karl held up the handheld *oculus* and made some adjustments. The screen was covered in points of light, not unlike the stars in the night sky. "As you can see, there is a significant amount of cash to be found in the Chicago area. I will adjust the gain until we only see large concentrations."

Points of light on the screen dimmed and disappeared. There were still many, many choices remaining.

Illych asked, "Now you pick one and translate it here?"

Karl shook his head and answered, "Of course not. This does not tell us which one is a bank or a retiree's life savings stuffed in their mattress. There is more work to make sure the money we steal is legitimate criminal cash."

Legitimate criminal cash? Illych rolled his eyes.

Karl continued, "To do that, we must translate to Chicago and visually confirm."

Illych wondered out loud, "Uh, Mr. Lark, that might not be safe. The two of us on the south side of Chicago? Me in a bright orange jumpsuit that says "Ft. Leavenworth" on the back, and neither of us armed?"

Karl said, "You misunderstand. We will not be knocking on the front door and requesting they turn over their illegally obtained funds. Instead, we'll translate nearby—perhaps onto a rooftop or some other isolated space—and use proximity to make a better determination."

Illych was starting to wonder how this was going to end.

Karl was working the *oculus* controls and scrolling through different options. "There, that is a likely target. And here is a nearby building that used to have a water tower, but the tank was removed, leaving a platform on stilts."

Illych asked, "When are we going to do this?"

Karl did not look up from the *oculus* screen as he ambidextrously worked its controls and the *ouiblet's* simultaneously.

"Right now." And everything went black.

●　　●　　●　　●　　●

It was dark and cold. Well below freezing. The view, however, was magnificent. Illych took in the nighttime

Chicago skyline for a brief moment before the nausea hit. Knowing it was coming, he was better prepared this time and remained standing.

The platform they were on was indeed high up on top of a tall building, and everything around them was easily observed. It was the dead of winter. The ground and roads in all directions were covered in snow, and the few visible trees were barren. Desiccated brown weeds poking from snowdrifts in an empty blacktop parking lot led to the conclusion they were atop a long-abandoned industrial building.

Across the street to the south were single-family homes and apartment buildings. More than a few had Christmas decorations up. Nothing ostentatious, just lights in a window or around a door.

Karl adjusted the *oculus* controls, waiting for Illych's nausea to end. Relief was short in coming, and Illych relaxed while filling his lungs with cold winter air.

Illych picked out the telltale trash and general run-down appearance and remarked, "This is what they call a 'not-nice neighborhood.'"

Karl pointed at one of the run-down properties. "That one."

Illych shrugged, "It's not a bank. And that's a nice Mercedes out front. It's safe to say there is no little old lady inside with a mattress stuffed full of money."

Karl nodded. "Much of the money is spread out on a horizontal surface in a haphazard way. Translating that would be difficult. However, there is what appears to be a duffel bag full of cash in a closet. I can translate it to us, and we can take a look."

Seconds later, a neon blue duffel bag appeared on the platform. Illych pulled the zipper open. Inside were rubber-banded stacks of cash, plastic-wrapped packages of white powder, and three handguns. He checked each weapon. They were loaded.

Karl wrinkled his nose at the drugs. "We can leave the drugs. Take the guns and the cash. I will translate what is left back."

Illych scooped up the cash and guns in his arms and watched the duffel bag disappear.

Looking at the loot in his arms, Illych smiled and looked at Karl. "Merry Christmas, Karl. This is my second Christmas gift so far today."

Karl looked up from the *oculus* and cocked his head. "Is it Christmas day?"

Illych nodded. "Yes, December 25th is today."

Karl shrugged and returned his attention to the *oculus* screen. "I had not realized."

Taking another deep breath of freezing air, Illych realized he was on the verge of shivering. "You know, Karl, all hell is going to break loose in that house when someone opens the bag and finds the cash and guns missing."

Karl's attention remained on the *oculus*. "One of the hazards of drug dealing. If I may ask, what is the first gift you received today?"

Illych responded, "Getting broken out of prison. You didn't know you were doing this on Christmas Day?"

Karl's voice took on an edge of irritability: "I am not a religious person. A 'Merry Christmas' is in order, then. Merry Christmas, Illych."

With a smile and a warm tone, Illych responded, "Merry Christmas, Karl."

With finality, Karl said, "We have what we came for. We are done here."

And everything went black.

●   ●   ●   ●   ●

Back at the lair, they counted the money. Over ten thousand dollars.

Karl said, "This should be enough for a motel tonight."

Illych looked down at his orange jumpsuit and stated, "We need to do something about this."

Karl used the *oculus-ouiblet* combo to check out a men's clothing store, translating in options for Illych. Once this mundane task was complete, he added up the price tags and dropped the clothing tags along with enough cash on a checkout counter with a note explaining what the payment was for.

Illych watched this all play out. The old man's quirkiness would take some getting used to. "This integrity thing you have going is admirable. But maybe you're a little over-the-top with it?"

Karl declared, "Without rules, the world descends into chaos. And the rules are not for just when someone is watching."

Illych smirked. There was regular uptightness. And then there was Karl Lark uptight.

●   ●   ●   ●   ●

Less than an hour later, Illych enjoyed his first night outside of prison in two years, in a motel, laid out on a bed, wearing new clothes, and having takeout delivered.

Stretched out on the bed, he drifted off to sleep with *It's a Wonderful Life* playing on the television.

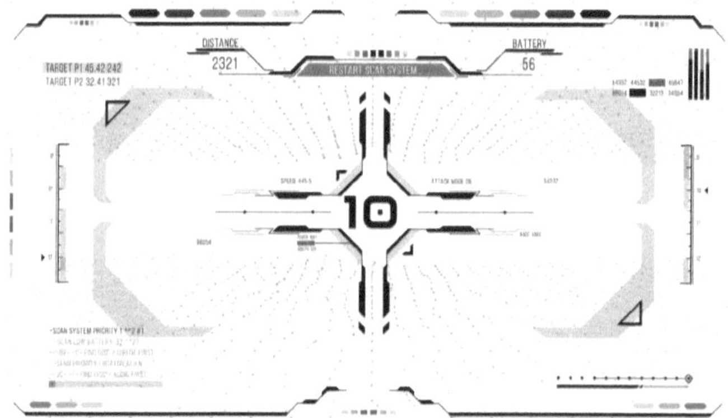

CHAPTER TEN

At a pre-agreed-upon time, Karl arrived at the motel where Illych had spent his latest night. They had been changing every day—a necessary, if tedious, inconvenience. At least until more permanent lodging for the ex-Green Beret was found.

The week after springing Illych from prison had been spent acquiring funds from unsuspecting drug dealers and loan sharks in the Chicago area. Followed by cash spending sprees purchasing needed equipment. In the case of firearms, they had taken the weapons in the dead of night while leaving a pile of cash in payment.

Karl found Illych ready to travel.

Illych greeted him, "I was watching the news this morning. That last place we robbed— when the owner found the cash missing, he went after someone he thought stole it. Ended in a shootout. Even SWAT was called in."

Karl shrugged and responded, "Unintended but understandable."

Illych asked, "I was thinking last night. Here I am staying in a comfortable motel room with a real bed and you live in that cave."

Karl nods.

"Why? You have the funds and access to pretty much anywhere. Why aren't you living in a nice place somewhere?"

"There is no harm in your knowing. My efforts to create the tools I use caught the attention of powers unknown. I used to live in my home, the place of my birth.

"Whoever they are, they tried to enter my home and figure out what I was up to. When that failed, they employed some means I still do not understand to attempt my capture.

"I was forced to flee and now I hide in that cave until I determine who *they* are."

Illych hefted his big green army duffel onto a shoulder. "Now I get it. So where are we off to today?"

Karl replied, "We will situate you in your next room, and then I will leave you alone for part of the day. I have an errand of a personal nature I must attend to."

Illych gave Karl a questioning look and asked, "Personal, huh? Where and when?"

Karl replied with a hint of frustration, "Today, soon. I will be translating to visit someone. It is a last-minute thing. First, I will need to make a call to set it up."

Illych refused to let it go. "What's this in regard to?"

Karl snapped, "It is personal and does not concern you. I am just sharing that I will be unavailable for part of the day."

Illych planted his feet shoulder-width apart and addressed the old man directly, "Wrong, Karl. Your safety concerns me. You brought me on as your bodyguard. Also, it's in my self-interest that you stay healthy. Going back to that cell isn't part of my future plans, so spill it. What's going on?"

Karl exhaled a sigh and replied, "All right, then, if you insist. It is a family thing. I have a grandniece that I gave up for adoption years ago. Her adoptive parents keep me up to date on her activities."

Illych's surprise played out on his face. That wasn't where he'd seen this discussion going.

Karl continued, "With the loss of my permanent residence and its telephone, they can no longer contact me through proper channels. As a workaround, I have crafted a simple communication device using technology similar to the *ouiblet*. The goal of the meeting is to give the adoptive parents the device. They will be able to alert me if there is something to discuss. Then I would get to a phone and call them."

Illych's tone was incredulous: "You have a grandniece?"

Karl frowned and shook his head. "That is what I just said. Are you listening?"

Illych smiled and said, "Yes, I am. And how did your grandniece end up being adopted?"

Karl's voice took on a note of frustration again: "The details are none of your concern."

Illych blinked and smirked. "Again, yes, they are. If I'm going to keep you safe, I have to know what's going on."

Karl was obviously frustrated. "Do you need to know for professional reasons or just impertinent curiosity? I had not expected to share my personal information this morning."

Illych shrugged. "Both."

Karl's shoulders sagged just the tiniest shift in surrender, and he said, "My brother was a drunk and a fool. A perpetual failure, he eventually married a despicable woman, and they produced a daughter. The mother was of unstable character and loose morals. I never understood my brother's interest in her. She eventually ran off, leaving my idiot brother with a daughter to raise.

"The daughter gave birth to my grandniece when she was only sixteen. Four years later, my brother and his daughter perished in a car crash. Two days after that tragedy, family services showed up at my door with Danielle. I knew instantly that her care was beyond me. An adoption agency helped me place her with a good family.

"As per the adoption agreement, once per year I meet with the adoptive father for an update. These are typically short meetings and, over the years, have been a positive experience. She has done well for herself. Top of her class in graduate school. Now she works as an analyst for the FBI."

Without pause, Illych followed up, "So, we're going to meet this adoptive father person?"

Karl responded, "Steve Mersen is his name. And why are 'we' going?"

Illych pointed at himself and stated, "Bodyguard. And you're giving him something to contact you with?"

Karl nodded and replied, "Correct."

Illych's voice was now sarcastic: "Would bad guys be able to summon you with this device?"

Karl snapped back, "That is what the *oculus* is for. To make sure only Steve is involved. Plus, I will have you with me as my bodyguard."

Illych smiled and retorted, "Touché. What could go wrong? Let's do it. Oh, and will I be getting one of these magical communication devices?"

Karl sighed while answering, "Yes, I have a second one for you. And it's not magic. It is science. Maybe just not science as most people understand it."

They translated out to a phone and made the call. Steve answered and agreed to meet in two hours at the same coffee shop as Karl's previous visit.

● ● ● ● ●

Illych and Karl translated near to the meeting destination and stayed out of sight, watching on the *oculus*. Nothing was visible that made either of them nervous.

Illych was the first to speak: "I have a question, Karl. You say Danielle works for the FBI. How is that going to play out with you associating with escaped prisoners and robbing drug dealers?"

Karl responded, "She is an analyst, a forensic accountant, not a field agent. And I have not met her in person in twenty-two years. It is unlikely we will have any interaction with her."

Illych's tone shifted to incredulous: "You've been keeping track of an estranged grandniece for twenty-two years and haven't met *in person?*"

Karl frowned but kept his eyes on the display.

Steve was right on time, and Karl left Illych with the *oculus* to watch. He then walked the remaining short distance to the coffee shop.

Upon entering, Karl could see that Steve's expression was a mask of concern. They shook hands. "Karl, your call was unexpected. Is everything okay?" Both men took seats opposite each other.

Karl replied, "Yes, I am well. I have taken a new job that involves travel. Quite a bit of travel, actually. It will be difficult to reach me by traditional means. I wanted to meet and provide a way for you to contact me."

Steve looked skeptical. "A new job at your age? And travel? Is this some sort of late mid-life crisis?"

Karl awkwardly smiled and replied, "Nothing of the sort. I will not be purchasing a red sports car or attempting to recapture my youth. A unique employment opportunity presented itself, and I have accepted it."

Karl took the device from his pocket and handed it to Steve. It very much resembled a beeper from the '90s. "It's satellite-connected. Just slide open the cover and press the button. It can reach me anywhere, and I will call when I am able."

Steve turned it over in his hands, examining the gadget. "Fancy. I'll put it in a safe place. In the unlikely event of an emergency requiring your immediate attention, I'll use it. Thank you for thinking of Danielle."

Karl nodded. "You are welcome. I must apologize for the abrupt visit, but my schedule is tight, and I must be going."

Karl rose and began to leave.

Steve also stood. "Safe travels, Karl."

Karl paused, nodded, and walked out the door. Not thirty minutes later, he and Illych were back in the lair.

Illych could not resist asking, "So you have a grandniece you check up on regularly?"

Karl put the *oculus* down on a workbench. "She is my only family, and I only check up on her once a year."

A now-smirking Illych kept going, "Yet you feel compelled to provide a channel for emergency contact, even under the current extraordinary circumstances."

Karl took a deep breath. "It is appropriate. Regardless, keeping up with family is exhausting. Hopefully, this channel of communication will never be needed.

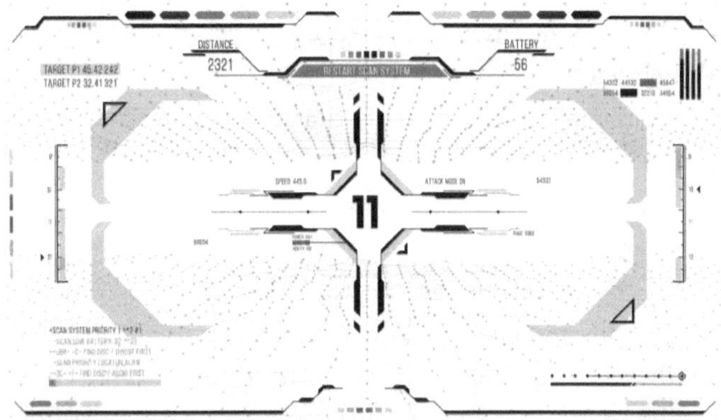

CHAPTER ELEVEN

Early in the morning, two days later, Karl arrived at the motel where Illych was staying and knocked on the door. Illych promptly opened it, ready to go as usual.

A rested Illych asked, "Where to next?"

Karl entered the hotel room as Illych closed the door behind him. "I have located a long-term solution as to where you can reside without the daily changes."

A visibly surprised Illych responded, "Really? You figured out how to overcome the people-getting-too-familiar problem?"

Karl nodded. "Indeed. A remote hunting cabin in the mountains. The owner accepts cash in advance for the entire year and does not ask questions."

With a questioning look, Illych asked, "Mountains? Which ones?"

Karl replied in a mildly irritated tone, "Rocky, does it matter?"

Illych shook his head. "Nope. Just curious."

Karl continued, "The cabin is without plumbing, electricity, or cell phone service. There are thirty miles of rough trails and back roads before reaching pavement. Then another twenty miles to the nearest town. The closest neighboring occupied residence is more than ten miles from the cabin. There is no chance of electronic surveillance, nor are there any witnesses who might remember you when asked."

Illych nodded and added, "I'm going to need some things before moving in."

Karl said, "I had considered as much. We will do that now."

The two men had been standing inside the motel room with the door closed and the window shades drawn.

And then the room was empty.

●　　●　　●　　●　　●

Later that afternoon, the pair translated close to the cabin in the mountains. Snow covered the ground. A strong breeze delivered frozen air. The area was wooded, but not densely so. A winter wilderness wonderland.

"Picturesque," Karl observed.

Illych filled his lungs. "Crisp, clean mountain air. Costs less than the motels, and the owner didn't haggle or even ask questions."

Karl nodded. "I am finding that a sheave of hundred-dollar bills solves many issues quickly and quietly. It is almost as if money is planned to work that way."

Nearby evergreens towered upward, reaching for the sky. The cabin was built into the side of a gentle slope. A single-room log cabin affair with a ribbed steel roof.

Karl called out as Illych strode down the slope to the cabin door. "The owner said he had only ever able to rent it out for part of a year. It's been empty for months."

Illych looked around as he approached the cabin. "Other than animal tracks, there've been no recent visitors."

There was no lock on the door, and it opened easily enough. Inside was a cast-iron potbellied stove, chairs, a table, and a triple bunk against the wall. One wall was dominated by a massive fieldstone fireplace.

Illych took it all in and proclaimed, "Nice, I'll take it."

Karl's expression was quizzical, "I do not understand. We have already taken it, so to speak."

"It's an expression. It means I like it." Illych dropped the two full military duffel bags he was carrying onto the lowest bunk. "It'll take some work to clean it up, but it's an improvement from Leavenworth or changing motels every day."

Karl turned to leave. "Yes, well, I will leave you to it then. You have your device for contacting me."

Illych nodded and held up a palm-sized box.

Karl said, "I shall return tomorrow."

Illych got the last word in: "Make sure you knock. It'd be unfortunate if I mistook you for a bear. Or better yet, call out Marco before you get too close. I'll know for sure it's you."

* * * * *

Karl returned the next day. Translating upslope from the cabin, he called out, "Marco!"

After a long pause, he repeated himself only louder.

The cabin door made a scraping noise and swung open.

Illych appeared and retorted, "Polo!"

Karl made his way down and entered the cabin. "Why do you make me say that silly word to announce my presence?"

A smiling Illych replied, "Because it works."

Inside, Karl could see Illych had been busy. There was a roaring fire in the fireplace. The room was warm, with firelight and daylight competing to illuminate the freshly swept and organized room.

Karl took in the improved situation and asked, "You are settling in?"

Illych closed the door against the cold and latched it. "I am."

Karl looked around, "This is better than the motels?"

Illych grunted a laugh and answered, "In the important ways. The lack of facilities takes some getting used to, though. Nothing that we didn't learn to deal with in the Army."

Karl nodded. "I'm sure." He took a seat in one of the rickety chairs. Illych sat in the other.

Karl spoke first: "I have been considering what to do next. Opportunities to explore and where to source funding."

Illych nodded while watching the fire in the fireplace. "Roger that."

Karl's eyes narrowed. "There must be services we can perform and receive financial compensation for. Like finding a missing object or person?"

Illych tilted his head back and replied, "Depends on what the limits are. We could sabotage things, kidnap people, or, for that matter, your *ouiblet* would make child's play of assassination-for-hire."

Karl nodded. "Agreed, but perhaps we start small and work up to the more involved activities. My understanding was that they have bail jumpers. Returning them to prison could be lucrative."

Illych shook his head. "Not that lucrative. And it seems almost unfair with the translation thing. Also, there's a lot of people contact involved. Not sure if that works for us. It could be an option, though. My vote is to explore stealing money and property from criminals. There are a lot more of them, and they have a lot of money. Sort of a Robin Hood thing, except we keep everything."

Karl said, "On the surface, that does appear to be the path of least resistance. I would prefer providing proper services, though. It feels more honest."

Illych frowned and asked, "Karl, what is this push for money? Even the small heists we have made so far have provided plenty of cash. The rent on this cabin is nothing to worry about. The lair costs nothing. Unless you are planning to start collecting Ferrari's, your expenses are not all that much."

After a pause, Karl responded, "There are things I would like to purchase for my research. Stealing everything, even from criminals, diminishes the accomplishment. I am also not interested in mere subsistence. The goal is not a wealthy lifestyle, but I believe there is a point between opulence and hiding out in the lair and here in this cabin that is more comfortable and less distracting."

Illych nodded. "Fair enough."

Karl took a deep breath. "That is enough money discussion for now. There is another topic I wish to discuss. An excursion we will pursue.

"Before your liberation from prison and before I created the *ouiblet*, I went to a park to test out the early version of the *oculus*. The test was a success, but I inadvertently found *something* at the same time.

"To be honest, Illych, it was so improbable that I do not trust my memory of it. The fantastic nature does not lend credibility. To confirm that I did, in fact, see what I thought I saw, we are going there together. You will give me peace of mind by doing so."

Illych blinked at Karl. *What fresh hell was this?*

Karl continued, "But first, I wish to acquire a book. This will require a short trip to visit someone. Are you ready to travel?"

Ilych stood and replied, "If you're ready, I'm ready."

Karl joined him in standing.

And they were gone.

●   ●   ●   ●   ●

Even though they had been comfortable inside the warm cabin, the change from having the frozen mountains outside to standing outdoors in warm sunlight and humidity was jarring. And there was green everywhere. Karl had translated them to a secluded outdoor spot somewhere tropical.

The nausea hit, and Illych bent over, putting his hands on his knees.

Through gritted teeth, he said, "I wonder if motion sickness medicine would help with this?"

Karl did not comment and waited patiently until Illych stood and nodded, indicating he was ready.

The pair walked out of a patch of overgrown, lush green foliage.

Illych looked around them as they walked. "Where are we? This is a lot of plants."

Karl said, "Florida. More specifically, a gated retirement community. The person I wish to speak to lives here."

Illych glanced Karl's way and asked, "Does this person know we are coming?"

Karl responded, "They do not. The man we are visiting wrote a book that no one was interested in. Then he was mocked about it for decades. Now he is elderly and will have no interest in discussing the topic."

Illych asked, "This retired guy has the only copy of the book?"

Karl nodded. "I searched for a copy. Even anonymously reached out to people in the old book business without any success. It appears every copy has disappeared."

The pair found themselves on a sidewalk surrounded by single-story buildings. White-haired elderly people were everywhere. Some with walkers, a few in scooters.

Illych looked at Karl and stated, "You fit in here, I don't."

Karl shrugged and responded, "If anyone asks, we can tell them you are my nurse."

Illych rolled his eyes. "Uh-huh. So, this guy we're looking for, does he have a name?"

There were a lot more women than men, and most of those they passed were looking at Illych.

Karl observed the attention given Illych. "Franklin Townshend. And you appear to be popular with the females. I can't say the visibility helps us."

Illych grinned. "Can't do anything about the ladies, Karl. So, you have a name. What about an address?"

Looking ahead, Karl said, "Yes, yes, we are almost there."

Illych was vigilant while looking for and not seeing potential threats. Maybe security would try to kick them out if they knew he and Karl were not members. Otherwise, this was just a walk in the park. Surrounded by a disturbing number of elderly people.

Karl pointed to a nearby home. "Here, this one."

A single-family dwelling. Just a square house with steps up to a small porch. Climbing the steps, Karl pressed the doorbell.

After a minute, a balding, diminutive, bent-over, elderly man opened the door. Looking at the oddly paired men on his porch through squinting, rheumy eyes, he croaked out, "Yes?"

Karl declared, "Franklin Townshend?"

Franklin scowled and replied, "That is me? Who are you two?"

Karl continued, "I have a scholarly interest I would like to discuss with you."

Franklin grumbled, "Pay to live in a place to get away from door-to-door salesmen, and they still get in. How did you two get in here?"

Karl looked . . . miffed, "I assure you that we are not here to sell anything. You wrote a book a number of years ago. I wish to ask some questions about it."

Franklin paused, clearly taken aback. "That book was nothing but trouble. Finally reached a point where nobody asks about it, and now you two show up. You need to leave before I call security."

Karl's features set, "Mr. Townshend, I have been to Townshend Park and have seen what is there."

Conflict played out over the old man's face as he asked, "You are not here to make fun of me?"

Karl tersely answered, "No, absolutely not."

Franklin pointed to Illych and inquired, "What about him?"

Without moving his gaze from Franklin, Karl said, "He is my nurse; nothing to worry about there."

Franklin's tone shifted to accommodating: "Fine, you can come in, but no funny business."

Karl accepted, "Thank you. We will do our best to not be humorous."

Illych shook his head.

The front door opened directly into the living room, and they all took seats.

Franklin asked, "What are your names?"

Karl responded, "My name is Karl Lark. My nurse here prefers to remain anonymous."

Franklin looked back and forth between his visitors. "Fine, whatever, Karl and Mr. Anonymous Nurse. I would offer you something, but there is nothing in the house. I never get visitors. So, what did you see in the park?"

Karl's voice took on a darker note: "It was the size of a child, with unnatural features. And it was green."

Franklin sat back in his chair. "That was it, all right. Still there after all these years.

"My family settled the land all around that park before there was even a US of A. They bought up even more land after the revolution. Ten generations of Townshends. Most of it is gone now. Sold off and the money reinvested. That is why I get to end my days here in the sunshine state.

"Nobody wanted the land that park was on, though. Finally, these government fellas showed up and offered some tax breaks if the family donated the property to make a park. Sweet deal too."

Karl asked, "Your family must have had a long history with whatever that thing is?"

Franklin smirked, "Hrrmph. Called it the *Gitchoo*. In two hundred years, six members of the Townshend family disappeared in them woods. Along with a lot of other people. The Indians, or Native Americans, or whatever you call them, knew to stay away. Walk there, and the Gitchoo will get you. The last Townshend to disappear was my grandfather. Went hunting and never came back. You can read all about it in my book."

Karl interrupted, "Unfortunately, I have been unable to locate a copy of your book."

Franklin looked right at Karl and said, "Well, you aren't trying very hard. The local library has a copy."

Karl shook his head. "No, not even the library. I checked. Searched extensively. The book you wrote has disappeared."

Franklin looked wistful, got up, and shuffled to a bookshelf. Grabbing a small hardcover book bound in green leather, he looked at it in his hands.

Walking over to Karl, he handed it to him.

Franklin's voice took on a defeated tone: "Here. When I published that, I was publicly mocked. My family almost disowned me for airing family laundry. I only wrote it because my grandfather disappeared. That is probably the only copy left, then."

Karl looked at the gold lettering on the cover and then carefully opened the book. "What can I offer you in exchange?"

Franklin waived his hands and pleaded, "Do *something* with it. Not many have seen the Gitchoo and lived to tell the tale. Maybe you can keep someone else from losing their grandfather. Everything I know is in that book."

Karl dipped his chin and replied, "Thank you, Mr. Townshend."

Franklin's grumpiness returned as he continued, "Now, you two need to leave. My nurse is stopping by, and she will wonder how you two got in here."

Illych and Karl rose together. Karl gently shook Franklin's hand before they left.

As they walked down the steps, Franklin called out, "If you find it and figure out what it is, please come back and tell me. It would be good to know before I shuffle off this mortal coil."

Karl nodded and clutched the book close. Turning onto the sidewalk, he set a fast pace to get back to the translation point.

A startled Illych asked, "What's the hurry, Mr. Lark?"

Karl did not pause to explain and continued his speed walk: "There is a reason this is likely the last copy of this book. I will rest easier when it is safely back at the lair."

As they approached the clump of vegetation that would soon hide their disappearance from this place, giggling could be heard from inside and out of sight.

Undeterred, Karl charged right in. Sounds of surprise and outrage emanated from where Karl had just disappeared into the foliage.

Illych could not believe what he was hearing. He shook his head and whispered, "He brought us in at a make-out spot. The make-out spot at an old-folks home."

Seconds later, an elderly couple with flushed cheeks, disheveled clothes, and distressed looks exited the overgrowth. They almost ran into Illych, which only enhanced their surprise. The two walked away with occasional backward glances.

And now they're going to wonder what the two of us were going to do in there together.

Illych found an impatient Karl, his foot tapping, waiting. He took a spot next to him and prepared for the translation.

Karl huffed, "I should have sent you in first. You would not believe what they were doing."

Illych took a deep breath and exhaled, "I can believe it. Keep popping into places unannounced, and you'll eventually see some things you weren't expecting."

A cross Karl said, "People have homes for that sort of thing."

And they were gone.

●　　●　　●　　●　　●

Illych threw another log on the fire. With a metal poker, he situated the burning wood. The coals crackled and threw off sparks that were caught up in the rising smoke, disappearing into the chimney.

Karl watched from a rickety chair. "I read Mr. Townshend's book last night."

Illych took the chair next to Karl's. "And?"

Karl replied, "There's a long history in that place. The Native Americans knew about the presence of something malevolent, and avoided it. The Townshend family inadvertently began participating in that history when they acquired a large parcel of land that included the area where all the disappearances occurred.

"Once they figured it out, the family knew to avoid the area. Unfortunately, once enough time had passed since the previous disappearance, someone would ignore the warnings and end up missing.

"I have seen what's in those woods. What I don't know is what is happening to these people. Is that thing carrying them off as food? Or is it some sort of slavery thing? What does it do with them?"

Illych interrupted, "What the hell did you see in those woods?"

Karl described what he witnessed on the day of the *oculus* trial run.

An incredulous Illych asked, "And you want to go looking for this thing?"

Karl frowned while answering, "Yes, to understand it. I have a plan based on what is in the book and my own observations. What is it? Why is it here? Why are people disappearing? Does this thing take them?

"As the creature may be potentially hostile, special precautions are in order. Once we locate it, I will use the *ouiblet* to place it in a cage. There is a nearby zoo with a steel box used to transport gorillas. We will borrow that and translate it into position. Once we find our objective, it will go into the cage."

Illych, now concerned about what they were about to get themselves involved with, asked, "Mr. Lark, what exactly *is* it? I've been all over the world and never needed a gorilla cage to hold anything."

Karl stared into the fire as he replied, "We are going searching for a fairy-tale creature, Illych. We are going to capture a *goblin*."

Back in the day, Illych would have considered what Karl was saying to be crazy talk. But that ship had sailed. If the old man said he saw a goblin, then he might have. Considering what had happened over the last week, he gave Karl Lark the benefit of the doubt. Honestly, if the old man claimed he could show him a unicorn, he might believe it.

Illych exhaled and asked, "When are we going goblin hunting?" And then thought to himself: *Might as well get this over with.*

Karl looked at Illych and replied, "How soon can you be ready?"

"To do the bodyguard thing you brought me in for?"

Karl nodded. "Correct."

Illych's expression and tone changed to serious: "Fifteen minutes."

"Then let us leave in fifteen minutes."

Illych changed from his mountain-man flannel into proper tactical gear. He had not acquired everything he wanted yet. But since joining up with Karl, his loadout capability had leveled up considerably.

Illych asked, "Do we expect there to be any shooting?" It seemed like an important detail to check into.

Karl shrugged and responded, "The goal is to capture it, not kill it. However, we are going after something that could be immortal and therefore may have unknown capabilities."

Illych held up a box of earplugs and said, "Put these in. We'll still be able to talk to each other, but we won't go deaf if I use this." He patted the rifle hanging from his chest on his tactical harness. Karl nodded and took a pair.

Illych briefly considered bringing a Taser, then shook his head and put it down. The electric snakebite was not the correct tool for the outdoors.

While strapping things on and confirming rounds were in the chambers of the large caliber firearms, handguns included, he asked another question: "Where exactly are we going to find this goblin?"

Karl replied, "Townshend Park. We're going to a place called Townshend Park."

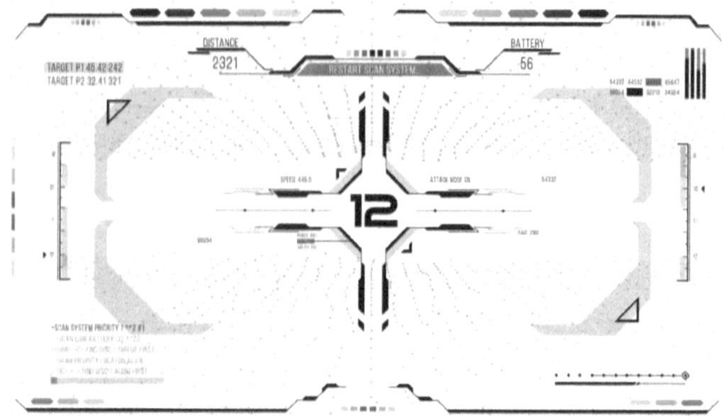

CHAPTER TWELVE

Illych and Karl translated straight to the Townshend Park parking lot. The last time Karl was here, it had been a cool fall day with red and gold leaves on the trees.

Now it was a frigid windswept snow-and-ice winter wonderland. Skeletal trees, long shorn of their leaves, surrounded the parking lot. Freezing wind gusts greeted their arrival. The sun was blocked by a gray cloudy sky that was threatening more snow. Everything they saw was cast white, black, and gray in the weak afternoon light.

They paused for a moment while Illych struggled through the translation nausea. Karl confirmed what he had observed with the *oculus* just moments before arriving. The park was empty. There was not a living soul to be found within miles of where they stood.

Illych indicated he was back to 100 percent, and Karl continued working the *oculus*. Much had changed since that inaugural test months ago. His skill in working his invention meant it did not take long to identify a portal near the geographic center of the park, similar to the one containing the lair or the one at Abyssal Park.

Karl pointed into the forest and said, "That way." The pair trudged through knee-high snow. At first, side by side, and then changing to Illych in the lead.

Karl called out what the *oculus* was telling him: "There is a portal, perhaps a half mile through these woods. It is centered in a clearing. I am seeing no sign of what we are looking for, though."

There was no hurry, and their pace was relaxed. Not wanting to be surprised by a fairy-tale creature, Karl kept his eyes on the *oculus*. He saw nothing but snow, barren trees, and frozen land.

Illych broke the silence, "Odd. A forest like this, no apparent recent visitors, and the only animal tracks I've seen are a single set of rabbit tracks. In the wilderness around the cabin, there would've been more, much more."

Illych slid his rifle from his shoulder to the ready in both hands. A high-powered semi-automatic with a high-capacity drum magazine. He had previously assured Karl it would drop a charging grizzly.

Arriving at their destination, they stopped just inside the tree line. Looking out, they took in the barren white circle inside the gray perimeter of the trees, perhaps a football field across and sloping gently down from their current position.

Illych commented, "I bet this is a nice meadow on a sunny day."

Karl nodded. "The *oculus* shows the portal is right there in the center." He angled the device so Illych could see.

Illych looked and asked, "So where's this goblin?"

Karl frowned and speculated, "Perhaps it's only around on certain days? Or maybe this is not where it resides? Maybe I did not really see it? Coincidence? I don't know."

Illych hissed and pointed, "Or a little green man could just appear out of nowhere."

They were close enough to see it contrasting with the snow, but far enough away not to be able to see detail. Roughly centered in the snowy circle was a distant greenish figure in colorful, patchwork clothes.

The figure was looking right at them. It took a few steps and paused.

With tension in his voice, Illych whispered, "Now might be a good time to get that cage ready, Mr. Lark."

Karl nodded and worked the *ouiblet* controls to deliver the cage. A metal box silently materialized to their left and settled into the snow.

The goblin crouched when the box appeared and then stood straight again. Now it was padding across the snow towards Karl and Illych at a casual pace.

"That thing isn't that far away. You might want to put it in the box now." The tension in Illych's voice pushed Karl to work faster.

The *oculus* outlined the approaching goblin, and the *ouiblet* was updated. Karl activated the controls.

And nothing happened.

His hands moved through the sequence again, and nothing. He repeated each action carefully and deliberately, making sure there were no mistakes.

Nothing happened.

Illych barked, "What's happening, Mr. Lark? We're running out of space here!"

The goblin was close enough to see detail now—solid black eyes and a steam-shovel mouth full of crooked, needle-like teeth. The closer it came, the more its hands formed a claw shape.

Karl voiced his frustration: "It's not working. The *ouiblet* can't seem to grab it. I've tried over and over."

They had run out of time. The goblin's loping approach changed into a sprint, and Illych opened fire. Each shot was impossibly loud in the silent winter forest. The gunfire was continuous, with cartridges ejecting in rapid succession without pause in a display of expert marksmanship. Illych was firing so fast as to make it appear the weapon was on full auto. Yet each round was delivered center of mass on the goblin with barely a miss.

The successive impacts slowed the creature, yet it kept coming. Each bullet took its toll, splattering the snow with green ichor. Its lifeblood eventually joined by bits of goblin separated by the volume of fire.

The bolt on Illych's rifle locked back, and in another demonstration of skill, the former Green Beret ejected the drum out onto the snow and smoothly inserted a magazine while releasing the bolt in one swift motion.

Illych raised the rifle to fire at the still-standing goblin, not more than ten strides away. The creature had stopped and was swaying unsteadily. Its thin body was torn apart by dozens of impacts, green ooze ran down onto the white snow.

Like a marionette with its strings suddenly cut, it crumpled to the ground and went still.

Both men stayed where they were and watched.

The green splatters on the snow were fading, evaporating away.

The goblin's corpse was now giving off a steaming shimmer. Its finer features lost their definition. The mass of it was decreasing before their eyes.

Karl's voice broke the silence: "Now I understand why there are no bodies of such creatures on display in a museum. This thing is melting or sublimating. My guess is it will be gone within the hour."

Illych kept his weapon pointed at the apparently now-deceased creature. "Ok, now what do we do since Plan A is no longer an option?"

Karl looked at the gorilla crate. "Well, we don't need the cage." With a quick work of the controls, the now-frozen metal box disappeared.

Karl indicated the center of the clearing and said, "And now we check out the portal."

"What if there are more of these?" Illych pointed to the rapidly disappearing goblin.

Karl started walking and explained, "I have the *ouiblet* set to get us both out of here in an instant. Another of those things appears, and we are leaving."

The short winter day was ending, and dusk was settling in. The weak winter sun edged behind the trees. Without the light, it felt colder, and the wind picking up increased the chill. The pair cautiously approached the portal.

Nothing popped out to greet them. Karl viewed the portal's inner workings on the *oculus*.

He shrugged. "For all intents and purposes, the door is open. Just one small adjustment."

The pair took one step forward and found themselves in a space not all that different from the lair—a spacious chamber with a domed ceiling. Toward the back, away from what could be called the front door, was an oval opening leading back to something.

The temperature was unchanged from the meadow outside, and the space was faintly lit by patches of some sort of glowing moss or fungus.

Illych attached a light to his rifle and turned it on. Its bright beam further illuminated the chamber. The light fell on a diorama of human-sized figures made from sticks. Their clothing was a bizarre combination of modern all the way back to Native American buckskin. Breaking the silence first, he asked, "What's all that?"

"It's not just that." Karl had been working the *oculus*. "This place is full of what I suspect that goblin has been collecting from passersby's over the years. Over there is a pile of rifles, flintlocks, and bows with flint arrows."

Illych kept working his light around. "Yeah, but what happened to the passersby?"

Karl moved his own light to a square shape, perhaps resembling an altar. Illych took several steps to look closer. The structure was made from carefully fit-together bones. The human skulls answered what kind.

Illych glanced at Karl and asked, "So that thing grabs people who wander by and are in the wrong place at the wrong time?"

Karl moved right next to the altar. "Yes," he answered, "and based on its speed and the remarkable amount of punishment it took to stop that thing, it is unlikely even a small group of hunters would have had a chance at escape."

The two men picked through the organized debris. They found some items of value, but most of it was garbage, decaying with age.

The doorway in the back of the chamber turned out to be an alcove. Whereas the walls of this place were rough gray rock, the alcove was smooth black rock. The center was a rectangular depression. Karl cycled through the *oculus* settings while trying to figure out what it meant.

Karl brought the *oculus* closer to his eyes and declared, "The goblin is not dead."

Illych swore while snapping his rifle into a firing position, "Where is it?"

Karl's eyes shifted to the depression as he pointed to it. "Right here, in this box. It is slowly reforming."

Illych moved backwards and readied his weapon. "How long?" he asked. "Do we have time to get out?"

Karl took a moment and then responded, "Seven years."

Illych barked, "What?"

Karl had an incredulous look on his face as he said, "Based on what I am seeing on the *oculus*, the creature will reform over a seven-year period."

Illych lowered his weapon. "We kill that thing, and it reappears seven years later?"

Karl nodded. "That is correct."

Setting the safety on his weapon, Illych commented, "No wonder a whole park was set up around that thing."

Karl said, "We are similar in thinking, Illych. I suspect this park was set up purposefully to minimize the likelihood of people meeting such a creature. And if someone did wander out here, it would only be a single person or a pair that would go missing. Eventually, the place got a reputation, and people stopped visiting. When I drove here the first time, I noticed how there were no signs at the highway exit showing where this park was. Even the sign at the entrance is almost impossible to see."

Illych detached the light from his rifle and used it like a flashlight, looking around. "Why not just kill that thing? Bows and arrows or muskets might be challenged, but modern weapons would put it down quick."

Karl took a breath and exhaled, "Risk of contact, and it would just come back after seven years. If they could not get through the portal—or were even aware the portal existed—the next best thing was to make this place hard to find."

Illych chuckled, "I get it. Even if they put up a big fence, people would just ask why there's a big fence, and sneak inside. This is the low-impact solution."

Karl said, "Franklin recorded in his book every disappearance he knew of. There was a pattern in his records. He did not see it, but I did. A cycle every seven years. Now we know why. Even if the thing is not destroyed, whatever is going on in that box repeats."

Illych shined his light into the depression. "What about burying the portal in concrete?"

Karl said, "I suspect that has been done in the past. Someone would eventually figure out where these things were coming from, and would create a mound over the portal to seal it in. But they would have to find the geographical location of the portal first. Not an easy feat."

The two men headed back to the main chamber. Karl translated the pile of potentially valuable items back to the lair, and both men exited through the portal into the frozen meadow. A pale half-moon reflected off the snow, lighting up the night. Away from an urban space, with no light pollution, the starry night sky twinkled overhead.

They trudged back to pick up the dropped drum magazine.

Illych pointed at their footprints in the snow. "See what's missing here? There are your boot prints, and those are mine. But none of these are from the goblin. It left no prints walking across the snow."

Karl looked out over the moonlit snow and said, "You are correct. My guess is that it would leave no footprints in dust or mud either. That is disconcerting on several levels."

Illych smirked and looked at Karl. "Do you remember the night you came to my cell to offer me a job, and I asked if the work would be interesting?"

Karl nodded.

Illych chuckled, "Well, Mr. Lark, this qualifies as interesting work."

After a pause, he asked, "Say, what happened with the translation thing? Why did the goblin not end up in the cage? That was unexpected."

Karl replied, "I was equally surprised. Whatever those things are, the *ouiblet* does not work with them. Its physical being does not fall under the modern concept of physics. This is problematic."

Illych shook his head. "Problematic? It was almost fatal."

Passing the spot where the goblin had fallen, the moonlight made the snow almost glow, and they could see that every trace of evidence of the creature ever having been there had evaporated out of existence.

Looking up at the moon, Karl said, "The *ouiblet* has its own mysteries. I do not claim to know everything. Fortunately, you were here to deal with the situation."

The two men stopped so Illych could bend down and pick up the previously discarded drum.

Illych stuffed it in a thigh pocket in his cargo pants, "Fifty rounds of .308 can solve a lot of problems."

Karl's voice took a note of questioning: "You did not hit with all fifty rounds?"

Illych replied while smiling, "That's the great thing about .308, you don't need to hit with every shot."

Karl prepared the *ouiblet* control.

Illych's was looking around now, his voice loud in the silent night air: "Karl, how many of these portal places do you think there are?"

Without looking up, Karl replied, "I have done some limited searching with the *oculus*, and I suspect there are thousands of them."

Illych stammered a bit as he exclaimed, "Wow! Really? Thousands?"

Karl nodded as he set up the *ouiblet* for their departure. "Thousands. Maybe tens of thousands. Perhaps even more."

Looking back to the center of the clearing, Illych asked, "How old are they?"

With their departure imminent, Karl looked at Illych and answered, "Unknown. Very old by human standards. I don't have enough information to know if they are natural or manufactured by someone or something in the distant past."

Karl paused and then said, "Enough speculating. It is time to go. Are you ready?"

Illych took a deep breath of the cold night air and nodded.

A moment later, all that was left in the clearing were footprints in the snow and fifty ice-cold, expended .308 rifle cartridges.

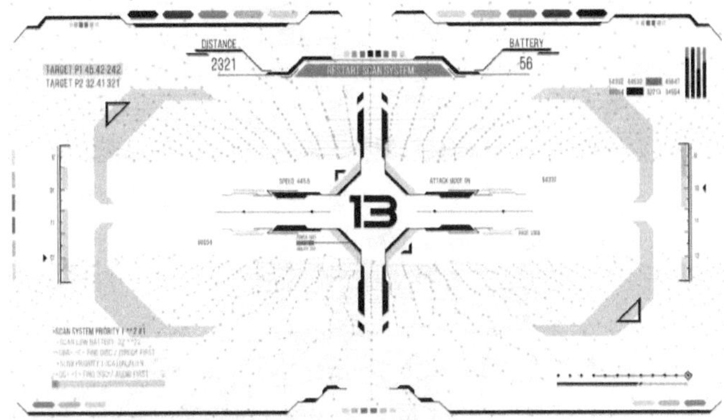

CHAPTER THIRTEEN

"Italian food is my favorite. And I work out enough that spaghetti is ok," Danielle said as she swirled more noodles onto her fork and relished the note of marinara in the air before filling her mouth with ambrosia.

Her blond-haired, blue-eyed friend Theresa beamed with delight. "Glad I'm not the only one. This is Chicago, and there are some really good Italian restaurants."

Danielle spoke through a full mouth, "This is fantastic! What a great way to end the day."

Theresa nodded, "You know who also has a great end? *Very* Special Agent David, who also happens to be in your part of the office. One of the benefits of being in IT is that I get to know where all the cute guys are."

Danielle's face wrinkled into a look as if Theresa had made a bad smell and said, "Ick."

An incredulous Theresa lifted her hand up and asked, "He's a handsome guy. Where do you get *ick* from him?"

Danielle looked from side to side like someone could be listening and leaned forward, whispering, "I was down in the third-floor evidence locker and checked something out for research. I took it onto one of those desks with the high sides, the ones where nobody can see you."

Theresa was listening intently, enthralled by the potential of whatever her dinner companion was about to tell her.

Danielle continued, "Dave was there with someone I didn't recognize, and what they were talking about makes me believe they didn't know I was there."

Theresa blinked in anticipation and exhaled, "And?"

Danielle said, "Dave was telling the other guy about a strip joint he goes to for lunch two or three days a week. Apparently, he thinks the food is not bad, and the ambiance is, as he put it, 'top-shelf.' His words."

Now it was Theresa's turn to make a face. "Eww, Dave's a strip club guy?"

Danielle sat back. "Yep," she replied. "And you'll never guess the name of the place. It's called The Pink Pole."

Theresa cackled loudly enough to disturb the other diners. "That is too much. Okay, now I get it. Dave is not an option."

Danielle shrugged. "I'm not worried about meeting guys. My apartment is right downtown, and it's a target-rich dating environment."

Theresa's voice took on a concerned tone: "Aren't you maybe a little worried about living downtown? You're an FBI agent and carry a gun, but that won't help if you're jumped by a crew of thugs."

"Not at all," Danielle said, shaking her head. "I don't walk around the place, and the building I live in has secure underground parking. I'm not taking risks. It's not in my nature."

Smiling, Theresa remarked, "No kidding, you don't take risks. Just look at your dating life."

Danielle laughed, "Eventually, but right now I'm the new person in the office and need to focus on my career. It'll take the right guy anyway. Most men find the gun intimidating. Add the FBI part, and they're looking for the exits."

Theresa smirked, "And the handcuffs—don't forget the handcuffs."

Danielle laughed and asserted, "No, they *really like* that part."

Both women roared with laughter loud enough to get looks from nearby tables in the restaurant.

Quieting back to a conversational volume, Danielle continued, "You would think accounting in the FBI would provide more dating opportunities. Talk about being in a man's world."

Theresa shook her head. "You're preaching to the choir, sister. I work in IT. It's all guys. Seeing you on your first day was an answer to my prayers: another woman in the office close to my age."

●　　●　　●　　●　　●

The gate to the underground parking raised after Danielle swiped her card. Looking left and right to make sure no one was lurking nearby—ready to dart into the garage on the down ramp—she tapped the accelerator and started in. Once past the gate, she slowed to watch it lower without anyone sneaking in. She was not usually so paranoid, but Theresa's ranting about being alone downtown made her more vigilant than usual.

With the gate down, she relaxed. The parking garage was well-lit, and there were security cameras. Nothing to worry about there.

Exiting her car, she grabbed her dinner leftovers and slung her purse with a 9mm Glock inside an easy-access panel over her shoulder. As safe as safe could be.

Taking a breath of the freezing night air, Danielle started walking and made it two steps before something like an electric snakebite lit up her entire being with pain. Paralyzed, she began sinking to the ground—the sensation was nonstop. Hands caught her, and she was lowered all the way down. She could see her purse right there in front of her as the world went dark.

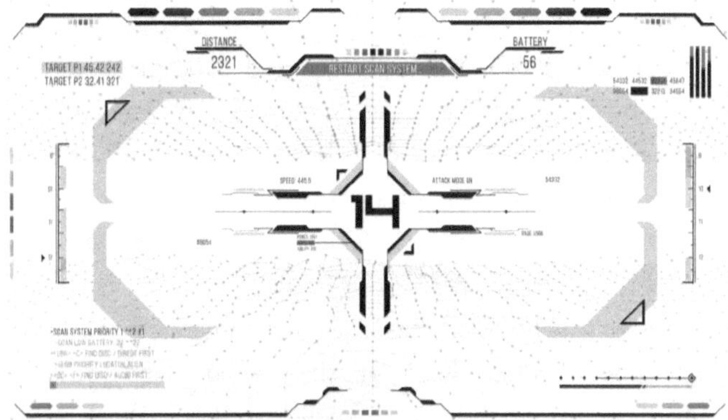

CHAPTER FOURTEEN

He kept a clock on the wall. It provided some time discipline, especially with regards to meals. Having no need to sleep made it difficult to remember when to eat. More than once, he had found himself light-headed from working continuously without sustenance for twelve hours or more.

Right now, the clock was telling him it was night. Or, at least it was where his abandoned home was. Not that there was any change in the extra-dimensional space Karl now called home. There was no light through the windows because there were no windows, or even the sound of birds outside to indicate the passage of time. Regardless, he was conscious of the late hour while sitting alone at a workbench. This knowledge enhanced the soothing peace and quiet of this place. There were no doorbells or telephones to interrupt the flow of his work.

Karl was startled as his peace and concentration were broken by a high-pitched pinging noise. He frowned. One of the beepers had been activated. It was either Illych or Steve Mersen, with Illych being the more likely of the two.

Karl exhaled a long sigh. *That is an irritating sound. Why is Illych contacting me at this hour?*

There was no good reason for his bodyguard to activate the beeper. Unlike Karl, Illych needed sleep, and his bodyguard was an early riser. At this late hour, Illych would be unconscious. Signaling in this way was likely not a positive development.

Scenarios rampaged through Karl's mind as he shuffled over to the shelf where the beepers were lying. He blinked in irritation at the noise as he moved to the devices with the goal of shutting the pinging one off.

Something had better be horribly wrong to justify this interruption. He would have words with Illych if this was because the former Green Beret used the last of his toilet paper.

Even if an FBI team was not storming Illych's cabin, by the time whatever problem this was had been resolved, half the night would be gone.

Picking up the offending device, he realized it's not Illych's beeper. Pausing for a moment, he processed the implications. There were only two of these devices, and it was the Steve Mersen beeper making the noise.

Based on past experience, it was likely to give him an update. Perhaps Danielle had been promoted. Or she'd gotten a cat. Something mundane. This channel of contact should only be used for emergencies. When they spoke, he would have to convince Steve that the beeper was not for everyday use.

Karl looked at the clock again. Except it was nighttime where Steve lived as well. This was an odd time to be reaching out . . .

Why is Steve Mersen contacting me in the dead of the night?

Karl shrugged. Regardless, he would collect Illych and go asking. He prepared to exit by shutting down everything that required shutting down. With the *oculus* and *ouiblet* controls in hand, he was ready to leave. At the last second, he remembered to grab a coat. It was cold in the mountains.

•   •   •   •   •

The translation dropped him within shouting distance of the cabin. His mild nausea passed quickly.

It was dark on the mountainside amid the tall trees. Snow crunched under feet, and a frozen wind made Karl glad for the coat.

Looking down the slope to the cabin, he could see firelight flickering in the windows and smoke rising from the chimney. Illych was likely home.

"Hello, the cabin!" His shout was small and quickly lost in the dark, frozen forest around the cabin.

Karl walked closer, taking his time while awaiting a response.

The scrape of the door being unbarred and opened carried across the intervening distance, followed by Illych's silhouette filling the doorway.

Illych called out, "Come on in, Mr. Lark. It's warm inside."

Karl crunched across the packed snow, walked past Illych, and went inside. Illych barred the door behind him. The fireplace was roaring, and it was genuinely toasty.

Gone were the rickety chairs and the triple bunk. One of the benefits of the *ouiblet* was the ease of furnishing the cabin. The minimalist wooden furniture had been replaced with two large, tufted, overstuffed leather chairs facing the fireplace. The bunks had been disposed of in favor of a proper bed. The past week's efforts to make this place long-term livable had been successful.

Illych sat in one of the chairs, and Karl took the other.

Yawning, Illych snarked, "To what do I owe an unexpected visit in the middle of the night?"

Karl said, "My apologies for the late hour. Something unexpected has occurred. Steve Mersen used his beeper."

Illych sat up a bit in his chair. "Your grandniece's adoptive father? Just now?"

Karl nodded. "Not thirty minutes ago."

Illych got a thoughtful look and asked, "At this time of night? Is that unusual?"

Nodding again, Karl answered, "Very unusual. He would not contact me at such an odd hour for no reason. I am here to collect you. We must go visit now."

Illych smiled and shook his head. "I should've known better than to sit down." Illych lifted himself from the chair and began changing into clothing that was more average streetwear and less mountain man. A sport coat hiding a shoulder rig and a handgun were the order of the day. The equipment situation had been steadily evolving since they had robbed that drug dealer while Illych was still wearing an orange prison jumpsuit.

In less than five minutes, a dressed and groomed bodyguard was ready.

Illych's expression settled into something serious as he sternly stated, "Let's go."

•　　•　　•　　•　　•

The *ouiblet* delivered them to a pitch-black, winter-cold place.

"Where are we?" Illych managed to get the words out while the translation nausea had its way with him.

Karl's calm and disembodied voice replied in the darkness, "A garden shed, and don't move. We're in a small space, and the floor is covered with things you might trip over. This is Mersen's neighbor's property."

Illych's voice carried a hint of irritation: "Why do we need to be this close? Can't you just do the snapshot thing? Hiding in the dark in a frozen garden shed is not cool."

Karl replied, "Snapshots can show specific items. A proper scan looking for, say, a police officer requires a more sophisticated approach. Hence, we are closer."

Illych's eyes adjusted to the dark, and the contents of the shed revealed themselves in the faint glow of the *oculus* display. Karl was not kidding. The floor of the shed was covered in paint cans, bags of fertilizer, and garden tools. A guy could get hurt stumbling around in here in the dark.

Karl angled the *oculus* for Illych to see. "There. See that car just across the street? Two men, just sitting there." More adjustment to the *oculus*, and he continued, "And see there? They have guns. The Mersen's are being watched."

Illych said, "I see, but why and by whom? From what you've said about these people, they're pretty vanilla."

Karl replied, "They are, for lack of a better expression, extraordinarily ordinary. Steve would not have contacted me without a reason, and the beeper is not something that can be accidentally activated."

The next few minutes were spent looking at neighboring houses, their layouts, and who was home. Karl was able to map out a path from the tool shed to the Mersen's back door, where it would be almost impossible for them to be seen.

Confident in his choices and with the *ouiblet* control in one hand, ready for an instant getaway, Karl navigated the stealth path to the Mersen's back door with Illych near his side.

Karl knocked lightly while viewing the men in the car highlighted on the *oculus*. Illych remained close by, taking up position in a corner shadow.

After his third try at knocking, the door opened, and the back door light revealed a haggard Steve Mersen in slippers and a robe. He blinked a few times while looking at his unexpected visitors.

Frowning, Steve asked, "I don't understand. Karl, why are you knocking on my back door in the middle of the night? Why not the front door?"

Steve's eyes widened when they found the almost-hidden shadow that was Illych. "Who is that?"

Karl extended his hand and lied, "By coincidence, my employer had placed me nearby. When the beeper went off, I was able to come right over."

Steve took Karl's hand, gripped it tightly, and shook it slowly.

Looking from Karl back to Illych, he said, "You just happened to be close by in the dead of the night and just came over? To the back door?"

Karl nodded and continued lying, "Yes, an unfortunate circumstance. We got the address wrong and arrived at your backyard neighbors. Decided to just cut through to save time. My apologies for the inconvenience."

Still looking concerned, Steve stammered, "Okay."

An awkward moment of silence followed.

Karl asked, "You rang? Or, in this case, *beeped*?"

Steve nodded and took a half-step back into the house. "Would you and your friend like to come in?"

Karl replied, "Unfortunately, no. We're pressed for time. Why did you contact me?"

Steve's expression shifted from just haggard to mournful. "Danielle's been kidnapped."

Karl froze, expressionless, for a few moments and then asked, "But she is FBI. How could she possibly be kidnapped?"

Steve exhaled and inhaled, "The FBI has not told us much. They know it happened when she arrived home Sunday night. Her boss figured something was wrong when she didn't show up for work Monday morning. After she didn't respond to calls, they sent someone to check. Then they found something that makes them think she'd been kidnapped.

"They were here all day, asking questions. There are even two agents watching the house. Honestly, the FBI did not share much, but it seemed they didn't know why either."

Karl remained frozen, and Steve paused and then said, "Karl, it has been over twenty-four hours. All the experts say that's bad. Her mother had to be tranquilized. Danielle is our only daughter. To lose her . . ."

Karl's voice came out almost robotic: "Thank you, Steve, for notifying me. I have work to do, but I will be in touch soon."

Steve had a stunned look on his face as Karl turned and walked away, Illych falling in behind. As soon as they disappeared from sight into the neighbor's yard, the *ouiblet* delivered them to the mountain slope above the cabin.

● ● ● ● ●

The two men silently entered the cabin. Illych piled wood on the fireplace coals until, once again, the silent room was toasty. The flickering, red-and-orange firelight filled the cabin, pushing back the darkness.

Illych sat in the unoccupied chair next to Karl, watching the old man. A long period of silence followed.

Karl broke the silence, stating, "This is unacceptable."

Illych nodded and inquired, "How so?"

Karl's tone was that of irritation, his words coming out in a clipped staccato: "Danielle could not possibly have done anything to justify kidnapping."

Illych raised an eyebrow and said, "I'm pretty sure that's not how that works."

Sounding more irritated, Karl snapped, "I care not one whit how it works."

More silence.

Karl continued, "Something must be done."

Illych nodded. "Of course. What do you have in mind?"

Karl's eyes were wide and unblinking. "Under normal circumstances, most people would wait for the FBI to resolve the situation."

Illych nodded in agreement. "Yep, most people would have to wait by the phone. There aren't a lot of options in a kidnapping."

Karl turned to Illych and continued, "But we are not most people. And we have options others do not. We are going to assist the FBI in finding Danielle."

Illych failed to see this discussion landing on helping the FBI, but he decided to share his thoughts regardless: "I am 100 percent on board with getting your grandniece back. But I'm also guessing the FBI will not appreciate our involvement."

Karl's face was shadowed in the red firelight, and in a dark tone, he snarled, "It does not matter. They are getting it whether they like it or not."

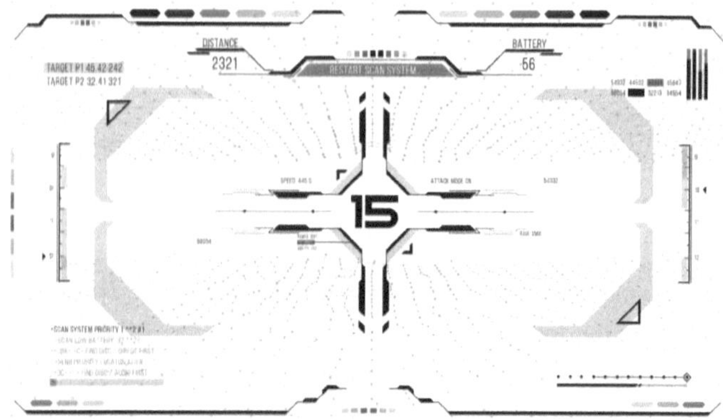

CHAPTER FIFTEEN

Karl left Illych at the cabin, returning several hours later. Illych opened the door, and both men took what were becoming their customary seated positions in front of a roaring fire in the fireplace.

Karl began, "Her supervisor's name is Jack Hemway."

Illych nodded. "Good to know. And how did you figure that out?"

"I called her adoptive father and asked."

Illych looked sideways at Karl. "On the phone?"

Nodding again, Karl answered, "Yes, I paid cash for one of those disposable cell phones and called."

Illych looked back at the fire. "Uh-huh, with their FBI agent daughter kidnapped, her parents' phone is likely being monitored."

Karl's voice betrayed irritation: "I threw the cell phone away afterwards."

"What I meant is they now know you know."

Karl shrugged. "Can't be helped. We need a place to start, and kidnapping random agents until we figure out the right one would not be efficient."

Illych coughed, "We are kidnapping FBI agents now? Isn't that where the problem started? Someone kidnapping your grandniece, the FBI agent?"

Karl's expression now showed his irritation as he explained, "We are not keeping them. I just need to borrow her supervisor for questions."

Now Illych let out a short laugh. "We are *borrowing* an FBI agent for questions? Do you have a plan for this?"

Now, with his facial expression brightening, Karl said, "Absolutely. We are going to start by setting the FBI building on fire."

Resigning himself to the strange place this conversation was going, Illych stated, "Are you sure burning down federal buildings is a good way to start the search for your kidnapped grandniece?"

Karl nodded. "Just a small fire in a storeroom. Enough to cause the building to evacuate. Then we grab Mr. Hemway on the street."

Illych asked, "Why on the street? Why not at his house?"

Karl took a breath and continued, "Because it is 5:00 a.m., and he is already at the office. Apparently, he has been there since they figured out Danielle had been kidnapped.

Some twenty hours now. My guess is that the situation will remain so, and it is unlikely he will go home for the rest of the day."

Illych nodded. This interesting job thing was getting even more interesting.

Karl added more: "As he leaves, we accost him at his car, or close to it. You use that Taser device, and we will translate him to a prepared private location while he is unconscious. He will only be out for maybe five or ten minutes, and then we shall question him."

Illych said, "Uh-huh, the Taser device. And you believe he'll be interested in answering your questions?"

Karl's tone shifted just the tiniest bit to petulant: "They are reasonable questions."

Illych shook his head. "When are we doing this?"

Karl stood and looked at Illych as he stated, "Right now."

Illych stood and stretched. Grabbing a three-quarter-length coat from a hook, he dropped the Taser in the right-hand pocket. No long rifle for this adventure, but he did holster a large caliber handgun and a knife in a shoulder rig under the coat.

Looking at Karl, he braced himself for what was coming next and said, "I'm ready."

●　　●　　●　　●　　●

The translation delivered them to a pitch-black room.

Karl hissed, "Stand still while I get the light."

A moment later, the bright fluorescent lighting made Illych squint.

The mop bucket, toilet plungers, toilet paper, and a lot of different chemicals in bottles told Illych they were in a utility closet.

Looking at his travel companion, Illych asked, "Where are we, Mr. Lark?"

Karl shifted a mop bucket with a foot and began picking through bottles on a nearby shelf. "This is a closet on the fifth floor of the federal building in Chicago where Danielle works."

Illych watched as Karl worked his way through the chemicals. He handed some of the bottles to Illych and told him to begin filling the plastic mop bucket. No sooner had this process begun than the tiny room was filled with an eye-watering chemical stink.

Karl handed Illych the last bottle and lifted the *oculus*. "There is nobody nearby." Opening the closet door, he shooed Illych out into the hall. The old man then turned and kicked the bucket over into the closet. The vaporous goo sloshed out, covering the floor. The wave of liquid hit the far wall and rebounded back, working the pool of mixed chemicals out into the hall.

Karl produced a flare from a pocket, ignited it, and tossed it into the room. The fumes catching fire before the flare landed in the goo. The enclosed space instantly transformed into a raging furnace. Both men squinted against the heat wash and backed away.

Illych was impressed. The old man was a hardcore arsonist.

Karl worked the *ouiblet* controls and proclaimed, "Time for us to go."

● ● ● ● ●

Two more translations in quick succession delivered Illych and Karl to the bottom of a stairwell in a parking garage.

Three total translations in such a short time put Illych on his knees.

Hissing from between clenched teeth, he shared his condition: "Mr. Lark, if I throw up, I'll make sure it lands on your shoes."

Karl ignored the threat and waited patiently. His own nausea effects were a mere nuisance.

Recovering, Illych stood and faced Karl. "Anything that makes you this sick can't be healthy. Am I going to get cancer or something from your *ouiblet*?"

Karl absentmindedly shook his head. "No, Illych, there are no permanent side effects. The illness appears to come from changes in electrical signal propagation. Different parts of your body are temporarily no longer synchronized with your brain. Recovery takes less than a minute."

A frowning Illych said, "You say it *appears* to come from that? How confident are you?"

Karl snapped, "Stop interrupting me! I am trying to locate this Jack fellow."

Illych shrugged and looked around, inspecting their surroundings.

Karl feverishly worked the *ouiblet*, his fingers moving with speed and dexterity.

Illych looked over at the ever-changing display. "How do you know who this guy is?"

Without taking his attention from the *oculus*, Karl said, "Earlier, while the *oculus* was translating in for snapshots, visual spectrum images were taken. His office has a name tag with a photo. Knowing what he looked like, I waited until a man with the same appearance entered his office and sat at the desk. Then I visually confirmed it was him."

Illych asked, "Can you show me what he looks like?"

Karl flipped a switch and moved a small joystick with his thumb. A grainy photo of a tired-looking, middle-aged man slouched at his desk was displayed.

Illych said, "He looks spent. Rough day, I guess. So, are we waiting to see if he's going to his car?"

Karl replied, "The fire alarms have gone off in the building, and it is being evacuated. Our target is likely part of the crowd. Separating Jack out will require some effort."

Looking at what was on the *oculus* screen, Illych was compelled to ask, "That's a lot of people. What are you looking for? Those aren't people's faces on the screen."

Karl took a deep breath and exhaled, "Jack was injured sometime in the past. His right leg has a distinctive pattern of rods, pins, and screws. Metal objects are more easily differentiated with the *oculus*."

Illych nodded. "Cool."

Karl agreed, "Indeed. And there he is."

A disembodied collection of hardware filled the screen.

Karl said, "From what I gathered in my intelligence attempts just prior to our setting the building on fire, the FBI people typically park their vehicles here. In the parking garage we are currently standing in"

They intently watched the screen to see where Jack was going.

The barest hint of a smile betrayed Karl's victory. "Yes, he is coming this way."

Karl opened the door and exited the stairwell. Illych was close behind. People were streaming in from the ground-floor entrances, and most were taking the parking garage elevators to their vehicles.

Illych made a rough estimate of the head count. "Considering the size of the building being evacuated, that's not as many people as I would have expected."

Karl remained focused on the faces passing by. "The smaller crowd is convenient, which is to our advantage. It is 7:00 a.m., and the normal day staff has not arrived. I also suspect most of the FBI personnel are in the field looking for Danielle."

Karl kept looking at the *oculus*, holding it low to try to be inconspicuous. An attempt at stealth that was only partially successful. They got a few looks from people as they passed by. Individuals in the crowd noticed the out-of-place and oddly paired white-haired elderly man and the much younger, serious-looking, tall, dark-haired man. This contrast drew attention to them, and Karl holding a strange device that resembled a box on a pistol grip further exacerbated it.

Karl whispered, "Here he is."

Jack entered looking very much like a man in need of sleep and a shower.

Karl said, "Perhaps he is taking advantage of the fire situation to go home for some rest?"

Illych whispered, "Now what, Mr. Lark? There are a lot of people around." With emphasis, he added, "A lot of federal law enforcement people."

Karl nodded. "Let's follow him to his car."

The pair drifted in behind the preoccupied Jack Hemway and joined him and several others on an elevator ride.

During the elevator ride up, Jack's eyes focused on Illych for an instant. Something like recognition formed on the FBI agent's features. This passed quickly, and the tired expression returned.

Illych felt sympathy for the guy. Jack was having a profoundly bad day and was suffering because of it. And his day was about to get a lot worse.

Jack exited the elevator, with Karl and Illych following close by.

Illych whispered, "A lot less people here."

Karls nodded and whispered back, "I think this is where the more senior people keep their vehicles."

The pair was keeping their distance when the car Jack was approaching beeped. Jack whirled to face Illych and Karl while drawing his weapon.

In a commanding voice, he barked, "Put your hands up! I am a federal agent."

Illych started to comply.

Karl said, "But why?"

Illych looked over at Karl, not believing what he had just heard.

Jack declared, "You two followed me onto the elevator. Drop that thing in your hand. Then get your hands up and turn around."

Illych could see Karl working the *oculus* one-handed. The image on the screen was focused on the sprinkler piping directly above Jack. The *ouiblet* control was in the old man's other hand.

Illych started to smile. Yep, Jack's day was about to get worse.

The *ouiblet* removed most of the cross section of the sprinkler water main right above Jack. A column of water as big around as the man's head torrented down. Brown and smelling of years of stagnation, the force of it slammed Jack to his knees. The agent's gun clattered away under a nearby car while the man struggled to keep from being flattened to the concrete floor.

Illych's posture changed instantly. His hands came down, and taking long strides, he closed the distance to the tsunami gushing over the overwhelmed man. Stopping just outside the splash distance, he activated the Taser.

Between the exhaustion, the unexpected near drowning in foul water, and now a tasering, Danielle's supervisor almost instantly collapsed unconscious into the expanding water pool on the concrete floor.

The water flow was not stopping, changing from brown to fresh water as the pipes drained and makeup water was supplied.

Illych was forced to wade in and retrieve the unconscious, sodden Jack.

Karl walked over and retrieved Jack's gun from under the vehicle while avoiding the foul water.

Dragging the FBI agent clear, Ilych asked, "Now what?"

Returning to stand near Illych and the unconscious Jack, Karl pulled a black knit cap from a pocket. "Put this on over his eyes. Just in case."

Illych confirmed the man was still breathing and then pulled the makeshift blindfold over his head.

And then they were gone.

●　　●　　●　　●　　●

Illych felt the nausea and looked at the unconscious man he was holding.

Lucky bastard. This was the only bad thing Jack was missing out on today.

The trio had translated into a small, square room with cinderblock walls and a concrete floor. A single, bright fluorescent light illuminated the space, and one wall was a garage door.

Illych took in their surroundings and commented, "Storage unit?"

Karl said, "Yes, new construction, just finished. Not opened for tenants yet. An enclosed space where we will not be disturbed."

In the center of the room was an old wooden chair.

Illych dropped Jack onto the chair. Karl handed him a bag of zip-tie restraints.

Illych commented while pulling out a few ties, "You planned ahead."

Karl watched Illych work. "After learning of Danielle's kidnapping and returning you to the cabin, I determined some preparations were in order. I anticipated we would be questioning people, so I acquired the necessary tools and location. This impromptu interrogation room is the result."

Jack was swiftly and securely zip-tied, and the mask over his eyes was removed. Illych searched the man and found no other weapons. The wallet showed their captive's family: his wife and two smiling children. Nice.

Blinking eyes and verbal mumbling announced Jack's return to consciousness.

Coherence of thought coalesced, and Jack asked, "Where am I?"

Karl responded, "My apologies for the inconvenience. There are some questions that I need answers to, and I did not feel it was likely you would voluntarily share."

There was a long pause, then Jack asked, "Who are you people?"

"Concerned third parties," Karl answered. "The location and safe return of Danielle are important to us."

Jack coughed to clear his throat. "Yeah, well, that is important to me too. You idiots have kidnapped a federal agent. Do you know what that means?"

Illych chimed in, "There seems to be a lot of that going around. Why don't you answer the man's questions, and we can all go back to not being around each other?"

Jack looked back and forth at his captors and grimaced, "You're that Green Beret that went missing from Ft. Leavenworth. I recognized you in the elevator. There are a lot of people looking for you."

Karl interrupted, "Yes, and in spite of that, here he is, and here you are. Perhaps you should take that into consideration when answering my questions."

Karl paused for emphasis and then asked, "Why was Danielle kidnapped?"

Jack appeared to think for a moment and shrugged. "There's no reason you can't know what we know. Honestly, I don't know why. She's only been with us for six months. Danielle isn't even a field agent. She works as an analyst. Forensic accounting."

Illych leaned in and tapped the man between his eyes with his middle finger. The bound man jerked his head from the unexpected contact. Jack said, "No need for that. I'll tell you what I know. Danielle is a good kid, and if someone else can help find her, I'm ok with that.

"When she was a no-show at the office yesterday morning, I called her. Danielle is always prompt, and her no-show, no call—it wasn't right. When she didn't answer her phone, I called the local PD to do a wellness check. Her purse, cell phone, and car keys were found next to her car in the parking garage under her apartment building. Someone disabled the security cameras and appears to have grabbed her when she arrived home from work around seven in the evening. Not only were all her possessions just left there, but there was also no evidence that she fought back.

"The FBI has a protocol for this kind of situation. We've been tearing Chicago apart ever since. Whoever did this grabbed her with no witnesses, no surveillance camera video, and left no evidence we've been able to find. This wasn't local thugs getting some cash for their next fix."

Karl considered this and said, "That is obvious. Perhaps this is related to what she was working on? Something she learned at work?"

Jack shook his head and explained, "Danielle works money laundering. Organized crime business dealings to legitimize illegal cash flows. Important work, but she is low-profile. No street work or court appearances. Nobody outside the FBI knows who she is. Danielle is a pretty girl, but she is not a candidate for human trafficking—too old and not vulnerable enough. Those people don't take people with guns. And there's no jealous boyfriend in the picture either."

Karl nodded and thought for a moment before asking, "Speaking of guns. Did she carry one?"

Nodding in the affirmative, Jack answered, "Yes, and it wasn't found with her other personal items."

Karl continued, "You must have contacts in the criminal world?"

Jack snorted, "Every federal law enforcement officer within five hundred miles has been having very frank conversations with anyone who might know something. The gloves are off, and everyone knows it. No rational player wants a piece of this. Whoever did this is not playing with a full deck."

Karl said, "Our discussion has filled in a number of gaps in my understanding of the situation. Thank you. Do you have a business card in case I should need to call?"

Jack's expression changed to genuine surprise. "In my wallet. What? That's it? No rubber hose treatment?"

Illych opened Jack's wallet and pulled out a business card. Fortunately, it was still dry, and Karl took it, tucking it away in a pocket.

Karl frowned. "Don't be ridiculous. You'll be returned so you can continue pursuing Danielle's kidnappers. If I have further questions, I will call. Thank you for your time, and good luck in your search. Illych, taser him again."

Jack interrupted his imminent unconsciousness by saying, "Wait, if you can get her back, you have my thanks. She doesn't deserve this."

Karl paused while looking at Jack and then nodded to Illych, who promptly zapped Jack into unconsciousness.

Karl growled, "You are correct. She did not deserve this."

●　　●　　●　　●　　●

Another translation later, and Illych dropped an unconscious Jack Hemway, just out of sight, in bushes in the backyard of his house to awaken mere footsteps from home.

Karl placed his handgun back in its holster. If it were not for his soaked and stinking clothes and marks from the Taser, Jack might have wondered if it all really happened.

Illych and Karl translated to the cold outside the cabin and trudged inside to figure out their next steps.

•   •   •   •   •

Illych stoked the ebbing fire until it roared, radiating warmth to every corner of the cabin. The two men settled into the comfort of overstuffed leather.

Karl stated, "It was an inside job."

Illych took his seat and asked, "How so?"

"It is logical," Karl said, shrugging before he continued: "Danielle is relatively new in the office. She is not a field agent and does not provide testimony. There are no external-facing activities. Her kidnapping is not a crime of convenience. Everything in her hands was dropped. That is why the gun was not found. It would have been under her clothes.

"No body, no ransom, no theft. She was taken for what she knows."

Illych nodded. "But what could she know?"

Karl looked at Illych and replied, "Mr. Hemway gave that away. Her work is in money laundering. She knows something somebody else has a compelling interest in."

Illych shrugged and asked, "Okay, let's say she was taken for what she knows. How did she get taken without a fight?"

There was a long pause before Karl answered, "That part I do not know. Perhaps someone she knows who could get close? Regardless, I am certain of the rest."

Illych stretched in his seat. It had been a busy morning and was likely to get busier. "What's the next step?"

"It will take time for her captors to get all the information from her. And they will want to double-check and confirm. Her interrogation will not be over quickly. This is good. We likely have time to find her."

Illych took a deep breath before asking, "That's great, Mr. Lark, but where can we start?"

Karl's voice took on a robotic tone: "With money. Lots of money that is not in a bank. Where there is illegal currency, there will be money laundering. We will go back to Chicago and find people with obviously ill-gotten gains and question them."

Illych, no longer surprised by Karl Lark's unique approach, asked, "Those people aren't going to be as agreeable as that FBI supervisor was. This will take more persuasion."

Karl shrugged and stated, "It is unfortunate that some people will not be agreeable to supporting freeing my grandniece. I am sure there will be ways to convince them otherwise."

Illych asked, "What about the FBI guy? Do you think he knows about this inside job possibility?"

Karl nodded. "Likely. It makes sense, and he is in the business of investigating organized crime. He may also not be in a position to do much about it."

Slouching in the comfortable chair and the heat of the fire, Illych asked, "Okay, Mr. Lark, not to beat a dead horse, but what now?"

Karl gave an emphatic reply: "Six degrees of separation."

Illych sat up and blinked. "What?"

Karl continued, "There is a theory that any two people on the planet are only six degrees of separation apart. One person knows another, who knows another, and so on. For example, everyone is only six people away from the President of the United States."

A mildly exasperated Illych said, "Or the Queen of England. So, who do we start with?"

Karl turned his head completely to look directly at Illych. "We shall find someone to ask where we could launder large amounts of cash."

Karl then stood and headed for the door.

Illych looked at the newly stoked and blazing fire in the fireplace, shrugged his shoulders, stood up, and followed.

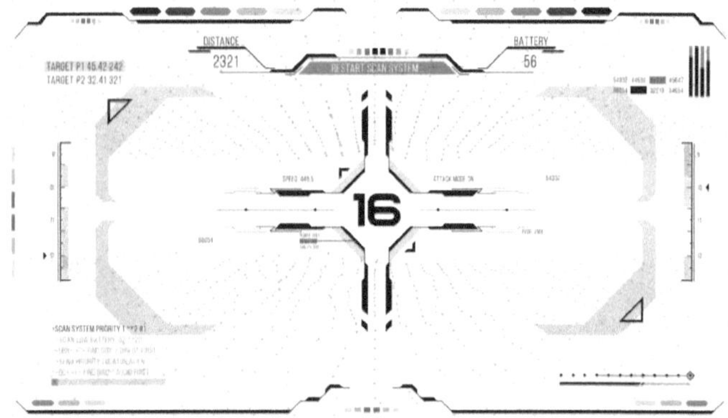

CHAPTER SIXTEEN

Chicago was cold in the winter. It was colder when you were perched atop a high-rise with no protection from the wind. Illych endured this while considering his situation.

The view of the whole city was fantastic from here. Not as amazing as at night, but inspiring even in the pale light of a winter morning.

Looking at Karl Lark intently focused on his *oculus*, Illych asked, "Can't we do this from the inside of a coffee shop?"

Karl gave a quick headshake and said, "No. The goal is to view the entire city as we begin. If our search forms a pattern, I can map it out from this image."

Illych's voice took on a hint of the incredulous: "In your head?"

His eyes still locked onto the *oculus*, Karl responded, "Yes, in my head."

Illych stamped his feet, confident no one was out on the roof of the skyscraper to hear him. "Assuming we don't freeze to death, what's next?"

Karl looked up from the *oculus* and out over the city. "We are going to look for a bookie."

Illych smirked. "A bookie?"

Not taking his eyes from the city view, Karl said, "Yes, as in someone who provides betting services."

Illych's smirk transitioned to a smile, and he asked "And where shall we find a bookie, Mr. Lark?"

Karl shrugged and replied, "I have no personal experience, but it is my understanding that this kind of activity takes place in bars. We must find a bar that shows sporting events and ask for a bookie."

Illych blinked while considering how weird this conversation was. "A bar that shows sporting events? You mean like a sports bar? You want to find a sports bar in Chicago?"

Karl visibly perked up. "There are sports bars in Chicago? Then let us go to one."

Illych shook his head, knowing what would come next.

●　　●　　●　　●　　●

Two hours of searching and several translations later—and nearly to lunchtime—the intrepid duo emerged from an alley and entered a nearby sports bar. Karl carried a small duffel bag over his shoulder with the *oculus* inside.

Karl speculated out loud, "This is early for such an establishment to be open."

Illych said, "They serve breakfast, and sports are global. There's a game on somewhere."

The central bar was surrounded by clusters of tables and chairs and supported multiple events simultaneously. The pre-lunch crowd was small but building as noon approached.

Karl looked around, almost to the point of gawking. "It is much larger than I expected. There are so many televisions with so many sporting events on display."

Illych nodded. There were a lot of televisions. And they were showing games from around the globe.

Karl was obviously out of his element, and Illych took the lead in finding them a seat at the bar. Pulling cash from a pocket, he ordered them each a beer.

Karl observed different patrons in turn, not unlike a boy looking at ants under a magnifying lens. "Which one do you think is potential bookie material?

Illych took a deep breath and exhaled, "I don't think it is going to be that easy. Let me work on it."

Illych got the bartender's attention. When he came over, Illych said, "Hey, my friend here and I have differing opinions on an upcoming Bull's game. We're looking to put some money behind our opinions. Know anybody who can help us out?"

The bartender looked back and forth between the oddly matched pair. "Betting is gambling, and gambling is illegal. Anyway, most of that stuff is online these days."

Illych produced a $100 bill and tossed it onto the bar atop the money for the drinks.

"Your tip."

The bartender looked back and forth between Illych and Karl and asked, "Are you guys cops? If you are, you're the weirdest cops I've ever seen in here."

Illych said, "We're not cops."

"Give me two more hundreds," the bartender replied, and Illych handed over the money.

The bartender nodded, tapped the money on the bar, and continued, "Sit tight. I might know a guy."

Illych sipped his beer. Never much of a drinker, his stint in prison had enhanced his appreciation for beer though. Two years without the option for something changed things—a lot of things.

Karl was giving off an uncomfortable vibe for anyone watching.

Illych said in a low voice, "Drink the beer, Mr. Lark."

Karl replied, "I do not drink."

Shaking his head in exasperation, Illych emphasized, "Today you do. Sitting there looking out of place while not drinking the beer in front of you is not helping us."

Karl picked up the bottle and took a sip. And then he took another.

His head tilted as if considering something. "This is almost agreeable."

Scenarios in which Karl Lark became intoxicated began to play out in Illych's mind. None of them ended in a good way. *Perhaps this drinking thing should be nipped in the bud now?*

He was getting ready to interrupt Karl's new interest when they were both interrupted by a middle-aged man with an overdeveloped smile.

The new guy stood close and said, "The bartender here says you guys have a difference of opinion and want arbitration, if you get my meaning. This may be your lucky day because I am in the arbitration business."

The man extended his hand. "My name is Jimmy. What should I call you guys?"

Illych replied, "This is Karl, and I'm Bob."

Jimmy pointed at each of them in turn and said, "Got it, Bob and Karl. What do you have in mind?

Illych pointed a thumb at Karl, smirked, and stated, "Karl here has a history of not following through on bets he makes when he loses."

Karl's head turned to look at Illych with an accusing stare.

Illych continued, "This has led to friction between us in the past. We agreed to work with a third party to keep this from happening again. Can you help us?"

Jimmy had a thoughtful look as he said, "What kind of money are we talking here? Arbitration is for serious people. You guys better not be wasting my time with small time numbers."

Illych shook his head and replied, "Anything less than ten thousand is boring. Does that work?"

Karl interrupted, "Do we get a receipt? That is a lot of money."

There was an awkward silence while Jimmy looked from Illych to Karl and back again. "No, no receipts. Look, you guys, I'll get back to you." The bookie hurriedly headed for the exit.

Illych hissed, "A receipt? You're asking for a *receipt*? You spooked him, and he ran away."

Karl was almost petulant in his reply: "Spooked him? How? That amount of money should involve receipts."

Illych noticed Karl's voice was not as clipped in delivery. "How much of that beer did you drink?"

Karl lifted up the bottle and slurred ever so slightly, "Just half."

Illych took the bottle from Karl and sat it on the far side of the bar. "That's enough. Now what do we do? Look for another bookie?"

Karl looked at the now-out-of-reach beer. "No, one is enough. This Jimmy will be able to give us what we want." Karl opened the duffel bag and focused on the *oculus* within. "Let's track him and find a good place to ask him questions."

The bartender had watched Jimmy's quick exit and was now giving them unfavorable looks.

Illych nudged Karl's arm with his elbow and quietly said, "Yeah, it's time to leave. I think Jimmy's quick exit marked us out to the bartender.

Karl closed the duffel bag and stood up. "Agreed, let's get out of here and follow Jimmy."

Once outside, the two quickly ducked into a nearby alley. Huddled around the *oculus*, they watched the movements of the departing Jimmy.

The bookie took a cab, stopped at a store, and then walked two blocks to what appeared to be his residence. Karl and Illych watched this all play out on the *oculus*.

Karl worked the *oculus* and *ouiblet* in preparation. "He's alone now. Let's acquire him and take him to the storage unit for questioning."

Illych coached in a gentle voice, "Or we can surprise him at his apartment and just ask him nicely. Then, if he is stubborn, we can take him to the storage unit and question him."

Karl paused for a moment and then said, "If it works, your suggested approach is more efficient. However, I suspect casual questions will not arrive at a constructive conclusion."

The pair translated to an unoccupied stairwell just down the hall from Jimmy's apartment. After waiting for Illych to recover, Karl opened the door, and the two men strode down the hall, quickly arriving outside the apartment.

Karl consulted the *oculus* and stated, "He is sitting watching television."

Illych nodded. "I can knock, or I can kick the door down. Your choice."

Karl looked up from the *oculus* and shook his head from side to side. "Neither is needed. The door is unlocked."

Illych smiled and pulled his pistol out from inside his jacket. "Convenient."

A twist of the knob and four great strides later, and that pistol was pointing at a shocked-looking Jimmy.

Illych said, "Hello, Jimmy."

Karl closed and locked the door behind him. "I have some questions for you and am hoping we can conclude our business quickly."

Jimmy looked back and forth at the odd pair. "I knew you two were trouble. What do you want?"

Karl said, "This bookie work that you do. Is there a lot of cash exchanged?"

Jimmy's voice became belligerent: "Yeah, that is how money gets made. People pay for things."

Karl continued, "You cannot be depositing this money in a bank."

Jimmy's voice got louder: "Hell, no. Can't trust banks. What's with the weird questions?"

Karl ignored the bookie's increasing anger and asked, "Then where does the cash go?"

Jimmy was waving his hands now and getting visibly worked up. "You two weirdos want to know where money goes?"

Illych interrupted, his voice controlled and cold: "Jimmy, answer the questions, or we'll move the conversation to the top of a very cold building with you naked and dangling off the side."

Jimmy nodded, the gravity of the situation deflating his anger. "So, yeah, if I have too much cash, you know, more than I'm comfortable with, I arrange for it to be deposited, but not with a bank. There are guys who do that. It is like a paper route, except instead of delivering papers, they are picking up the cash."

Karl stated, "And where does the cash go?"

Jimmy was looking back and forth between Karl and Illych. "You guys are crazy if you're planning on robbing those people. Look, I have a territory. I work my bookmaking and hand over the rent for the territory. I am not ratting those people out."

Illych said, "No ratting, Jimmy. We're looking for something, and the people you know can help us out. Share where they are, and we're out of here. Make us *their* problem."

A loud pounding on the door made all three men jump. An irritated feminine voice called out, "Jimmy, you said you would leave the door open."

Looking back to Jimmy, Illych continued, "What's it going to be, Jimmy?"

The pounding continued, followed by an angrier version: "Let me in. You said to come over." Kicks to the door followed the pounding.

Jimmy explained, "I'm having a friend over."

Karl commented, "That doesn't sound like a friend to me."

Jimmy retorted, "Yeah, well, maybe it's more fun that way."

Illych and Karl stared menacingly at the bookie.

"This is the address." He scribbled it on a scrap of paper and handed it to Karl. "Now get out of here."

Illych looked directly at the bookie and harshly informed him, "Jimmy, if this turns out to be useless, we'll be coming for you. And that naked-on-top-of-a-freezing-high-rise scenario will play out."

Jimmy waved his hands and acquiesced, "No, no tricks. That's the place you're looking for. Now get out."

Illych's free hand pulled out the Taser, and Jimmy did the dying chicken dance on the couch until he was very unconscious.

The voice outside the door continued, "You call me over and don't let me in? I can hear the TV, you bastard! I know you're in there. It's that whore from down the hall, isn't it? I'm comin' in whether you like it or not." There was a loud crash of something substantial throwing itself against the door.

Karl turned Jimmy's head so they could translate without a chance of being seen.

Another loud crash at the door.

Karl was feverishly working the *oculus*. "We must go before the wrath of that woman finds us here."

They disappeared seconds before the door crashed in.

●　　●　　●　　●　　●

Karl and Illych were watching from a rooftop, several houses down and across the street from the address Jimmy provided. Finding the address and a vantage point from which to surveil it had taken only a few minutes, and now they were looking out onto a classic ghetto scene.

Karl looked at the poor condition of the street and houses. Trash was everywhere. He then stated the obvious: "This address is in a terrible neighborhood."

The mid-afternoon sun did not provide any warmth, and the wind was bone-chilling cold. The rooftop offered no cover.

Illych whispered to himself, "I don't know, but I've been told Eskimo pussy is mighty cold."

Karl turned to look at Illych and disdainfully said, "I beg your pardon."

Illych smirked and replied in a playful tone, "Just a cadence we sang when I was in the Army. Seemed appropriate."

Karl's face turned disapproving. "How is a vulgar chant appropriate?"

Illych shook his head.

Their target was a two-story, cinder-block structure. It might have been a home or small apartment building at one time. Now, half the windows were boarded up, and the ones that were not had bars on them. Outside, down by the street, stood three men warming themselves around a barrel with a fire inside.

"I'm guessing those three are lookouts or guards. Outside in this weather is a terrible job." Illych observed.

Karl shifted the *oculus* so both men could view the inside of the house.

Karl angled the *oculus* to share with Illych and stated, "There is plenty of cash."

Illych said, "You know, Mr. Lark, Jimmy might have lied. These could be competitors or some problem he wanted solved."

Karl shrugged with indifference. "The clock is ticking on my grandniece, and these characters can get me closer to her freedom. I do not care if they are specifically guilty of what happened. They are obviously not good guys, and I am in a hurry. Do you have an issue with what must be done?"

Illych's face took on a flat, serious look. "No issue, Mr. Lark. My guess is the men down there are not Boy Scouts late for church, and I have two years of frustration to let loose and vent on someone. These guys will work as well as anyone."

Karl made more adjustments and said, "Three outside by the fire. Gatekeepers. And then three inside. I am guessing the three outside will not be as helpful and are likely to raise the alarm if we just walk up. Let's eliminate them and take one of the three inside for questioning."

Illych gave Karl a skeptical look. "I'm good with a gun, but after shooting those three, the ones inside will be ready for us. Not a plan for success."

Karl nodded. "Agreed. But perhaps there is a more effortless approach."

Illych watched the *oculus* screen as Karl zoomed in on a car half a block down. Out of the corner of his eye, he saw the car disappear from its parking spot at the same time it vanished from the *oculus* display.

His gaze switched to the men down on the street, only to see the car reappear ten feet in the air, halfway between where it was and its intended target. Gravity took over, and the car fell to the ground with a crash somewhat muted by the snowdrift it landed on. None of the three men saw this happening. The loud noise made them jump, though. Turning to look, they saw the car that used to be down the block was now much closer, bouncing on broken suspension with a broken windshield. Illych could hear a faint "What the…?" carried on the wind.

A frustrated Karl hissed, "My mistake. Should have been fifty feet up and one hundred feet over. Switched them around and missed a digit. That was ten feet up and fifty feet over. Correcting."

The car disappeared again. Then it reappeared so high up that Illych had to look up slightly, even from their elevated position on the roof. Gravity took over again, and the car plummeted downward. His eyes followed its descent.

The three men's shock at the car's sudden disappearance was evident in their body language and head movements. One of them actually looked up just as the car's fall came to an end. The men were crushed flat, as was the burning barrel.

Sparks and glowing coals shot out from under the vehicle as its suspension bottomed out.

With no snow to dampen the noise, the crash sound was shattering, and car alarms began sounding from several directions.

Illych was incredulous at what he just saw: "Who looks up in that situation?"

Karl flatly stated, "Those men will no longer be an obstacle."

Illych said, "No kidding, and we've also completely lost the element of surprise. The men in the house will be ready for us."

Karl did not miss a beat in his reply, "I have a plan for that. And my apologies for this."

Illych had just an instant to feel a hint of anxiety. "Apologies for wha—"

The *ouiblet* delivered them to the side of the house, behind barren shrubs and overflowing garbage bins.

Illych doubled over and hissed, "No warning, Mr. Lark?"

Karl said, "We are pressed for time. My apologies again. This may be loud.

The sound of shattering glass, breaking wood, and collapsing drywall came from inside the house. The plywood on the window above them was sucked into the building.

Illych recovered as Karl announced, "The men inside have been disabled. We must enter now."

Karl walked out from beside the house to the front yard and headed straight for the front door, which had been blown into the house. Illych followed, pistol in hand.

Illych cautioned, "Karl, maybe you should stay closer to the wall."

Without pause, Karl strode forward. "The men inside have other concerns than our presence. We must get inside quickly, though."

As they turned the corner, the level of destruction began to register. Every window was shattered and blown inward.

Karl walked up the steps and boldly entered right through an open doorway. The door itself had been torn free from its hinges and laid off to one side.

The lights inside conveniently remained on. Entering, they were greeted by a scene from a disaster movie. Shattered window glass covered everything. Chunks of drywall ripped free from the walls and the ceiling covered much of the floor.

In the middle of the chaos of broken glass, shards of drywall, and swirling dust were three men writhing on the floor. Each was clutching his chest and in obvious distress.

Illych had seen a lot of destruction and death, but this was just . . . *weird*. "Jesus, Lark, what did you do?"

Karl's voice took on a hint of pride: "I instantly removed all the nitrogen and oxygen from the room. Every last atom. I estimate the pressure on each window from outside the house exceeded three tons. Each. The external air pressure blasted the door, windows, and parts of the walls inward.

"The air would have been ripped out of the men's lungs. Quite painful and probably damaging."

One of the men was choking and indicating he could not breathe.

Of the three men, one appeared less damaged than the others.

Karl pointed at the healthiest and said, "We will take him. Can you take care of the others? We do not need witnesses."

Illych shrugged and fired twice. The shots were deafening in the enclosed space. The remaining man's expression was of pure terror.

"Illych, please use the Taser. We must travel from this place," Karl said, walking to the wall switch and flicking off the lights. The room went dark.

The buzzing of the Taser indicated to Illych that his hearing was recovering from the gunfire.

Karl walked back to stand by Illych and the prone man, who was now very unconscious.

And then they were gone.

●　　●　　●　　●　　●

A bleeding and seriously wounded man was zip-tied to the chair, his eyes covered, in the empty storage unit. No sooner had they secured him than he started mumbling.

Illych called out, "He's waking up."

Bound Man slurred, "Why can't I see?"

Karl said, "You are blindfolded."

Bound Man grunted, "Uh. At least I'm not blind."

Karl began, "What is your name?"

Bound Man said with bravado, "Call me Tee."

"Well then, Mr. T, I—"

Tee yelled, "Do I look like I wear a bunch of gold chains? No, mister, just *Tee*." Illych snickered, and Karl looked perplexed for a moment.

Karl said, "Understood. You are Tee."

Karl leaned closer and continued, "Well, Tee, I have some questions. If you can answer them quickly, you will be returned. Do you understand?"

Tee nodded. "Uh-huh."

Karl asked, "Your residence is a collection point for money?"

Tee coughed and spat, "I ain't about to tell you my business."

Karl frowned. "Unfortunately for you, Tee, the path to your freedom from this situation will be delivered by your sharing information with us. We are not interested in you. Only in finding the next person."

Tee coughed again: "I don't feel so good. My chest hurts."

Karl calmly said, "You are suffering from extreme, sudden decompression, and your lungs have sustained serious injuries. Medical attention will be required soon if you are to survive."

Illych gave Karl a questioning look. Karl leaned close and whispered, "I'm not a medical doctor, but the decompression must have damaged his lungs."

Tee's voice took on a more raspy and wet sound: "Get me to a doctor, and then maybe we can talk about your questions."

Karl took a breath and exhaled, "Tee, I am not a patient man. If you will not share information, you will be disposed of, and I will go looking for someone else to answer my questions. Are there others in your line of business in the Chicago area? My guess is dozens, maybe even hundreds. And I will work through every single one until I get answers."

Tee coughed and flecks of blood covered his mouth. With resignation, he said, "What do you want to know?"

Karl said, "The money that comes to you, where does it go?"

Tee replied without delay, "I take my percent and call it in. They send a truck."

Karl looked at Illych and asked, "Who is '*they*?'"

Tee gave a half-shrug. "I don't know. I mind my business and don't ask. Take my percent and do my job."

Karl asked, "Who recruited you?"

Tee coughed a nasty, wet cough and said, "That guy is dead."

Karl's voice was shifting to frustration: "Tee, I need to know who is in charge of the money. Who is in charge?"

Tee gave out a coughing laugh. "That's all? Just read the newspapers, man. Last year, the cops arrested a guy they say is the big boss. His lawyer got him off, though. You should talk to him—the lawyer. I bet he knows."

Karl nodded. "Thank you, Tee. You have been most helpful."

Tee asked, "Can I go home now? I need a doctor."

Karl picked up the *oculus* and replied, "Working on it now."

Tee smiled, showing red teeth. "Thanks, man." Instantly, he was gone from the chair.

Illych shook his head. "I'm never gonna get used to that. Did you send him home?"

Karl said, "I did. He was translated three hundred feet above the place we took him from, and he fell to his death."

Illych blinked and said, "Mr. Lark, you implied the guy would get medical attention if he gave up the information."

Karl stated, "I lied. He could not be allowed to survive and tell anyone about our questions."

Illych shrugged. "That's cold. It makes sense, but very cold."

Karl was working the *oculus* for the translation Illych knew was coming. "Our goal is to locate and secure the safety of my grandniece. All other considerations are secondary."

Illych took a breath and prepared himself. "So now what? Did Tee there give us enough to work with?"

With everything set, Karl looked up from the *oculus* and locked eyes with Illych. "Indeed, he did. We will find this lawyer and have a conversation with him."

●　　●　　●　　●　　●

Returning Ilych to the cabin, Karl announced, "I am going looking for the next person we need to interview. I shan't be long." The old man promptly disappeared.

Illych shrugged. He was sure whoever they were zip-tying to a chair next would not describe the experience as an *interview*. Closing the cabin door behind, him he looked at the bare whisp of embers in the fireplace. *Time to get that roaring again, and then get some shut-eye before whatever Mr. Lark comes back with next.*

Seven hours had passed by the time Karl knocked on the cabin door, announcing his return.

Illych called out, "Door's unlocked."

Karl entered from the chilly air and announced, "I have found him."

A recently-awoken Illych was sitting in front of the fire, cleaning a handgun. Closing the door behind him, Karl took a seat. "The search was not too difficult. Finding a prominent, successful attorney whose cases make money laundering headlines was child's play."

Illych didn't even look up from his work as he stated, "Seven hours is a long time for child's play."

Karl took a deep breath and explained, "Indeed. Such people go to great lengths to hide their residences. Finding where this particular lawyer lived was an involved process. Ultimately, I was successful. This was followed by scouting the residence and formulating a plan. Another few hours were needed to assemble the necessary items to support the plan. Person, location, plan, equipment—all that is left is coming here to collect you."

Illych completed the reassembly of the pistol, stood, and stretched. "That took a long time. I even had time to get some sleep. So where is this pillar of the community we're going to interview?"

Karl was focused on the fire while he said, "Penthouse suite on top of a high-rise in downtown Chicago."

Illych began grabbing his gear and putting on a coat as he asked, "Do I need anything specific for this? A rifle?"

Karl shook his head and replied, "Other than the Taser and your handgun, no. I have already gathered the needed items.

"There is an empty set of offices in a building across from our destination. We can view the situation and discuss. Ready?"

Illych gave a nod . . .

● ● ● ● ●

They translated onto the floor of a building being remodeled or otherwise under construction. Scaffolding, paint buckets, and plastic sheeting were scattered about. Karl pointed out through the floor-to-ceiling windows, across the canyon between buildings, to the nearest high-rise.

"The top ten floors are penthouse suites, one set stacked vertically in each corner for a total of forty residences. Each corner has its own elevator, requiring key card access at each level. There is also a stairwell for each corner, also requiring key-card entry at each individual suite level. This is apparently a full concierge building, as there is also a service elevator for staff to access the suites without disturbing the residents."

Illych sighed, "So this is how the other half lives."

Karl said, "More like the tenth of a percent, but yes, these residences are quite luxurious."

Illych studied the glass tower and asked, "So, who are we about to terrorize in the dead of the night?"

Karl said, "An attorney named Alexander Haskins. Quite successful. Has his own law firm and represents people with complex legal issues simultaneously burdened with a high net worth."

Illych smiled slyly. "You have a plan?"

"Yes, we will translate into a closet where the elevator opens onto Mr. Haskins suite. I will then use the *ouiblet* to disable both elevators."

"And the stairwell?" Illych asked.

Karl's expression brightened just the slightest as he answered, "I have something special planned for that. You will see when we arrive."

Illych looked at Karl. "Are you going to do that air removal thing to this Alexander fellow?"

Shaking his head, Karl said, "Unfortunately, no, we may need to question him for some time. The perfect vacuum approach could accelerate his expiring before I am satisfied."

Illych was thinking of contingencies now. "And if he has a gun?"

Karl was looking at the *oculus*. "I checked. There are no firearms in the residence."

Illych turned to look back into the construction zone inside the building. "Very thorough."

Karl gave a curt nod and replied, "Thank you."

Crossing his arms, Illych looked at Karl and inquired, "So, we teleport in?"

Karl did not pause his fiddling with the *oculus* as he corrected him, "*Translate*—there is a difference."

An admonished Illych said, "Understood, so we translate in. Disable the elevators and stairs. Then walk in and have a conversation with Mr. Haskins."

Karl's eyes left the *oculus* and went level. "Yes. Should he prove uncooperative, we take him to the storage unit for a more robust interrogation."

Illych made a face like he smelled something bad. "Ugh. Mr. Lark, I'm not torturing a guy with pliers and a blowtorch or whatever you have in mind."

Disdain flashed on Karl's face. "Nothing like that at all. The *ouiblet* opens up numerous options for persuading someone reluctant to respond to questioning."

Illych stood up straight and returned to looking at the intended target building. "This is what I get for asking if the work would be interesting."

Karl looked at Illych and asked, "Shall we?"

Illych nodded.

●　　●　　●　　●　　●

Their destination was pitch-black. Illych only knew the translation was complete when the nausea hit. While he recovered, Karl found the light switch.

Karl began working the *oculus* with his left hand and the *ouiblet* control with his right. Illych could see the elevator cable on the *oculus* screen. Ghostly images of people inside flashed across the screen as a small chunk of the cable was translated away. The focus then shifted to the next elevator.

An incredulous Illych declared, "Did you just cut that cable with people inside?"

Karl did not pause. "Do not be concerned. All elevators have a safety system that locks the elevator in place in the event the cables are cut. The people inside are perfectly safe."

The same scenario played out for the service elevator.

"And now for the stairwell." Karl worked the *ouiblet* controls again.

A large, heavy-looking crate marked *CS Gas, Riot Canisters* appeared in the closet.

Karl looked at Illych, stating, "I found these in a police warehouse. They had many, many of them and will not likely miss this one. Please drag it out into the entryway. We will use it to prop open the stairwell door."

Karl opened the closet door, revealing a richly appointed foyer beyond.

Illych started dragging the box out. "You know, Mr. Lark, we spend a lot of time coming out of the closet. People are going to talk."

Karl regarded Illych for a moment before asking, "Humor?"

Illych shook his head and answered, "Only to some."

With the stairwell door blocked, the crate was opened, and Karl grabbed a canister. Walking to the stairwell railing, he pointed downward and said, "See that central space between the railings. We are going to drop these down there, hopefully distributing them randomly between floors. These canisters generate a considerable volume of gas and will fill the stairwell. This will hinder any efforts to interfere with our questioning of Mr. Haskins."

The unlikely duo spent the next twenty minutes bombarding the levels below with canisters spewing noxious gas. By the time the last canister fell into the fogged stairwell below, both men's eyes had begun to water.

Pushing the crate back out into the hall, they allowed the door to close.

After a final review of the *oculus*, Karl stated, "Let's go talk to Mr. Haskins."

Illych drew a pistol from inside his coat.

Curiously, the door to the penthouse was unlocked.

A concerned Illych asked, "Is he expecting guests?"

Karl shrugged. "If he was, they are likely now feeling discouraged in getting here."

The inside was a communal space with rooms to the left and right. The building corner was floor-to-ceiling glass.

Karl was watching the *oculus*. "His bedroom is to the left, and he appears to still be sleeping."

Illych took the lead while Karl followed with the reclined form of their target highlighted on the *oculus* screen.

The bedroom door was mostly open, and they entered quickly. The man on the bed continued snoring softly. Illych took up position with his weapon pointed at the bed's occupant. Karl found the light switch and flipped it on.

A tanned middle-aged man with a full head of steel-gray hair raised his hands to his eyes.

Alexander blinked and squinted, finally adjusting to the light. He looked back and forth between the white-haired elderly man by the door and the dark-haired, serious-looking man pointing a gun at him from beside his bed.

"Who are you two?"

Karl replied, "We are concerned citizens who wish to ask you some questions."

Alexander was apparently the unflappable type. "I have business hours."

Karl did not pause as he continued, "Unfortunately, time is pressing, and these are not the typical consultation questions."

Alexander sat up, revealing he slept in briefs.

Apparently unimpressed by the armed men entering his house in the middle of the night, he informed them, "This is breaking and entering. If you leave now, you may avoid arrest and prosecution."

Illych interrupted, "Mr. Lawyer Man, start talking. We've been asking people questions all day, and some of them can no longer answer anything. I wouldn't put it past the old man here to shoot out a window and count how many Mississippi's until you hit the ground."

Alexander wrinkled his nose and asked, "What's that smell?"

Karl responded, "That is tear gas. The elevators and security system have been disabled. The stairwells are now pressurized with CS gas. We can have our talk without any concern of interruption."

The gravity of the situation was now sinking in on Alexander Haskins. "You guys are serious about this?"

Karl and Illych nodded.

He continued, "And if I tell you what you want to know, you'll leave, and I don't go out the window?"

Karl nodded. "This is why we are having the conversation here. If we have to move you to another location, it will be a one-way trip. Unless you are directly involved, in which case falling from a great height will be the least of your concerns."

Alexander shrugged and sat back against the headboard. "What do you want to know?"

Karl asked, "Who owns money laundering in the greater Chicago area?"

Alexander laughed, "That's all? You planning on a hostile takeover?"

Karl disagreed: "Nothing of the sort. We represent a third party who wishes to resolve a poor judgment call on someone's part. The goal is to find that someone and convince them of their error."

Alexander looked thoughtful for a moment and then said, "This has to do with that FBI agent being kidnapped, doesn't it?"

Karl nodded. "Indeed, it does."

Alexander took a breath and shook his head, "Can't say I am surprised. The FBI was at my firm today with questions.

I can assure you that none of my clients, no one I know, nor anyone they are associated with or employ, are involved."

Illych snorted, "You pinky promise?"

Karl had a skeptical expression. "Mr. Haskins, why should I believe you?"

Alexander elaborated, "It's bad business. *Money laundering*, as you call it, is an established, good business. All parties involved know each other and have a vested interest in the status quo. Everyone gets paid. The politicians and police know the arrangements. On top of that, the FBI keeps track of the whole business."

A surprised Karl queried, "The FBI knows the entire operation?"

Alexander continued, "Of course they do. It's in everyone's interest that money operations are stable. Otherwise, gang wars and all kinds of problems manifest. And that's bad for business."

Karl was now obviously thinking about what has just been shared: "There are no open disagreements? No interested parties?"

Crossing his arms, Alexander said, "If someone internal did this, they'll be found out and then never heard from again. Kidnapping an FBI agent is stupid. It's bad publicity and degrades trust with the feds. Again, this is bad business."

Karl speculated, "What about ambitious individuals looking to increase their position? That has to happen all the time?"

Alexander said, "There are always low-level people jockeying for more. There are mechanisms in place for this. Just recently, a distributor was not happy—" Alexander froze, his magnificent tan lightening by a few shades.

Karl noticed, "You look like a man who just realized something?"

The concerned expression remained, and Alexander said, "Yeah, I need to make a phone call."

Karl leaned closer and advised him, "No, Mr. Haskins, you need to talk."

Alexander looked back and forth between the two men standing in his bedroom and capitulated, "Fine. There is what you might call a 'territory manager.' His name came up in some meetings. He's been pushing to move up and isn't realizing he's reached the limit of his talents. I've never met the man and don't know where to find him."

Karl's expression turned dark. "You have the name?"

"Jerry Alba."

Karl's head cocked to one side, sizing Alexander up before asking, "Is this an attempt to get us to leave quickly?"

A shake of his head showed Alexander was being truthful. "I have to check on this one, but honestly, I don't believe he has the talent to pull this off. For now, it's all I've got."

Mr. Lark stepped back away from the bed and said, "Mr. Haskins, this will be checked out. If we need more information, there may be a repeat visit."

Alexander frowned. "I should bill you guys."

Illych blinked and coughed while keeping the pistol trained on the lawyer. "Is it me, or is the gas smell getting worse?"

Karl looked at a ceiling vent. "I suspect the building ventilation is distributing the gas in unanticipated ways. We must be going."

His eyes now watering profusely, Alexander Haskins looked back and forth between Karl and Illych. "I don't know who you guys are, but next time just call my office instead of doing terrible things to my neighbors and the building I live in. My receptionist will know to pass through the callers who announce themselves as the 'Tear Gas Guys.'"

Karl regarded Alexander for a long moment and then said, "Thank you for the consideration, Mr. Haskins. Illych, taser him."

Illych moved swiftly, surprising his victim, and Alexander let out a yelp while convulsing on his bed.

Karl and Illych left the bedroom, closing the door behind them.

Karl commented as they walked to the middle of the room, "This was less helpful than I had hoped. I assumed the syndicate running the money laundering operation would be at odds with the FBI. Instead, it's likely a known situation. Which also means Danielle also knows the complete operation as part of her job. And she likely has been kidnapped for that information."

Karl and Illych's eyes were flowing, and both men began coughing.

Illych hacked out a comment: "I think we overdid the CS gas, Mr. Lark."

Karl nodded while holding his free hand to his mouth for a cough. "It served its purpose. Time to go."

Illych asked, "What's next?"

Karl removed the *ouiblet* control from a pocket and started working both it and the *oculus*. "A change of clothes and then a conversation with Mr. Alba."

A faint curl of CS gas marked where the two had just stood.

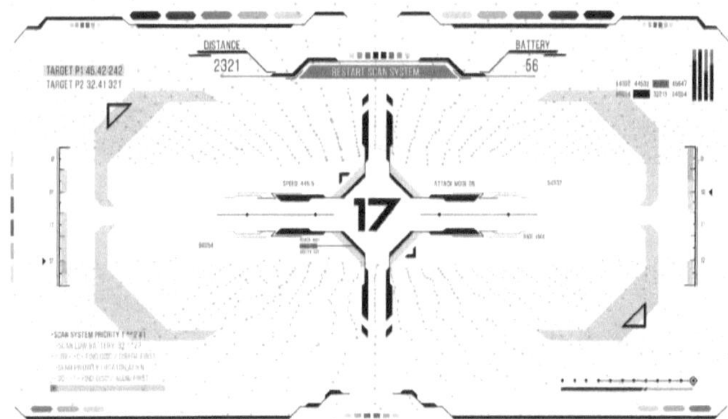

CHAPTER SEVENTEEN

Illych found himself alone on the now-familiar slope outside the cabin. He looked around for Karl. It was the middle of the night, but the stars provided ample light to see that he was alone on the snow.

Illych considered, *This is new. Either he split us to separate destinations or something horrible just happened and I'm on my own.*

Shrugging his shoulders, he started towards the cabin. He was hungry, and his clothes stank of CS gas. Time to clean up and relax. Nothing to do but wait and see if the old man turned up.

●　　●　　●　　●　　●

Not an hour later, Karl appeared on the same slope, walked down to the cabin door, and knocked.

Illych's muffled voice called out, "Come in."

Karl entered and closed the door behind him. The fireplace had a roaring fire, and the reddish-orange light competed with the bright white of a gas lamp to illuminate the inside of the cabin.

Illych had changed into fresh clothes and was sitting at the table, eating steak. Between bites, he asked, "I made extra. You want some?"

Karl shook his head, walked to his preferred chair, and took a seat.

Illych paused to ask, "What was the separate arrival trick all about?"

Karl replied, "Trying something new, and it seemed like a way to save time. There is no reason to escort you back here. I assume you can find your way."

Illych cut his next bite. "You might warn me next time. I wasn't sure if something went wrong. Like a moving-the-decimal-place type of thing."

Karl exhaled, "An oversight on my part. Now, if you are done voicing your concerns, can we discuss business?"

Illych spoke with his mouthful, "As long as I can do it from here. This is good steak, and I like it hot."

Karl ignored the unorthodox speaking arrangement and continued, "I have this Jerry Elba's home address. It was much easier to find compared to Alexander Haskins. It was as if that man did not want people to know where he lived."

Illych commented, "That easy, huh?"

Karl nodded. "Perhaps, if Mr. Alba is home."

Pausing before his next bite, Illych asked, "Are we leaving right away?"

Karl shook his head, "Please finish your steak. It's been a busy night, and I wish to sit here comfortably and collect my thoughts. Then we will go."

Illych finished enjoying his dinner, then collected his coat and tools of the trade. The two men stood close together.

Illych looked at Karl and nodded.

●　　　●　　　●　　　●　　　●

Karl and Illych translated to a wooded lot across the street from a large American home surrounded by an expansive snow-covered yard. Accent lighting illuminated the many impressive features of the home.

Illych commented, "Nice house. Apparently, crime does pay."

Karl was looking at the *oculus*. "Yes, Mr. Alba lives well."

Illych asked, "Is he inside?"

Karl, working the *oculus* controls, replied, "Indeed, he is. And despite the fact it is the dead of the night, he appears to be in a hurry. Ah, he is packing. Perhaps Mr. Alba intends to leave."

Illych smirked. "Can we do the air vacuum thing again?"

Karl shook his head, "Too risky—it could kill him."

A disappointed Illych said, "That didn't stop you at the cash-drop house."

Karl said, "That was different. There were three of them. It was likely one of them would have survived long enough to answer questions. Here we have only a single thread connecting us to the next step in our search."

"Okay, but are we sure this is the guy?" Illych asked, looking directly at Karl. "We've got the word of a lawyer that this Alba is who we're looking for. What if the guy in the house is his housekeeper or something? Or Haskins gave us a fake lead? You know, to make us go away?

"I'm just saying, before we go full hardcore—like drop a car on this guy or whatever you have in mind—we should make sure he's the guy. Emphasis on *the*."

Karl looked up with a thoughtful expression. "If the attorney misled us, I will be very disappointed. We will confirm this is Jerry Alba first. Once confirmed, we will question him."

Illych wondered how careful Karl was really going to be. "So how do you want to do this?"

Karl stated, "There is a car in the garage he is placing things into. I estimate that shortly he will be driving away. Let's stand outside his garage door and greet him when he leaves."

Illych shrugged, and Karl plotted a path on the *oculus* to the garage door. The two men followed it to the driveway, confident they could not be seen from the house.

The wait was short, and the driver's eyes went wide when the garage door opened to reveal two men standing in his way. He found himself staring down the business end of Illych's large caliber handgun while Karl walked around to the driver's door and called out, "Get out of the car."

Composing himself, the driver's side door opened. Karl and Illych now realized Jerry Alba was a big man. Tall and muscular, he looked like a physical match for Illych, if not more so. Levering himself out of the driver's seat, he addressed the pair, tone menacing, "What's this? Who are you two idiots?"

Karl barked in a commanding voice, "Please turn around and re-enter your house."

The man, who might be Jerry, sneered, "Why, because of pistol boy here? What is it going to take to get you out of my driveway?"

Karl said, "Answer a few questions quickly, and we will be gone in minutes. I must warn you, though. Should you attempt to flee, my companion here will shoot you. And then we will question you."

The man looked at the business end of the pistol and relented, "Uh-huh."

Karl waved a hand toward the inside door. "Let us go inside, Mr. Alba."

The big man's eyes narrowed. "You know my name." A statement, not a question.

Illych smiled. *Question answered.*

Jerry turned and walked slowly into the house. Illych maintained his distance with his weapon aimed and ready. As they entered the hallway connecting the rest of the house with the garage, Karl activated the garage door closing. He then directed, "This door right here—open it."

Jerry pointed at the door and asked, "How did you know this was the door to my basement?"

Karl's speech took on a clipped aspect: "You need to talk less, Mr. Alba."

As Jerry opened the door, his free hand grabbed a poster-sized picture frame from the adjacent wall, leveraging it free and pushing it towards Illych. Before the pane of glass reached its target, Illych fired. The gunshot was cataclysmically loud in the enclosed space of the hallway. Jerry cried out and sprinted down the hall. After a few steps, he fell, clutching his left hip.

Illych coolly commented, "I winged him."

Karl nodded, acknowledging his marksmanship. "Excellent shooting."

Turning to Jerry, Karl said, "It is unfortunate you chose this path. We now have to drag you down the stairs, which, with your injury, will likely be painful."

Illych grabbed the big man's arm and dragged him to the stairs. "You can either crawl down the stairs or I'll push you down. And if you try to grab things and make this difficult, I'll start shooting other parts of you that won't kill you. Capisce?"

Jerry nodded reluctantly. "*Capisce.*"

Obviously in severe pain, the big man worked his way down the stairs, leaving a blood trail on every step.

Karl and Illych followed. The basement was fully furnished. Full bar, all wood, with shelves of liquor bottles. Pool table, big-screen television, and a collection of overstuffed leather chairs and couches. The epitome of a man cave.

Illych whistled, "This is nice."

The man-cave floor was deep-pile carpet, and Jerry was staining it with a ruinous blood trail as he dragged himself along.

Illych said, "Pick a chair, Jerry." The wounded man pulled himself up, wincing as he settled in.

Karl started the questioning: "Mr. Alba, you are an ambitious man? Aspirations for expanding your material wealth?"

Jerry glanced at Illych and asked him, "Why does he talk like that?"

Illych rolled his eyes, shrugged and shook his head.

Karl continued, "Why are you in such a hurry to leave?"

In spite of his wound, Jerry spoke loudly: "A little birdie told me my name came up with the feds, and I needed to disappear for a while."

Karl continued, "And why did your name make the list?"

Jerry blinked in pain and said, "Some FBI chick got grabbed, and my name got associated with it."

Illych could see Karl's expression shift for a fraction of a second. If he'd blinked his eyes, he would have missed it. For the briefest instant, something cold, almost reptilian, manifested. It occurred to him that this Alba fellow might want to be more careful with his words about Mr. Lark's grandniece.

Karl exhaled, "Yes, an FBI agent was kidnapped. What do you—"

The question was interrupted by a crash upstairs. A door being broken open? And the sound of booted feet on the floor above. A lot of booted feet.

Illych said it first: "What the hell?"

Karl grabbed the *oculus*. A commanding voice could be heard from upstairs: "FBI! Show yourself!"

Karl's other hand was now holding the *ouiblet* control.

Now the loud voice was at the door at the top of the stairs: "If someone's in the basement, declare yourself!"

The tactical officers opened the door and tossed flash-bang grenades down the blood-trail-covered stairs. A brief moment after they detonated, the basement was stormed.

All they found was an empty room with a bright red blood trail on the carpet leading to a fresh pool of the same on a leather chair.

"We must have just missed them. They have to be close."

Many miles away in a storage unit.

The stress of being shot, the blood loss, the cognitive dissonance of translating, and the additional discomfort of the translation nausea were causing Jerry Alba to have a full-on anxiety attack. He was writhing on the floor, screaming. "Who are you people? What just happened?"

He then curled into a fetal position and moaned, "I feel sick."

Illych leaned against a wall to weather the feeling of nausea.

Karl waited patiently while Illych and Jerry recovered.

Illych hauled Jerry up onto the chair. The big man did not resist at all, obviously weakening from blood loss.

Karl started in on him: "Answer my questions quickly, Mr. Alba. What do you know about the kidnapping of the FBI agent?"

Slurred words followed. "She knows—she knows everything. If you want a bigger piece of the pie, you have to know."

Karl hissed, "And who wants the bigger piece?

"Everybody wants a bigger piece, man." Jerry appeared to be fading, and his eyes drifted closed.

Karl slapped the man. The suddenness surprised Illych.

Karl moved closer to Jerry, bending over inches from the man's face, and demanded, "I need a name, Mr. Alba. *Who* wants a bigger piece?"

Jerry's eyes snapped opened with a return of focus.

"The big man wants more." Jerry Alba's eyes closed and did not open again.

Illych asked, "Who is the *big man?* Is that even an answer?"

Karl stood up straight and replied, "I believe it was, and I know just who to ask."

●　　●　　●　　●　　●

Alexander Haskins sat at his desk in his magnificently appointed office, looking through listings for a place to live. Having arrived still wearing the sweatpants and T-shirt from his rescue only a few hours ago, he was able to shower and change into the emergency suit he kept in the office.

The lunatics who'd showed up in his penthouse in the dead of the night pumped the stairwell full of so much CS gas that the entire building had to be evacuated. The paramedics had cleared him, but his throat hurt, and the red in his eyes made him look like a drug user.

The stench permeated everything. It would be a month or more before he could return to living in his home while the mess there was cleaned up.

At least he had the good sense to not mention his visitors to anyone. Blame would have fallen on him, and there would have been many, many more questions.

The police were investigating who had vandalized his building with police-inventory CS riot canisters. His contacts in Chicago PD informed him the serial numbers had been traced to a missing crate at a police warehouse.

Those same police contacts had also shared that there was a raid last night to arrest Jerry Alba, executed only a few hours ago. He'd only told last night's home invaders about Jerry and no one else. The raid so close behind his visitors leaving last night meant someone else was figuring out what was going on.

This was good. It was likely the missing FBI agent would be found, dead or alive, in the next few days, and he could get on with his life without having to be concerned with any unexpected visitors pointing guns at him.

The phone on his desk rang. It was his assistant. "The Tear Gas Guys are on line two," she stated, her words concise.

Not even twenty-four hours. They were back in less than a day. Taking a deep breath, he picked up the phone and said, "Haskins."

Karl Lark's voice was on the other end: "Good morning, Mr. Haskins. We intend to avail ourselves of your expertise perhaps sooner than you would have expected."

The lack of sleep and outrageous outcome from last night's visit drove the anger in his voice: "Who are you? And why should I tell you anything?"

Karl calmly explained, "If I tell you my name and you are not judicious with whom you share it, there are others who will want to talk to you. They are possibly less pleasant house guests than I am."

Alexander snarled, "Those were riot canisters you used in the stairwell. They're meant for the outdoors. The stairwell was positively pressurized by all the gas. Anyone who would have tried to climb the stairs would have died. The entire building had to be evacuated. People are in the hospital. The poor bastards in the elevator suffered lung damage."

Karl's voice remained calm: "This is unfortunate. Should I assume everyone will fully recover?"

Exasperated by Karl's nonplus tone, Alexander yelled, "Yeah, no one is permanently injured. Regardless, your breaking and entering my home almost killed people. Speaking of my home, the CS gas damage is permanent. The building is in the process of having its occupancy permit pulled. Who knows when I can move back in."

Karl responded in the same flat tone, "You sound angry, Mr. Haskins; normally, I would give you time to calm down and call back later. Unfortunately, matters are pressing. We had a chance to talk to Mr. Alba."

Alexander blinked and said, "You did? I heard the police were looking for him."

Karl said, "Indeed, we had barely made his acquaintance when the police arrived and forced us to relocate him elsewhere."

Knowing where this was likely going, Alexander felt the need to ask, "How is Jerry doing?"

Karl shared, "Unfortunately, Mr. Alba has expired. He made an unwise attempt to escape, and suffered as a result."

There was a long pause as both parties remained silent.

Karl then continued, "Mr. Haskins, before Jerry passed, he shared a straightforward comment: '*The big man wants more*.' Can you elaborate?"

The lawyer part of Alexander's brain formulated his response carefully: "I'm not sure. Maybe."

For the first time in this conversation, frustration entered Karl's voice: "It has been some time since I or my companion have had proper sleep. Perhaps you will help us bring this issue to resolution, and then you can begin looking for your new residence."

Alexander said, "Not over the phone. As much as I would prefer not to, this should be face-to-face."

His voice returning to its monotone, Karl responded, "Understood. Do you have a place in mind to meet?"

Alexander said, "I do, but again, not over the phone."

There was a pause, and then Karl declared, "This is not a concern. Go there. We will find you." The line went dead.

Alexander put his head in his hands and considered his options. He had resources and knew some serious people. Based on recent events, he concluded that bringing others in might not land this nightmare in a better place. Grabbing his coat, he told his assistant he'd be out for the rest of the day.

Go there. We will find you. And how was it they would find him? The implications of that statement—*We will find you*—were chilling.

Who were these people?

If he was lucky, this would be his last time meeting the odd couple.

●   ●   ●   ●   ●

Alexander was on his way to the coffee shop he liked to visit whenever he felt the need to get out of the office and clear his head. A stiff, frozen January wind cut through the cold canyon between buildings, making his eyes water. This wasn't a day he would choose to go out for coffee. Days like this were when he sent someone.

The welcoming warmth and scent of the coffee shop were much appreciated as he entered. Breathing deeply, he stomped his feet to clear off the snow. Looking around, he felt a spike of relief when he realized his tormentors were nowhere in sight. Deciding a coffee was called for, he stepped towards the barista. If the dynamic duo was a no-show, it could be a celebratory drink.

Out of the corner of his eye, he saw the tall, serious-looking guy from last night walking towards him down the hallway from the back of the store. From all the way back, where only the employees went. The barista noticed as well and stared at the man, indecision playing out across her face.

Illych tossed a hundred onto the counter. "There's your tip. Find something else to do." The barista grabbed the bill and shuffled away.

Illych strode up to Alexander, leaned in, locked eyes and said in a low voice "You're being followed. Let's go." A head nod indicated to walk to the back he had just come from.

Resigned to his fate, Alexander led the way. They arrived in the back and turned a corner to find the old man standing there. In his right hand, he held a box with a computer display mounted on a pistol grip.

Alexander shook his head. "You two are the weirdest pair. What's your story?"

Karl said, "No time for that, Mr. Haskins. We need to leave."

A bolt of pain shot through the attorney, and everything went black.

●　　●　　●　　●　　●

Karl and Illych looked at the unconscious form on the chair.

Illych said, "At least you sprang for a hotel room. That storage space was getting ripe."

Karl surveyed the room while saying, "There were literally dozens of others that were empty, and the place does not open for several more days. We could have just moved to another bay. But it seemed appropriate to try a more congenial approach with Mr. Haskins."

Illych walked to the small fridge and pulled out a soft drink. "This is better; there's a mini-bar."

"Please stay focused," Karl admonished with a frown, "our guest is returning to us."

Alexander blinked and tried to stand. "What did you do to me?"

Illych held up a pistol-like device and answered, "Stun gun. High-voltage—knocks you out for at least ten minutes."

A blinking Alexander looked around and said, "Where a—"

Illych finished his sentence, "Hotel room."

Looking at his hands and feet, "I'm not tied up?"

"Nope," Illych stated, showing a large-caliber pistol in his other hand.

Karl interjected, "You may be useful for future consultation. The consideration for your comfort is based on the assumption that you will behave. And as soon as you answer the question, you may leave. Do you understand?"

Alexander looked back and forth between his captors. "Uh huh. I get it. Who is the *big man*? That's what you want to know?"

Karl did not reply.

Alexander continued, "Yeah, one of the suburb territories is run by a guy who is sometimes referred to as the *big guy.* I don't know why, or who started it. Ambitious fellow. I have a hard time believing he organized kidnapping the FBI agent, though. These guys who do that work are aggressive, and the police give them a lot of leeway. But the FBI will take one of these territory guys down without a second thought if they get out of line. They're still small fish in a big pond."

Karl interrupted, "Why, Mr. Haskins, would someone like that kidnap an FBI agent with detailed knowledge of the money laundering situation in the Chicago area?"

Alexander's eyes narrowed. "Wait, what? I knew about the kidnapping. I wasn't aware of the money laundering part."

Karl said, "Yes, the agent kidnapped is an analyst focused on money laundering."

Alexander took a breath and sat back. "No one that I work with would do that. It's bad business. Has to be a freelancer trying something."

Karl was staring directly at Alexander now. "Based on Mr. Alba's comments, this *big guy* may be involved. We would very much like to ask him some questions. Who is he?"

Alexander moved a hand slowly, reaching towards the inside of his coat and elaborated, "His name is Francis Helena. I've never worked with him directly, but my assistant will have a contact number. May I call her on my cell?"

Karl nodded.

Pulling the phone from inside his suit coat, he dialed his assistant. "Hello Trish, I need the number for Francis Helena." Alexander made a writing motion with his hands.

Karl slid the pen and pad with the hotel names on them in front of him.

"Uh-huh, excellent. Thank you." He hung up, tore the top sheet off, and handed it to Karl. "That is his cell number and home address. May I go now?"

Karl nodded. "Our collaboration is complete, for now. Thank you for your time, Mr. Haskins. You are free to go."

Alexander stood and walked towards the door. He put his hand on the knob and asked, "What, no warning not to discuss this with anyone else?"

Karl was focusing on the *oculus* and answered, "I find it unlikely our discussion qualifies for attorney-client privilege. You have already been warned about revealing our meeting. It is not *I* who you need to be concerned with."

Shaking his head, the lawyer opened the door and walked out. As it closed, he could be heard saying out loud, "Time for a vacation to the Caribbean. I've had enough—" The rest was cut off when the door shut.

Illych broke the silence: "Now what? Are we going to get this Francis guy?"

"Eventually, I would like to observe his movements first. See if they give clues to where Danielle may be."

"You think we're getting closer?"

"Six degrees of separation. We have interviewed four people in the same industry, and this conversation has delivered a fifth. It is likely we are getting close to the kidnappers."

Karl looked up from the *oculus* and declared, "Mr. Haskins has left the building, and so shall we."

Illych braced himself for what was about—

●   ●   ●   ●   ●

Illych sat in a comfortable chair, enjoying the crackling fire while sipping coffee. Mr. Lark had dropped him off after the Haskins interview, and he was now waiting for him to return. In the meantime, he'd taken a nap and was now basking in the heat coming from the open hearth.

Karl knocked and entered.

Illych looked up and asked, "What's the next step? Another kidnapping?"

There was a hint of disappointment in Karl's reply, "Not yet. The FBI is already at Mr. Helena's residence."

Illych sat up straighter. "They got him first?"

Karl shook his head while taking his seat. "Apparently, they have not. Our mutual target had already fled. Knowledge of the work we have done over the last few days has apparently worked its way upstream."

Illych settled back into his chair. "I'm sure you didn't come back to the cabin for the coffee. What's next?"

Karl nodded. "Indeed. The next steps have already been executed. Mr. Haskins gave us an address and a phone number. Once I observed the FBI at his home, I called and left a message on his phone."

Hearing this, Illych frowned. "There's no way he's using that phone. You know that, right?"

Karl exhaled, "Agreed, however, his business will require attending to. While I am by no means an expert, my educated guess is that those managing a money laundering operation do not enjoy holidays off. If Francis Helena does not take care of business, he will likely be driven out of business. Business requires communications, and this number is a long-standing point of contact."

With just a hint of sarcasm, Illych deadpanned, "Logical, Mr. Lark."

"Thank you, Illych. I try."

Illych continued, "Tell me about this message. What did you say?"

"An offer was made to meet and discuss resolving the issue."

Illych shook his head. "You called a guy who knows he is being hunted and offered to meet in person?"

Karl paused as if tapping his well of patience. "I also explained that, as an interested third party, I am willing to compensate him generously for the return of Danielle Mersen."

Illych was a little incredulous. "To be honest, Mr. Lark, I'm not sure where this is going. How is this guy getting in contact with you?"

Karl responded, "I purchased a temporary phone with voicemail. Like all things electronic, it can be monitored by the authorities. Regardless, we will be able to set up a meeting before anyone monitoring can react.

"If Mr. Helena is reasonable, he can acquire much-needed funds—something he desperately needs right now. I would think avoiding the FBI long-term is an expensive path."

Illych said, "Yeah, but by calling him like that, he knows you're having a hard time finding him."

Karl continued, "That is a statement of the obvious. My purpose in visiting is to prepare you for the type of meeting that will likely happen shortly."

Illych leaned his head back and closed his eyes. "And I now consider myself warned and will be ready when you need me."

Karl stood and headed for the door. "Excellent. I shall likely return soon."

Karl walked out into the evening twilight, leaving Illych to ponder where this would all end.

● ● ● ● ●

The knock on the cabin door woke a sleeping Illych. Karl entered, speaking before Illych was even fully awake. Something about meeting Francis Helena soon.

What Karl said snapped Illych fully awake, "Wait what? He's *eager* to meet? That's suspicious."

Karl shrugged. "We exchanged messages. He had someone leave a note at a pizza shop. I was to pick it up. Once there, I called Mr. Helena, and he called the pizza shop person to give me the note. It is all too cloak-and-dagger for my tastes. And time-consuming. The good news is that he is willing and eager to meet. An old abandoned school is the chosen meeting place."

Illych asked, "You just walked into a pizza joint and announced you were there?"

Karl frowned while saying, "Of course not. I translated to the alley behind the pizza shop and watched the people inside when I called in. Anyone other than one person heading for the back to give me the note, and I would have been gone before the door opened."

Illych stared at the fire in the fireplace. It had died down while he was napping. There was a chill in the cabin. Or, perhaps, it was just Mr. Lark. "The abandoned school thing sounds suspicious."

Karl nodded in agreement. "Indeed. We will thoroughly check it with the *oculus* and remove any threats that may disrupt our meeting."

Illych lifted himself from his warm and comfortable chair and walked to the wall with various weapons hanging on it. "I'm bringing something heavier for this." Illych grabbed the same rifle he'd used to put down the goblin at Townshend Park. Hefting the weighty weapon, then with a practiced pull and release, the bolt sheared the first round from the drum magazine.

"Just in case."

●　　●　　●　　●　　●

Karl translated them once again into a lightless space.

Illych whispered, "What is it with you and pitch-black closets?"

Karl gave a mildly indignant reply: "This is not a closet. It is—or *was*—the janitor's office."

With a flick of a switch, the light on Illych's weapon illuminated the mess that had been an office. Trash was everywhere. There were several pieces of broken furniture. Colorful graffiti covered the walls. Very little was left indicating this was once the heart of a school's janitorial staff. Only a wrinkled and aged pornographic calendar suggested that people used to work here. Illych walked over to it and flipped through, stopping to admire April.

Karl was methodically moving through the school with the *oculus*, meticulously checking each room.

Pausing at one point, he said, "There, that is where we are meeting. Looks like our counterpart is early. And he is alone. There is not another living person in the entire building. And he does not have a phone with him. As a matter of fact, other than the *oculus* in my hand and the light on your rifle, there is no functioning electricity or electrical device in the entire building. This place is dead."

Illych hefted his rifle. "Let's go meet Francis."

Completing his checks, Karl announced while nodding, "Agreed, this may be our one chance to get information from Mr. Helena."

The man on the *oculus* screen did not move much while Karl and Illych traveled the litter-strewn halls and stairs to the classroom where they were to meet. Outside the room, Karl stood to one side of the door and called out, "Marco."

A male voice from inside the room replied, "Polo."

Illych shook his head.

The wooden floor creaked as they entered.

Francis was sitting on a child-sized desk, smoking a cigar. He was dressed in a white suit with garish gold chains hanging from his neck. Bald, muscular and tan, he looked the part of a criminal overlord from a '70s television show.

There was a long pause as the three men sized each other up.

Francis broke the silence: "You the guy that's lookin' for me? For that kidnapping everyone's talking about?"

Karl nodded. "Others have shared you may have information about the kidnapping."

Francis barked, "Who others? I might want to talk to them too."

Karl took a few more steps into the room. "The *who* does not matter. And most of them are no longer available."

Francis' expression shifted to concern. "No longer available, like *dead?*"

Karl replied, "The ones who make the questioning difficult do not survive."

Francis nodded and looked around the room. "You know, I went to school here. It was condemned ten years ago. Used to sit at one of these little desks." He puffed the cigar, making a cloud of smoke.

He continued, "Okay, I get it. But see here, I didn't do it, and I ain't part of it."

Karl's expression remained blank as he said, "You are more cooperative than I would have expected. My hope is you have more to share than just your word that you did not do it."

Francis gestured with the cigar to emphasize, "That's me, Mr. Cooperative. When people are disappearing and the FBI is breaking down your front door, it can make a guy cooperative."

Impatience crept into Karl's voice as he asked, "Tell me what I need to know, Mr. Helena, so we can all go about our business."

More cigar waving as Francis queried, "My name stays out of this?"

Karl nodded. "You shall remain anonymous, of course."

Another puff of the cigar, "I think I'm being framed. On the night of the kidnapping, I get a call. A guy I know wants to meet. I go there, but he's not there. The next day, I see on the news that FBI chick is kidnapped. The place I went to meet is right outside that building. If there's a security camera, it shows me right there when the kidnapping went down."

Karl asked, "Do you have enemies who would benefit from framing you?"

Now the cigar gesturing was even more energetic. "In my business? Do I, and a lot of them."

Karl's tone shifted to dark: "That is not good enough. Who would benefit from you being blamed for the kidnapping, and would benefit from a more complete understanding of the Chicago area money-laundering racket?"

Francis looked surprised. "What does money laundering have to do with this?"

Karl filled in the blank, "The kidnapped FBI agent is an analyst focused on money laundering."

Francis went quiet while his mental processes played out on his face, eventually arriving at a realization, followed immediately by obvious fear.

Karl saw this and asked, "What did you just figure out, Mr. Helena?"

A somewhat more nervous Francis said, "Like I said, you have to keep me out of this."

Karl blinked in frustration. "This has already been agreed to."

The cigar waiving was back, and Francis continued, "I run a good business, always make my money and deliver. No screw-ups, no complications. And I stay out of the local stuff. No dipping into the drugs, gambling, girls, whatever—stay neutral. No conflicts of interest. Take care of anyone who has cash. Keep out of the turf fights.

"An offer was made to buy me out. Happens all the time. Some punk thinks they know the business and how much it takes to buy in. I just send them on their way.

"But with these wars going on? You know, Iraq and Afghanistan. There are some hard cases hungry to get in. Some of them are organized. Real badass types, afraid of nothing. Anyway, one of these groups comes to me, tried to make an offer I couldn't refuse. It got rough, but they got the point. They moved on. Or at least, I thought they did.

"You have to understand. Nobody I work with did this kidnapping. Bad business brings the kind of attention nobody wants. Pull a stunt like that, and word gets out. Then nobody ever sees you again. These hardcase guys, though, they don't know the rules. Or maybe they just don't care."

A now very focused Karl asked, "And where can I find these men?"

Francis' body language shifted to relaxed, and he took a draw on his cigar before answering, "Well, that's the thing. I can see you're a businessman, and we should discuss my finder's fee first."

Illych observed this new direction in the conversation and wondered if it would play out the way this Francis character thought it would. In anticipation, he shifted a few steps off to one side of Mr. Lark, opening up the situation for a clear shot.

Karl took a step closer to Francis, and through a granite expression, stated, "Share what you know, and I will consider a finder's fee." Karl's hands were working the *oculus* and *ouiblet*. The motion did not go unnoticed by Illych.

In a belligerent tone, Frances said, "How about I walk out of here, or you show me a taste of what I can get, and then I give it up?"

Francis Helena disappeared.

A surprised Illych asked, "Okay, Mr. Lark, where did he go?"

Karl took a deep breath and exhaled, "Ten thousand feet."

Taking a step closer to Karl, Illych asked, "Say again?"

Karl replied, "Mr. Helena is free-falling from ten thousand feet. I found his sudden switch to hardball negotiating off-putting. He was translated to an altitude of ten thousand feet. Perhaps after falling nine thousand feet in the freezing night air, he will be more agreeable. And twenty-seven seconds is now."

For an instant, Francis appeared in a semi-standing position with his face contorted in abject terror. He then slammed straight through the wooden classroom floor.

Illych took a half step backward in surprise. A moment passed while the two men processed what just happened.

Karl and Illych made their way to the splintered hole and shined a flashlight down. Francis had punched through the hardwood floor. The light showed the room below had a concrete floor. What had recently been a person was now a broken and twisted mass, the white suit splashed with red. All that was left was a very dead money launderer in a crumpled and broken, bloody lump.

Karl frowned. "Oh my. This is most unfortunate."

"Good god, Mr. Lark! What the hell?"

Karl looked at the *oculus*. "Inertia."

Illych's expression shifted quizzical as he exclaimed, "What?!"

Karl smirked. "Objects in motion tend to stay in motion. The *ouiblet* can compensate for inertia and momentum. Unfortunately, in the rush to get Mr. Helena back before he hit the ground, I missed the inertia compensation."

Illych blinked. "And then he appears in front of us and hits the floor? How fast was he going when he appeared?"

Karl was studying the *oculus* display. "Terminal velocity was likely approaching one-hundred-fifty miles per hour. He landed between two floor joists and punched straight through. The concrete floor below finally stopped him."

Illych grinned. "It's never the fall that kills you; it's the sudden stop at the end."

Karl nodded and replied, "An accurate summary."

Stepping back from the hole, Illych asked, "Now what do we do? He died before giving us a name."

Karl replied, "He told us the kind of people we are looking for. Others will know who they are. This is an unfortunate setback. However, Mr. Helena was never leaving this place alive."

A surprised Illych said, "You planned to kill him?"

"Not when we arrived. But once Francis told us he was being framed for the kidnapping, I knew he could not be allowed to leave alive. Once the kidnappers know their patsy is no longer a suspect, they will likely kill Danielle. This is a guess on my part, but I am loath to take the risk."

Illych took a deep breath and sighed, "And now what?"

Karl stated, "We go looking for out-of-place ex-military types with criminal ambitions."

"Wait a second, Karl, before we translate out. Are you sure that thing is safe? This *ouiblet*? There was that miscalculation with the car, and now *that*." Illych pointed to the hole in the floor.

Karl's tone was more admonishment now: "It is perfectly safe. These things happen when speed is needed. The normal planned translations you and I go through are nothing to be concerned with. Now, before we leave, I must remove Francis' remains. Can't have him being ruled out as the kidnapper before we find Danielle."

Illych said, "I get it, Mr. Lark. I just don't want to end up halfway in a wall."

Karl shook his head. "Halfway in a wall is unlikely. The worst-case scenario is translating to a location and finding ourselves in the path of a falling object or an automobile driving in an unexpected location."

Illych prepared for the imminent translation, "You know, your bedside manner sucks."

Karl locked in the *ouiblet* controls and curtly replied, "I am not here to provide comfort."

They were gone before Karl's parting words died out.

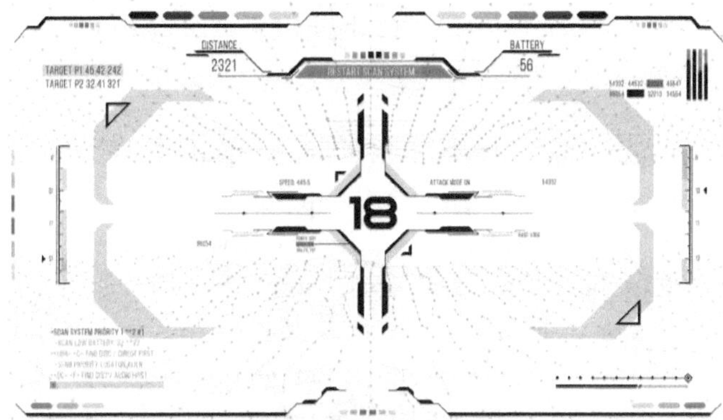

CHAPTER EIGHTTEEN

The pair translated into a hotel room with a pair of queen beds and a small communal space. Anticipating the nausea, Illych leaned against a wall and wondered where they were and why.

He watched Karl walk over to the dresser. On top was a cell phone with its battery pack removed and sitting beside to it. Karl assembled the phone and activated it. As soon as it was active, he dialed in a number.

Karl started speaking just as Illych's nausea receded: "Hello, Mr. Hemway, this is the interested third party from yesterday."

Even from several feet away, Illych could hear a loud male voice on the phone. Karl replied, "Agreed, it is a bit late for a call."

Karl patiently listened to the FBI agent's diatribe before responding, "Yes, Mr. Hemway, I am sure your experience was unpleasant."

More loud talk from the phone, and Karl frowned. "Complaints and threats are not appropriate. I am calling to set up a meeting. There are questions I wish to present."

Karl held the phone away from his ear as Jack said something so loud that Illych could hear individual words that made him smile. Bringing the phone close again, Karl said, "No, I am not crazy, and please refrain from using such language. We can either meet voluntarily, or you will be collected. Please choose."

Apparently, the G-man settled down because Illych could no longer hear what was being said. Karl calmly replied at one point, "Excellent, and your cooperation is appreciated. I will text you the meeting location shortly. It goes without saying: It is important there be no outside interference."

Karl listened some more and then replied, "Buy Treasury bonds if you want guarantees, Mr. Hemway. No one on my part intends you any harm."

Another short listen, and then Karl said, "Thank you, Mr. Hemway. In ninety-minutes then." He ended the call, sent a text, then removed the battery. Walking over to the miniature hotel wastebasket, he dropped both inside.

Illych was chuckling. "Sounds like the G-man is not looking forward to round two."

Karl took a deep breath and exhaled, "He is not. Regardless, he has agreed to meet." He then began working the *oculus* and *ouiblet* controls.

Illych knew what was coming next.

●   ●   ●   ●   ●

Illych looked at the inside of the cinder block cell they had just translated into. "Our destinations have been upgraded from closets to public toilets. Only first class, huh?"

Karl said, "Stop complaining. This provides for our undetected entry and exit. The surrounding terrain is open for a quarter-mile in all directions. Mr. Hemway is coming to us, and the *oculus* will detect any situations we would wish to avoid long before they become a problem."

Illych questioned, "And where exactly are we?"

Karl was watching images shift and change on the *oculus*. "This is a municipal park not far from Mr. Hemway's residence. We are currently inside the men's room. The park is closed for the winter, and everything is locked. An excellent location to translate into without being seen. This building is dead center in the park, providing easy visibility of anyone approaching."

Their breath formed clouds in the frozen air, and Illych was glad he'd worn his winter coat from the previous meeting with the unfortunate Mr. Helena. The two men huddled around the *oculus'* glowing screen and waited. Karl, scrolled the perimeter continuously, looking for change. A car soon parked on a nearby street. A lone figure got out and began walking across the snow-covered field.

"This appears to be him now." Karl zoomed in and changed the *oculus* settings. The pattern of metal pins in Jack Hemway's leg appeared on the display. "Confirmed."

When the figure was close, Illych unlocked the bathroom door from the inside, stuck an arm out, and waved the FBI agent in.

Jack entered, stamping snow from his boots. "You guys know it is freezing cold out? And how did you two get in here without me seeing you? I got here not ten minutes after you called, and have been watching this place the entire time. When the meeting time arrived, I parked closer and walked over to check. Figured you had bailed on our meeting. Then this door opens and your arm comes out."

Illych shrugged. "Ninja skills."

Karl said, "Let's stick to the discussion at hand. Are there any developments in the last twenty-four hours you would like to share?"

Jack snarked, "Other than waking up in my backyard soaking wet and half-frozen to the ground? Or getting called out to a midnight meeting in January? You know I bring my kids here in the summer."

Jack paused for emphasis while glaring at Karl, then continued, "The investigation is focusing on a Francis Helena. He is an ambitious operator in the money laundering space. It appears he grabbed Danielle to squeeze her for information on his rivals. We have video showing his presence near where she was kidnapped. Unfortunately, he's disappeared . . ." Jack's voice trailed off as he looked back and forth between Karl and Illych. "Did you two—?"

Karl nodded. "Mr. Helena is no longer a concern. Based on our conversation, he is not responsible for Danielle's kidnapping."

Jack looked skeptical and asked, "You're sure of this?"

Karl nodded and answered, "We met. He offered up who he thought the kidnappers were for a fee."

Jack's voice had a hint of hope in it: "What did he say? Did you give him what he wanted?"

Karl deadpanned, "There was an unfortunate accident, and Mr. Helena is no longer with us."

Illych smiled and shook his head.

Karl continued, "Before he expired, he shared that he suspected some ex-military types who have only recently entered the business. He called them 'hard cases.'"

Jack nodded. "I know who he's talking about. They are on the "potentials" list."

Karl's head cocked to one side. "This is why I called you. Who are they?"

Jake brought a hand up with a pointing finger and said sternly, "The FBI can handle this. There is no need for your vigilantism."

Illych rolled his eyes. He knew where this was going.

Karl's expression took on the reptilian look as he spat back, "You may use this information as you please. However, I require the name. Additionally, if your actions cause Danielle's death, you will never see the sun rise again—ever."

After a long pause, Jack kicked at the wall in frustration and capitulated, "Fine. Kyle Haenal. They call him Curly."

Illych interrupted, "His last name is *Haenal?*"

"Yes, Haenal, H-a-e-n-a-l, Haenal."

"That's unfortunate," Illych commented.

"How so?" Karl responded, "Does that last name mean something?"

Illych and Jack gave each other a knowing look.

Karl shook his head and continued, "Why the nickname?"

Jack raised his hand in frustration and explained, "He's bald. Maybe a Three Stooges reference. Who knows?"

Karl paused for a moment and then asked, "One last question. How do you think this person learned of Danielle?"

Jack said, "That is the million-dollar question a lot of people are asking. How could anybody know about her being a recent addition to the team? If this Curly is the kidnapper, there's no reasonable way he should have ever known about Danielle."

Karl waved him off dismissively, "Thank you, Mr. Hemway. I have what I needed. You may leave now."

Jack looked back and forth between the two men and the surrounding bathroom. "God, I hope I never see you two ever again."

Noticing Karl and Illych were not moving to also leave, Jack asked, "You two are just going to stay here?"

Karl frowned. "That does not concern you. Leave."

Jack exited out onto the surrounding tundra and began trudging away. Karl monitored him on the *oculus*. When their departed guest was a football field away, the bathroom was empty.

● ● ● ● ●

Arriving back outside the cabin, the pair entered. Karl took a seat in an overstuffed leather chair. Illych stoked up the fire. There had been so many visits in the last two days that the pile of firewood next to the fireplace was depleted to almost nothing.

Taking the other seat, the two watched the fire catch and roar up into the fresh wood.

Illych spoke first, "I hate to say this, but she has been gone forty-eight hours now. I've seen enough of those investigation shows to know that's bad."

Karl responded in a monotone, "The good or bad part does not interest me. The unusual circumstances of her kidnapping and the unique information she possesses point towards her still being alive. Even forty-eight hours is not long enough for her to recall and share everything. Even assuming Danielle is motivated to do so.

"Then there is the money part. These people are in this for the money. A lot of money, even by their avaricious standards. They will not give that up easily.

"They also planned this in advance. Their ability to elude the FBI this long, even misdirecting them at one point, points to this being executed by clever people. There is just something inside all this that does not make sense. I can feel it."

Illych looked over at Karl and said, "What do you mean? Inside?"

Karl's eyes narrowed. "The *why* makes sense. It is the *how* that I cannot understand. How did they kidnap her without her fighting back?"

Illych leaned back in his chair and offered, "Maybe they have some of this science-fiction stuff like you do. A *ouiblet* of kidnapping or something."

Karl stared into the fire, considering the prospect. "Agreed, there is a very real possibility others in this world have capabilities not commonly understood. That could be what we are up against."

The two men sat in silence for several minutes until Illych said, "So, we're going looking for Curly?"

Karl nodded. "Yes, and I fear we must act quickly or the FBI may find him before we do."

Illych snorted, "More quickly than we already have? Chicago property insurance rates are going up in the wake of the destruction of the last two days."

Karl watched the flames roll over the burning wood. "An unfortunate by-product of our search. I will leave now to consult public records and determine where Mr. Haenal lives and what he looks like. Then I will return to collect you, and we will pay him a visit."

Illych nodded and watched as Karl left.

He then shook his head and mumbled to himself, "Can't we just call him Curly?"

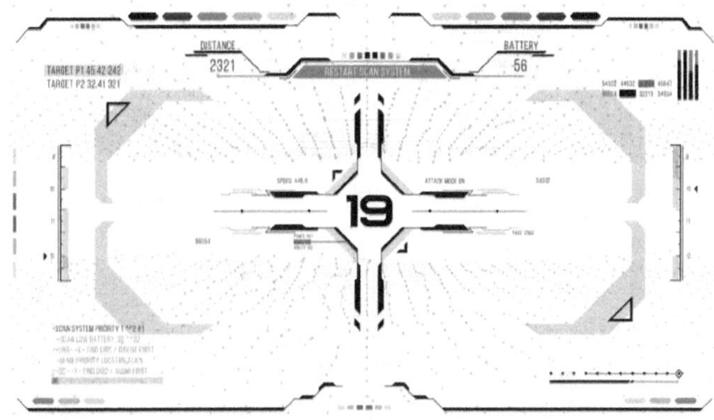

CHAPTER NINETEEN

Karl Lark returned in less than two hours. Awakening Illych with a knock on the door, they were gone in minutes.

They translated onto the roof of a building across the street from Curly's home. Once again, Illych got to take in the Chicago city lights in the dead of the night.

Breathing in the freezing air, he toughed out the nausea while looking down at their goal. "A strip club? This guy lives in a strip club?"

Karl was already working the *oculus* and nodded. "He owns the building."

Illych looked at the windowless, three-story cinder block building. The only indication of what went on inside was a pink neon sign forming the words *The Pink Pole*. "So, what's the plan?"

Karl replied, "We need information about what is going on inside. Mr. Haenal's habits. Perhaps we separate one of his men from the herd and interrogate him?"

Illych's voice shared his doubt: "How do we know which guys are with him? It's not like they wear uniforms."

Karl glanced up and said, "We may have to try more than once. The situation does not support precision."

Illych was looking at Karl now. "And if we grab the wrong guy?"

Karl shrugged, "I will attempt to minimize collateral damage until we are sure we have the right person."

The pair sat, watching the comings and goings of the patrons. There was way more activity than Illych would have expected considering it was three a.m. on a frozen January night. Between the patrons' activities outside and what the *oculus* showed going on inside, they both received an education on strip club activities.

Illych broke the silence at one point: "Have you ever been in one of these, Mr. Lark?"

Karl did not break line of sight to the *oculus*. "I have not."

Illych smirked, "Figured."

Minutes of silence later, Karl pointed at the *oculus* screen. "There, those two going out the back door into a dead-end alley—that man and woman. It's reasonable to assume regular patrons cannot use the service entrances. He's a candidate for being one of Mr. Haenal's colleagues."

An uncomfortable five minutes passed as they watched the pair engage in activities unfamiliar to Karl.

Illych shook his head. "This is like watching the worst adult movie ever."

Karl seemed intrigued. "Is what they are doing even legal?"

Illych took a deep breath before answering, "Between consenting adults, it is. I'm more impressed that this is happening in a Chicago alley in January. How are they not worried about frostbite?"

The woman straightened her clothes and reentered the building. The man lit up a cigarette and stood in the middle of the alley, staring out towards the road.

Karl's hands blurred into action with both the *oculus* and the *ouiblet* controls. "I will translate you directly behind him, and you can taser him."

Illych got the Taser out. "Wait, what about what happened to the car and the hole in the floor? This is one of those on-the-fly things."

Karl hissed, "There are no moving objects. This is just point-to-point."

Illych's voice betrayed his concern: "Are you—"

" — sure?"

Illych found himself standing arms-length behind the man in the alley. His spoken word caused the man to abruptly spin around. The look of surprise at finding someone right behind him was immediately replaced with one of discomfort as the Taser delivered unconsciousness.

Grabbing the man before he fell, Illych held him upright and covered the man's eyes with his hand. He looked up to where Karl was hidden and nodded.

And braced himself for translation.

● ● ● ● ●

"Who are you *dicks*?"

The man from the alley was zip-tied to a wooden chair in the middle of an empty storage unit. He glowered up at Karl and Illych as he leveled his acrimony. They, in turn, stood and casually regarded him as he regained his faculties.

Karl responded, "I don't understand the modern fascination with vulgarity. It is so common as to indicate a benefit, yet I do not see one. Hopefully, you can refrain while you answer our questions."

Their captive looked at Karl and then to Illych with a baffled expression: *Is this guy for real?* The man quickly blurted out, "I don't know anything."

Karl's head tilted just slightly. "How can you say that? We haven't asked any questions yet."

Sitting Man barked, "Don't matter. Still don't know anything."

Karl paused, frowned, and asked, "Do you know the owner of the establishment you were at just prior to our kidnapping you?"

Sitting Man gave an exaggerated shake of his head and said, "I ain't saying nothin' against Curly."

Karl continued, "Good, you do know him. What is your name, by the way?"

"Billy. Call me Billy."

Karl gave a tight-lipped smile. "Thank you, Billy," he said with a nod of his head, continuing, "It is important we move this conversation along as I have deadlines that need to be met. Now that we have established you know Curly, tell me how you know him."

Billy's expression betrayed confusion at the question.

Karl said, "Do you work for Curly?"

"Yeah, everybody works for Curly."

"What is Curly's business?"

"Don't ask me about Curly's business. Nobody asks that."

"Has he been busier than usual lately?

"Curly is always busy. He is a man with a plan."

"When Curly is not at the strip club, where does he go?"

"Nobody ever sees Curly leave."

"He never leaves the club?"

"Sometimes he leaves, just nobody sees it."

Karl walked over to a corner, waving Illych to join him, and whispered, "I don't believe this man has useful information. He's not a good candidate for questioning."

Illych shrugged and whispered, "Can't win 'em all, Mr. Lark. Please tell me you're not planning on killing this idiot."

Karl looked at their bound captive for a moment and then back to Illych. "No, Billy will wake up somewhere that will keep him out of the equation long enough. Please taser him."

Billy had been watching the two whisper, and apprehension was visible on his face when they walked back. Illych moved around behind their captive while grabbing his Taser from an inside pocket.

Billy tried turning to see what Illych was doing while speaking: "You guys are going to kill me because I don't know nothin'?"

Karl said, "Not today, Billy, Rather, I have decided to send you to a place that will keep you out of trouble for a while."

Billy's voice bordered on the histrionic: "That's not funn—"

Illych tasered Billy and cut the zip ties. Once their captive was no longer restrained, he stood back and watched Billy disappear.

Illych asked, "Somewhere to 'keep him out of trouble?' Is that a euphemism for something?"

Karl replied, "No, I have the coordinates for a secluded spot in a popular amusement park in Florida. It seemed appropriate considering Billy's mental age."

Looking at Karl with a raised eyebrow, Illych said, "The only part of that, Mr. Lark, that makes no sense, is why you already know where a secluded spot in an amusement park is."

● ● ● ● ●

Billy awakened and found himself lying on blacktop in a dead-end walkway behind a building. It was dark out, but much warmer than Chicago. The fact that the temperature was well above freezing and there was no snow told him he was somewhere else. Not even questioning why, he stumbled out of the alley and looked around. There were amusement park attractions and tributes to cartoon characters.

Billy smiled. He was alone in a huge amusement park.

● ● ● ● ●

Still standing in the storage unit, Illych asked, "Now what? This six-degrees-of-separation thing is slow going. In the case of Billy, it was a dead end."

Karl's expression became a death glare, and he stated, "No more trying to figure out an elegant approach. It is time to get Curly. We shall return to the observation point where we located Billy and re-acquire Mr. Haenal."

Illych braced himself for what was coming next.

●　　●　　●　　●　　●

Illych was getting cold and starting to wonder how a skinny old guy like Karl didn't have hypothermia setting in yet. "It's been over an hour of watching this guy. The sun will be coming up soon. He's not coming out. And he's always surrounded by people. A lot of people. What's the plan?"

Karl was silent.

Illych's voice betrayed his concern: "You know we can't do the building-on-fire trick like with the FBI? As crowded as this place is, it could turn into a Greek tragedy in there."

Agreeing, Karl nodded. "Correct, fire is not the solution. We will kill the power to the neighborhood and watch what Mr. Haenal does."

Illych asked, "Uh, when?"

"I have found the switchgear for this neighborhood. So, now."

The power to the strip club and nearby buildings was cut, and the surrounding streets went dark.

Karl watched the events inside the club unfold. "The emergency lights have kicked in. The music has stopped, but the number of people leaving is less than expected."

Illych smiled and playfully said, "Perhaps we now have the answer to what happens in a strip club when the power goes out."

Karl shook his head. "There. Our target is leaving the main club area and going upstairs to his residence. Perhaps we will join him."

Illych cautioned, pointing at the *oculus* screen, "Let's wait and see how many people join him first."

Curly was not alone. Several people followed him upstairs, and the party started all over.

Karl angled the *oculus* for Illych to see better. "Look at the size of his bathroom. That is the answer. When it looks like he will be headed there, we translate in and grab him."

Illych looked at Karl and nodded. "Yeah, I get it. That much drinking, and he'll feel the call of nature. And most people do that alone."

Karl was thoughtful for a moment, then said, "Another option is I translate out everyone in the room. Disposing of everyone except for him. Perform the interrogation, and then end Mr. Haenal. It would all be very quick."

Illych looked at Karl and said, "Karl, I understand we're in a hurry, but most of those people have nothing to do with your grandniece's kidnapping. I get this is a strip club, and trying to find a good guy in this group might be a stretch. But murdering half a dozen people to expedite the process is more blood thirsty than I'm comfortable with."

Karl said, "Agreed. I am just verbally exploring options. But yes, we should not commit mass murder for the sake of expediency. Let us try the bathroom plan."

Illych nodded. "No matter how awesome this private party is, everyone uses the head."

Not ten minutes pass, and Curly detached himself from the group and walked towards the bathroom. Illych translated into position inside the walk-in shower, and Karl translated himself inside a closed towel-filled closet with barely enough room just inside the door. For a minute, Illych was standing alone in the dark, waiting. Karl watched the *oculus* in case they needed to abort if another person joined in.

The *oculus* showed Karl the pistol in Curly's waistband and Curly stopping on his way to the bathroom to grab something that did not clearly register on the *oculus*. Karl had no way to share any of this with Illych while they waited.

The door opened, Curly entered, illuminated his path with the light from his cell phone, and closed the door behind him. Taking his position at the toilet with his back to the shower, he opened the front of his pants.

Illych saw none of this. Only the increased light. He could hear the urination, but saw no one was standing at the toilet.

Recognizing the signs any man would understand as the moment of vulnerability ending, Karl took the initiative, opened the closet door, and stepped out to confront Curly.

Curly saw the old man, gave it a shake, and started to zip up.

Both Karl and Illych expected to see a man facing the toilet.

But no one was there.

Karl switched back and forth between looking with his own eyes and viewing with the *oculus*. He saw the man on the screen. And then back to the toilet. No one was there.

Illych was peering out of the shower at what should definitely be a man standing by the toilet, and saw nothing as well.

Curly's disembodied voice was loud in the bathroom. "Figured you'd be coming for me."

The *oculus* display showed Curly pulling his pistol from his waistband.

The disembodied voice continued, "I'd explain it to you, but you wouldn't understand."

The gun raised while Karl fumbled for the *ouiblet* control.

Illych charged out of the bathroom stall and tackled what Karl's eyes told him was empty air. The gun went off, and the dark room flashed with an instant of daylight. Illych was grappling with *someone*, who then broke free and shoved Karl hard up against the wall. The door opened and closed. The dropped cell phone was still giving off a faint light, and Illych's upright form was visible.

The plan had failed; Curly was running, and they needed to leave now.

● ● ● ● ●

Illych and then Karl arrived back at their previous observation point.

Illych voiced his confusion as soon as Karl appeared, "What happened back there?"

Karl was experiencing the feeling that something extraordinary had just occurred. "I don't know. The *oculus* showed Curly was there, but when I walked out of the closet, I couldn't see him."

Illych was breathing deeply from his brief encounter with Curly: "Same here. I heard the door open. Then came the sound of peeing. The toilet was right in front of me, but nobody was standing there. I heard you open the closet door, followed by a voice coming from right in front of me saying, 'You wouldn't understand.'"

Karl said, "I do not believe it was just the dim lighting that confused us. Mr. Haenal grabbed something just before he entered. It didn't show up clearly on the *oculus*."

Illych said, "Yeah, well, when he said that part about us not understanding, I took a chance and charged the voice."

Karl nodded. "Your initiative is appreciated. Yes, there is more to Mr. Haenal than I expected. He is not a run-of-the-mill street thug. This experience may also explain how Danielle was kidnapped without evidence of a struggle. Fortunately, the *oculus* can find him, and he can be tracked as he leaves this place. Let's see where he goes."

It was not a long wait until Karl and Illych watched on the *oculus* as Curly exited the club into a waiting car.

Karl declared, "Following him on the *oculus* is straightforward."

Illych asked, "What's the range on that thing?"

Karl fiddled with the *oculus* controls and zoomed out. "Approximately twenty kilometers."

Illych nodded. "So, like thirteen miles."

Karl didn't answer and remained focused on Curly's movements.

Illych pointed to the screen, "Looks like he's headed to the lake."

Minutes passed as the car did indeed arrive at a boat marina.

Illych frowned, "There are no boats, and the lake is frozen. What's he doing?"

Curly exited the car alone and jogged through drifted snow out onto a pier and then to a solitary boathouse. Fumbling with the lock, he eventually dragged the door open in spite of the drifted snow and ice. Upon entering, Curly secured the door behind him and moved quickly towards a locker opposite the door.

He began pulling gear from the locker, including a sledgehammer, which he promptly used to smash a hole in the ice.

Illych was incredulous: "Is he doing what I think he's doing?"

Karl said, "I believe we are watching the elaborate escape plan of a paranoid man. It makes sense. However Curly achieved his magic trick back in that bathroom, he likely did not invent the capability. More likely, he found it or it was gifted to him. Regardless, knowledge that such capabilities exist would weigh heavily on a weak mind."

Illych chuckled and countered, "Hah, if he's paranoid about invisibility, wait until he finds out about the *oculus* or *ouiblet*."

Curly donned a wetsuit—presumably insulated—air tanks, and flippers. Strapping a bag containing his clothes to his chest, he then pulled a large torpedo-shaped device out of the locker. The *oculus* showed it included a pair of handles and a small propeller.

Illych ran his hands through his hair. "Is this guy for real? This is right out of a spy movie. Why? Just why?"

Karl commented, "Because once he is in the water, there is no way to pursue him or track him. That torpedo device will pull him along at speed for miles in any direction."

Illych said, "Ok, I understand; this is his getaway plan. But where's he going?"

Karl shrugged while watching the *oculus* screen intently, "I am sure we are about to find out."

The pair watched in fascination as Curly was pulled along under the ice. Keeping close to the bottom, he maintained a good speed.

Illych chuckled again. "Look at him go."

Karl pointed on the screen, ahead of the fast-moving Curly, "He is making for the river."

There was a close call when Curly pulled a hard turn and narrowly missed colliding with something large and half-buried in the riverbed.

Illych asked, "Why don't you just grab him from here and translate him to a storage unit?"

Karl replied, "There are risks with translating moving objects, as with what happened to Mr. Helena. Also, I want to see if he will lead us to Danielle first."

Curly slowed, obviously looking for something. A landmark? Underwater mark?

Backtracking at one point, he found what he was looking for. An underwater tunnel pipe that was big enough for a man to walk upright. Curly navigated inside slowly.

Karl zoomed the *oculus* out. The building was a renovated former factory. The first floor had restaurants, bars and shops, and was a fully developed commercial enterprise. The upper floors were apartments or condos. A properly gentrified development.

The basement levels were a different story. A maze of sunken rooms, bricked-up spaces, and fire doors locked long ago.

Curly surfaced inside a half-submerged, sunken dungeon and pulled himself from the water. Abandoning the air tanks and torpedo machine, he took the bag with his clothes, pulled open a door, and walked down a hallway to another door.

Stopping there, he stripped out of the wetsuit and dressed.

Using a key, he opened the door to enter another hallway. This one appeared to have been renovated.

Even on the *oculus*, Karl and Illych could see Curly's gait was that of a man unconcerned with his environment. Walking several blocks, he eventually crossed a street at the corner and was challenged by two men. They exchanged greetings—a complicated handshake—and Curly was allowed to continue.

Midway up the block, he turned to a building rising up more than a dozen stories and took the car ramp going down to underground parking. Still walking like he had all the time in the world, he entered a stairwell and began descending.

Karl occasionally zoomed the *oculus* view out, looking at the buildings and people near their target. Some of what he observed, showed this was what Illych would call a *bad neighborhood*.

The number of flights of stairs traveled down was impressive, and Illych commented, "He's still going down."

The *oculus* displayed that under the buildings and streets of Chicago was a whole underworld of basements, interconnecting tunnels, and utility corridors, all haphazardly arranged.

It was into this maze that Curly entered. Turning into different corridors, he made his way through to a door he had to unlock. Then a long walk along a singular tunnel brought him to his final destination. He knocked on the steel fire door.

On the other side of the door were two men in a domed chamber the size of a small house. An alcove on one side was walled up, with only a narrow door for access. Inside was a solitary figure.

Illych sensed Karl tense up, and broke the silence. "Is that her?"

Karl said, "I can't tell from here for sure. It is a female of the appropriate height. Danielle has no identifying characteristics that I am aware of. I will attempt to take a visual photo of her with the *ouiblet*."

The screen on the *oculus* soon showed a hooded figure lying on a cot.

Illych observed, "These guys are serious about hiding her identity."

One of the men responded to Curly's knock, opening the door. Handshaking and man hugs followed.

Curly's arrival triggered activity. One of the men opened up the alcove and brought out the person inside. They set her in a wheelchair and the man wheeled her out through the door and back the way Curly had just came from.

Illych said, "They're moving her."

Karl scrolled ahead on the *oculus*. "Yes, but where?"

Curly remained behind with the man who'd opened the door. They sat at the table and appeared to be drinking and playing cards.

Illych frowned. "This is an odd time for Curly to be doing some R&R."

Karl kept shifting the *oculus* back and forth—from the man with the captive in a wheelchair, weaving their way through the underworld maze, then back to Curly playing cards.

Illych blinked while running a hand through his hair and observed, "That's just peculiar. He stops to play cards. I don't get it."

Karl and Illych were focused on the puzzling card game when Curly stood, pulled a handgun from his waistband, and shot the man multiple times.

Understanding the situation now, Illych nodded and said, "Ok, now I get it. That guy is a cutout. No loose ends. Looks like Curly is serious about keeping secrets."

Karl nodded, and they watched Curly exit and quickly walk away.

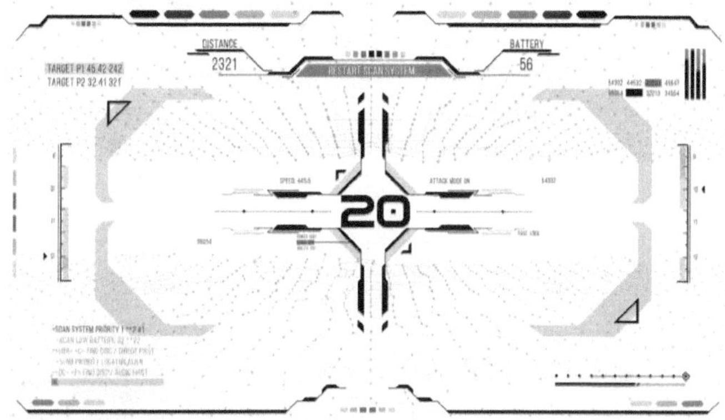

CHAPTER TWENTY

Karl switched the *oculus* back to the bound captive in the wheel chair and her handler. They arrived at the same underground parking Curly first walked into not all that long ago. The man pushing the wheelchair was met by someone, and they loaded their captive into a van. The new person stayed close to the captive.

Karl zoomed in with the *oculus* and stated, "The new arrival is a medical professional. He is checking her blood pressure. Now he is injecting her with something. My guess is they need her compliant for traveling."

Illych was impressed. "A doctor? That seems a bit much, doesn't it?"

Karl shook his head. "Not at all. Keeping a person docile or unconscious requires a high degree of skill with pharmaceuticals. Both in the application of the drugs and in the care of the individual. The profession of anesthesiology exists for a reason."

"So, this is a good thing?"

Karl took a deep breath and nodded. "Indeed, this is a very good thing. This level of attention indicates she is a valuable asset worthy of the best care. Her remaining healthy is part of their plan. At least for now."

Illych looked at Karl and asked, "So it's safe to say this is Danielle?"

Karl replied, "It's highly likely this is my missing grandniece."

Illych waited for more, and when Karl did not elaborate, said, "Can't we just grab her now with the *oculus* and drop the others from ten thousand feet into the lake?"

Karl shook his head in dissent. "Were she in imminent danger, I would exercise that option. However, it's important she not miraculously appear in an emergency room somewhere. People will ask questions, and the peculiar nature of her situation could lead others to connect her to me.

"To everyone involved, we are aggressive third parties. There is no credible indication of the *oculus* or *ouiblet*. Any witnesses who could share their experience with translation are dead. Danielle's escape will be scrutinized to the most severe standard. Her just appearing somewhere with no explanation as to how will not do."

Karl declared, "If law enforcement does not find her, Danielle must escape on her own."

Illych was processing this unexpected turn of events. "Well, Mr. Lark, assuming this is her, she's being loaded onto a truck. There are no cops in sight, and her being drugged makes her ability to escape unlikely. How's this going to play out?"

Karl snapped, "I said she must escape on her own. I didn't say we cannot help her. She's not in imminent danger. Now we look for a way to assist."

Curly joined the group, and once they were all in the van, it traveled up the ramp and out onto the street.

"We have a problem here," Karl said flatly.

Illych looked at the *oculus* and then at Karl.

Karl elaborated, "The *oculus* has a range of thirteen miles. We have not moved from our observation point at the strip club, but Curly has relocated some eight miles away. Now they appear to be headed north on the highway."

Illych chimed in, "They're moving out of range."

Karl nodded. "They are moving out of range. We must relocate closer. This will require taking the *oculus* away from the moving van, finding a new observation point to relocate to, translating, and then re-acquiring the van on a highway full of vehicles."

Karl's face tightened, his hands a blur of motion on the *oculus* controls. He gave no warning of the translation. The two just appeared on a frozen, snow-drifted roof. The nausea amplified by the surprise of the translation.

Illych gritted his teeth and mumbled, "An amazing way to travel, except for the aftertaste."

Karl did not respond, his focus still on the *oculus*. He was shifting and zooming in on vehicles that resembled the cube van.

Illych resumed his position next to Karl and watched a display of control-operation that would have made an arcade gamer proud.

"There, I have them," Karl exclaimed, "they have continued north."

The pair watched the ghostly *oculus* display for several minutes. The van took an off-ramp.

Karl observed, "They are going to the Midway airport. They plan on flying her somewhere."

The van made its way to a hangar and pulled inside, the hangar doors closing behind them. Karl and Illych watched an obviously unconscious woman being manhandled onto the plane, physician in tow. After their captive and the doctor were safely out of sight, Curly and the other man exited the plane. Curly opened the hangar door, and his companion drove the van outside.

After parking the van, the driver headed back inside the hangar and made a purchase from a vending machine before taking a seat at a table.

For a moment, the *oculus* screen shuddered and went blurry, and then recovered.

Illych asked, "What just happened?"

Karl said, "If my guess is correct, Mr. Haenal is going to dispose of another witness."

Curly left the hangar and joined the man in the office. The *oculus* showed the two men as ghostly outlines, their location and position, standing versus sitting. Karl zoomed in tight on Curly. His outline was different, less defined—more blurry and faint.

The man in the office did not react to Curly's entrance. The money launderer walked right up behind the sitting man, whose body jerked and promptly slumped to the ground.

Karl shifted the *oculus* to register thermal, and the blood from a mortal wound became obvious.

Karl filled in the blanks: "He walked right up to his victim and cut his throat."

Illych frowned. "In broad daylight? Tough to pull that off with complete surprise."

Karl smiled in realization, "*If* the target can see him."

Illych looked up from the screen to Karl and asked, "This guy's doing the same thing he did back in the strip club bathroom? Where he's there, but we can't see him?"

Karl nodded and answered, "Correct. This reinforces my belief that Mr. Haenal possesses a unique capability to move unseen to most observers."

Illych eye's opened wide. "This Curly guy can make himself invisible?"

"That is my working hypothesis at this point."

Illych pointed at the *oculus*. "But you can see him on that."

"Indeed, and that is an important distinction."

Illych continued, "What does that mean? His not being invisible on the *oculus*."

Karl took a deep breath and said, "It means we must be very careful in personal encounters with Mr. Haenal."

Curly returned to the jet, and the pilot started it up. In short order they were taxiing to the takeoff position.

Karl and Illych were huddled on a frozen roof, watching the plane take off with its four passengers on board.

The implication of the jet taking off registered with Illych: "Mr. Lark, if the *oculus* has a range of about thirteen miles, and that jet will be traveling at the speed jets travel at, how do you plan on tracking it?"

Karl Lark's reply was calm and devoid of anxiety: "I will not be tracking it."

Illych looked quizzically at Karl and waited.

"Flight plans. The pilot filed a written flight plan. It was still visible, and the *oculus* took a picture."

Illych nodded in appreciation. "Convenient."

Karl shrugged, "Not everything must be difficult."

Illych conceded, "It's difficult enough that when it isn't, I'm surprised."

Karl nodded in agreement.

"So, where are they going?"

"Mexico."

Illych raised an eyebrow, "Mexico is a big place. Where in Mexico?"

Karl showed him the image of the flight plan on the *oculus*.

After a pause, Illych shared, "I may have been in Ft. Leavenworth for the last two years, but I still know that is cartel country."

"Regardless, that is our destination."

"What about customs? How are they getting Danielle in without customs catching them?" Illych regretted it the instant he said it.

Karl stared back at him.

"Yeah, I know. *Look at where they're going.* It felt silly even while I was saying it."

Karl pointed at the flight plan on the *oculus* screen and stated, "This is a five-hour flight. During that time, I will scout out an observation point near the destination airport. But before that, I have a request."

Illych was intrigued. "A request? What do you need?"

Karl answered, "I wish to become proficient in the use of firearms, and I am asking you to teach me."

Illych smiled. "You're thinking we're gonna be doing some shooting?"

Karl nodded. "Possibly a great deal of it."

Illych was now looking forward to one of life's true pleasures. With a smile, he said, "Mr. Lark, it will be my pleasure to give you a crash course in the safe handling and operation of firearms."

●　　●　　●　　●　　●

They translated into a sunny, cold, clear, blue-sky day near the cabin. Snow crunched underfoot as the two walked the short distance to enter.

Opening the door, Illych said, "We can do the training here. There are enough firearms in the cabin. Let's grab a few, some ammo and a couple of empty cans, and walk up the hill. There's a space I've been using to sight in my weapons and brush up on my skills. Two years in prison is a long time to go without proper target practice."

Karl entered the cabin behind Illych and announced, "I have been studying up on weapon options. Most of the research points to larger calibers being an appropriate choice."

Illych said, "I agree because of our unique circumstances. For most soldiers on the modern battlefield, the rifle is something they lug around and very rarely use. The real damage is done by artillery and bombs. It's not like the old days when infantry would square off and properly shoot it out. For what we're doing, mano-a-mano gunfighting, it's important to not have to shoot someone more than once."

Taking this information in, Karl nodded and said, "Understood. Larger calibers in both handguns and rifles."

Illych added, "Handgun is .45 ACP, long guns are either shotguns or .308 or similar."

Inside the cabin, Illych began pulling weapons from pegs on the wall. Karl was outfitted in a shoulder holster with a modern version of the M1911 on one side and spare magazines on the other. Illych put on the same, grabbed the rifle from the goblin incident in one hand and an olive-drab ammo container in the other.

The pair then exited the cabin to trudge up the hill, their breath condensed in the frigid air.

After setting up some cans and walking back an appropriate distance, Illych asked, "Have you ever fired a weapon before?"

Karl answered, "A handgun once and a rifle twice."

Illych gave Karl a skeptical look. "You went shooting once with a handgun?"

Karl shook his head. "No," he said, "I fired a handgun a single time. One bullet. Two bullets with a rifle."

There was a pause before a quizzical Illych asked, "And what did you think?"

"They performed as expected," Karl deadpanned.

Over the next hour, the two fired over a hundred rounds spread across handguns and the rifle.

Illych watched Karl's dexterity with the weapons increase rapidly. "You're a natural. Both with the pistol and rifle."

Karl replied, "It's geometry. Two points make a line. Although hitting targets over distance is challenging with the handgun."

Illych chuckled at him. "Yeah, it's not like in the movies."

"Thank you, Illych. I am now comfortable with the operation of firearms. We can move on to the next part of the plan."

"And what is that?" Illych asked.

"We find an observation point at that airport in Mexico,where Danielle is arriving in a few hours."

"What about equipment? Do we have time to get more?"

Karl gave Illych a questioning look and asked, "Our armaments situation is insufficient?"

Illych elaborated, "There's a specialty item that I used on occasion back in the Army. And there's a place where we can get it and a few other toys."

With a questioning expression, Karl inquired, "Are these expensive? We can't just be stealing things."

Illych's voice changed to a hint of anger and a darker tone: "No need to pay for these. The Army owes me for two years in Leavenworth. They can charge it to that."

"Agreed. And where do we find these specialty items?"

Illych explained their destination. Karl did some reconnaissance with the *oculus*.

And then they were gone.

    •   •   •   •   •

The pair arrived in a warehouse with rows of floor-to-ceiling shelving. It was not an overly large building, and a single night-light provided enough illumination to safely walk about.

Illych leaned against a gray-colored industrial shelf unit to recover from the translation nausea.

Karl was standing in the middle of an aisle between the industrial shelving. "Now that we are here, what is this place and what are we looking for?"

Illych produced a penlight from a pocket and began inspecting crates and plastic equipment cases on the shelves. "This warehouse belongs to a third-party contractor who supplies the Army with some of its more customized gear."

Karl was staring at the *oculus* screen. "There are no cameras inside here with us, but should we exit this room, we will run afoul of many cameras." Expanding the *oculus* view outwards, he said, "And there are armed security personnel nearby."

Illych smiled and said, "This will take only a few minutes.

"Here, two of these." Illych grabbed two heavy-duty plastic cases from a shelf and started a pile at Karl's feet.

Karl turned the *oculus* on the cases and asked, "Handguns? Why? We have those already."

Illych went back to working through the shelves. "We don't have them like this. Those are special, fully silenced handguns. I grabbed two so I would have a backup." Finding what he was looking for, he hefted a wooden crate marked *9mm Parabellum, sub-sonic (1000)* from the shelf.

Illych placed the crate next to the plastic cases and added, "These pistols require special ammo, which is what's in this crate."

Standing up, Illych straightened out and took a breath, adding, "One more thing, suppressors."

Changing aisles, he quickly found what he was looking for. Several plastic cases were removed from the shelf, placed on the floor, and opened. They contained cylindrical and rectangular devices approximately the size of a human fist.

One of the cases was dumped out on the floor, and Illych began grabbing select items from the open cases and the mess on the floor, tossing them into the empty case.

Closing the half-full case, Illych walked back to Karl and added it to the other items.

"This stuff will get someone into trouble, so I'll do this..." Illych walked to a dusty flat shelving support and placed both hands on it, emphasizing his fingertips. "Now they'll know who came in here and robbed them."

Karl shrugged. "Do you consider this full compensation?"

Illych stood close to Karl and his newly acquired booty. "Not even close."

Karl did one last check with the *oculus* and activated the *ouiblet*.

And then they were gone.

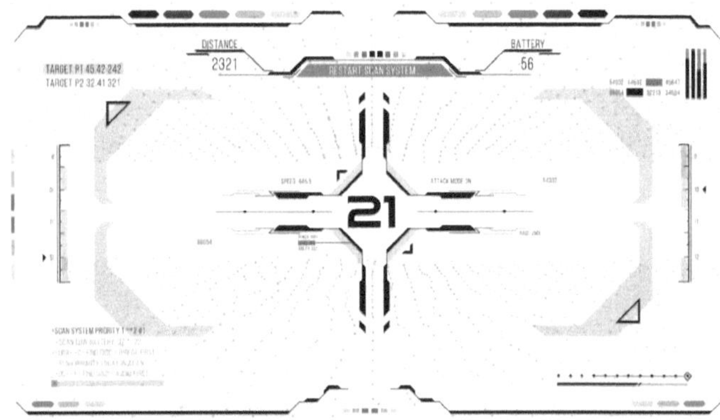

CHAPTER TWENTY ONE

They arrived near the cabin, and Karl left Illych to prepare for Mexico.

Karl was gone just over an hour and announced his return by knocking on the door.

Illych called out, "It's open."

Entering, Karl found Illych in tactical gear, ready to travel.

Still standing in the doorway, he said, "Were you expecting me?"

Illych shrugged. "I waited an hour and got ready. The clock is ticking, and I figured you weren't going to be gone much more than an hour."

Karl gave an acknowledging nod and said, "I have secured a novel location to observe the arrival of Danielle's flight."

Illych replied, "Novel, huh? As in unique?"

The hint of pride in Karl's reply told Illych that *unique* was the right word choice: "Indeed. Due to the range limitations of the *oculus*, it is advantageous that we start as close to the airport as possible. And while there is no shortage of nearby abandoned buildings—or even empty storage containers to temporarily occupy—I have chosen another, more innovative approach."

Hearing this, Illych's eyes narrowed. "Ok, Mr. Lark, what is it you're trying to avoid? You've never skipped out on a closet arrival before."

Karl frowned. "It's hot in Mexico. Which is, in and of itself, off-putting. Additionally, the wildlife in that part of the world is particularly hazardous."

Wildlife? Illych had to ask, "Lions, tigers, and bears?"

Karl shook his head. "No, snakes, spiders, and scorpions. Every abandoned structure I considered was lousy with one or more of them."

Illych smiled. "*Lousy?*"

Karl took a deep breath and exhaled, "It is a word, and I am using it correctly."

Illych closed his eyes for a moment and then opened them. "I get it. You don't like creepy crawlies. So, what's your alternative?"

The hint of pride in Karl's voice returned: "I used the *ouiblet* to remove a sphere of stone deep underground, beneath the airport. The *ouiblet* works most efficiently with the spherical shape. The excavated material was dropped in the Gulf of Mexico."

Illych asked, "How deep underground?"

Karl was now monitoring the *oculus* and replied, "One hundred feet. It seemed a safe number."

"We are going to be hiding in a hollowed-out void under a hundred feet of solid rock?"

Karl stated, "Yes."

Illych blinked and asked, "And that freaks you out *less* than creepy crawlies we can probably just sweep away?"

"Yes."

"What about air?"

Karl responded, "That is an excellent question. Removing the stone leaves a vacuum similar to what was applied in Chicago. However, in this case, the stone has sufficient structural integrity as to not explosively fail. Then the *ouiblet* translates in a sphere of air. The sphere is big enough that the air volume will allow us to breathe comfortably for hours."

Karl paused and then asked, "Are you ready?"

Illych's eyebrows shifted up. "Am I ready to be instantly transported over a thousand miles to a sealed chamber, deep underground, to await the arrival of bad guys so we can take their candy?"

Illych smiled and nodded firmly as he lifted his rifle from the nearby table. With his voice full of determined excitement, he exclaimed, "Sure, I'm ready."

●　　●　　●　　●　　●

The perfect sphere they translated into was illuminated by a single LED camp light. Other than the lamp at the bottom of the sphere, it was completely empty.

Illych took a deep breath while the nausea did its thing. Leaning down, he ran a hand over the concave surface. "That is really smooth—feels like glass."

Standing next to him, Karl's eyes had not left the *oculus*. "Indeed, the *ouiblet* translates a perfect sphere. Right down to selecting individual atoms."

Illych looked up and said, "And the airport is right above us."

Karl nodded. "Directly. If the flight is on schedule, there is still time remaining to explore the area with the *oculus*."

Illych speculated, "What if where they are taking her is not within thirteen miles of our hidey-hole?"

Karl snapped, "Then we will risk rapidly translating along her travel path so as to not lose sight of her."

Illych continued, "Uh-huh. How big is the airport?"

Karl's voice returned to its signature monotone: "It's a good size. Cargo flights mostly. The nearby town has a number of legitimate manufacturing facilities, and some of their products are air freighted."

Over the next hour, Illych found he could walk at a good pace in a circle around the base of the sphere. Karl remained seated on the rising curve off to one side, intently focused on the *oculus*, watching for the flight to arrive.

Karl called out, "The aircraft is on time. Same profile. Same number of passengers."

Illych joined Karl in watching the screen. The plane landed and taxied to a hangar, coming to a complete stop inside.

The exit stairway was let down, and the pilot exited and left. Curly, the doctor, and their captive remained on board, apparently waiting for something.

The wait was short as two SUVs arrived. One remained outside while the other drove into the hangar and parked beside the plane. Two men got out and climbed the steps inside.

Illych and Karl watched this all play out in real time on the *oculus*.

The two men grabbed the woman and carried her from the plane.

The woman, now with the mask removed, was walking on her own. She was pushed into the back of the SUV. Her captors joined her, one on each side. They drove away, joining the other SUV and forming a convoy as they left the airport.

Karl said, "I have her picture. The fast *oculus* was translated in, and I was able to get a visual." Karl held the *oculus* up a little higher to show Illych. A grainy image of a woman appeared.

Illych leaned in close. "Is that her?"

Karl nodded. "Yes, that is Danielle."

"She's a redhead?"

Karl shook his head. "Not naturally. I believe that is a fashion choice."

Illych gave a low whistle: "The picture quality isn't so good, but your grandniece is quite a looker."

Karl turned his head to look directly at Illych. "Please do not share your interest in Danielle's appearance with me."

Illych shrugged. "Well, hey, I've been in prison for the last two years."

Curly and the doctor left the hangar, got into a pickup truck parked outside, and drove themselves into the nearby town.

Karl dexterously shifted back and forth between the convoy and the pickup, driving in almost opposite directions.

Curly and the doctor parked in town, and the two men entered a nearby building.

The pair of SUVs drove a few minutes more to an isolated group of buildings several miles outside of town.

Karl ignored the Curly situation for now and stayed focused on Danielle.

The SUVs pulled into a compound of sorts. Ringed by raised earth berms around most of the cluster of buildings and a chain-linked cyclone fence for the rest.

Danielle was taken out of the center SUV. Apparently having recovered somewhat from the drugging, she pushed back when grabbed by one of the men. Illych and Karl both tensed up, wondering if this was about to get out of hand.

The man she pushed and the other who'd brought her there instead sandwiched her between them, tolerating the physical attacks and grabbing her arms. Essentially, they lifted her up and walked her into a nearby building, through the door and down the entire length of the long, shed-like structure. All the way out to the other side. Attached to the end of the building were concrete stairs down to a short, sunken corridor that ended in a steel door to a low-ceilinged concrete box. Without pause, they pulled open the door and pushed her down on a cot. One of the men pointed at her to stay. Taking a few steps back, they closed the door, leaving her there.

Karl did the *oculus* snapshot thing on the woman in the cell. The image on the *oculus* was of a haggard, unkempt Danielle.

Karl stated, "It appears Danielle has been situated for now."

Illych asked, "Why not grab your grandniece now?"

"She is safe. They still need to interrogate her. That gives time to engage Curly and get to the bottom of this invisibility thing."

Illych took a step back and asked, "What happened to 'all other considerations are secondary?'"

Karl's eyes were glued to the *oculus* screen. "Mr. Haenal must not escape."

Illych blinked and shook his head, "Okay then. What's this place he and the doctor are at?"

Both men watched as the display zoomed in on the building where they had last seen Curly.

Illych pointed to the many bottles on shelves, "That's a bar."

The *oculus* showed a lobby with women standing around or sitting on couches. Karl's head tilted just the slightest. "Actually, it appears to be a house of ill repute."

Illych leaned in closer. "A brothel?"

Karl nodded. "Correct. Curly and the doctor are celebrating."

Time passed while the two men huddled together, watching events unfold in the brothel.

Illych broke the silence: "Do we have to sit here and watch this?"

Karl replied, "I agree this is not what I want to use our time for, but we are waiting for an opportunity to approach our target. Fortunately, they do not seem to need much time."

Moments later, Karl abruptly leaned closer to the *oculus*, "What just happened? There was a distortion."

Illych replied, "Maybe Curly is using his invisibility thing?"

Karl nodded. "Possibly. I can see him here. He has left the room he was in and appears to be going to visit the doctor."

Karl and Illych watched Curly open the door and walk in on the doc and his female companion in *flagrante delicto*. The man reacted to the door opening and started to get up. The woman just leapt from the bed and ran out the door.

Curly produced a long-barreled pistol. The *oculus* registered the thermal blooms of rounds being fired.

Karl thought out loud, "Guns are loud, especially in enclosed spaces. Why are all the people in the building not reacting?

Illych pointed at the long barrel of the pistol and answered, "Suppressor. That's why the pistol looks so long with such a large-diameter barrel. A quality silencer with sub-sonic ammunition. And I'm willing to bet there's loud music in that place. Too bad the *oculus* doesn't do sound."

Karl shrugged and observed, "The *oculus*, like the *ouiblet*, has limitations."

The pair watched as Curly left the dead doctor and walked away. The strangest part was him walking down halls past people who did not react to the obvious gun in his hand.

Illych called it, "He's doing the invisibility thing. See how no one notices he's there?"

After ending the life of the last person from Chicago who could connect him to Danielle's kidnapping, Curly navigated downstairs and out a back door.

Illych shook his head. "This Curly guy is one cold-blooded, bloodthirsty dude."

"Agreed," Karl said, "he cannot be allowed to be near Danielle."

"What's the plan?"

"We take him now."

Illych's voice shared his surprise: "Translate him now? He's out in public. A lot of people are going to see a bald gringo disappear into thin air."

Karl shook his head. "Not quite yet. Remember how the goblin creature could not be translated? I am concerned about attempting the same while he is using his invisibility ability. He is in public, and it might not work. Or there could be other unintended consequences."

"Yeah," Illych mused, "it would be bad if he got the Helena treatment before we were able to question him."

Karl continued, "He must be getting transportation. Walking five miles through the desert to the compound will not be his first choice. When the opportunity presents itself, we will move. Are you ready?"

Illych put his hands on the rifle hanging from his harness and replied, "Ready."

Curly walked down the street, apparently with nobody able to see him. At one point, he ducked behind a van, out of sight. The *oculus* did the glitchy thing again, and he walked out into view.

He then entered a shop, obviously now visible, and spoke to a man. Another man came out of the back. He and Curly walked out to a parked truck. The man handed Curly the keys to the vehicle. Their target got in and drove away.

Karl waited until the truck had travelled far enough to be out of sight of the town. Illych watched in real-time as Karl worked on targeting the *ouiblet* on the moving truck's engine. A critical part was then removed.

The truck abruptly slowed, and Curly pulled off to the side of the road.

"That was not a clean sabotage," Karl admitted, "but it was effective. If someone takes the engine apart, they will see a mess. It is now time for us to have a conversation with Curly."

Illych said, "It worked out that he stopped on a deserted highway out of sight from the town and the compound. Now what? And what about the invisibility thing?"

Karl was working the *oculus* and *ouiblet* controls as he answered, "He must be disabled so we can search and remove it. Then we take him somewhere to discuss recent events."

Illych racked the slide on his rifle, "Roger that."

Karl brandished a Taser and turned to Illych. "I will know Curly's location from the *oculus* even if he goes invisible."

Illych nodded.

Everything went black, and then it was bright desert as far as eyes could see. Illych squinted and tried to suppress his reaction to the nausea. He looked around for Curly.

There was the buzz of a Taser, and in his peripheral vision he could see Karl standing next to *something* doing the now-all-too-common dying-chicken dance.

Illych rushed the vague shape that was Curly and got his hands on him. Pushing him to the ground, he frisked the man, pulling weapons away and tossing them into the nearby ditch. Under the man's shirt was a harness. Feeling around, he found buckles. Creepily similar to a teenager on a date trying to undo a bra clasp, he eventually freed the harness and pulled it off. Curly's form gained definition and became visible in the normal way.

Illych held up the harness. It was made from hard leather straps. In the middle of the chest space was a device made of a gray material, almost metallic or carbon fiber-looking.

Karl observed, "I didn't know what to expect, but I suppose that makes sense." He waved for Illych to hand it to him. Karl then set it on the ground and stood back. Moments later, the *ouiblet* disappeared the artifact.

"I put it somewhere safe for later research. Now, let us take Mr. Haenal somewhere and talk."

A moment later, all that was left was a mysteriously disabled truck baking under the desert sun.

●　　●　　●　　●　　●

Curly was zip-tied to a chair. The ties were viciously tight, the discomfort assisting his return to consciousness.

The sitting man's eyes blinked and focused. This was followed by a strong inhalation of air.

Karl said, "Hello, Mr. Haenal."

"Where am I? How do you know my name?"

"Good, your cognitive functions are returning."

Curly struggled against his restraints, exclaiming, "These ties are too tight. They really hurt."

"The hope is that the discomfort keeps you focused."

Curly stopped struggling.

Karl said, "You understand then. Conserve your energy. Why did you arrange for Danielle Mersen to be kidnapped?"

Curly smiled and snarled, "I didn't arrange for crap. I took her myself. She never even saw me coming."

"The artifact? You were invisible?"

Curly looked down at his bare chest and nodded.

Karl stepped closer. "You have a unique opportunity here. Danielle is alive and relatively uninjured. I have taken your invisibility artifact. You are no longer a threat. Even if you tell people what you have seen, the most likely outcome is your being locked up in a mental institution. Give me answers, and I will deliver you anywhere you wish to go."

Curly shook his head. "Yeah, right. That's not how these things end."

Karl's voice changed to a cutting whisper: "Mr. Haenal, you have cost me a great deal of time and concern. What I want now are answers. Make that quick, and you walk. Otherwise, I guarantee you will tell me. It will take longer, but you will talk."

Illych shook his head and added, "Look, friend, this guy is getting wound up to do some next-level weird stuff to you. I've seen it before, and trust me, you *don't* wanna go there. Whatever you were planning is toast—just talk and walk."

Curly looked back and forth between Karl and Illych. His face relaxed. "What do you want to know?"

"Where did you find the artifact?"

"Iraq. My unit was patrolling some crap province. We entered a village, and Haji came at us. The rest of the platoon pulled back. My squad was point, and we got cutoff. We took a building and holed up, waiting for armor support. It wasn't looking good. Half the squad was dead, and the rest of us were wounded.

"The badly wounded were moved to the center of the building. The rest of us kept firing. News came over the radio that the armor was delayed. That's when we figured out that the wounded were all dead. Throats slit. As was the guy who was caring for them.

"While the rest of us were focused outside and shooting, somebody slipped in and killed the wounded and our medic. Only four of us were left, and then it gets quiet outside, like they know something's in there with us.

"We shift positions and wait. Time is on our side. Every minute, an M1 main battle tank gets closer to ending the situation. One guy, Morales, makes a choking noise, and we all look. His throat's been slit from ear to ear, and blood is pouring out.

"Jackson, this big black dude from Mississippi, panics and starts shooting into corners. I call out to the fourth, Miller. He doesn't reply and instead stumbles closer with his throat slit too. Jackson completely freaks and runs for it. He sprinted out the door and the bad guys open fire. He didn't make it twenty feet before they cut him down.

"I figured this is it. There are maybe seconds before whatever it is gets me. So I start pulling grenades out. Pulling the pins and tossing them into corners, danger close, and all that. I got all six going before the first popped.

"I was out for a while, don't know how long exactly. Shrapnel cuts everywhere, lots of blood, but nothing fatal. Lying next to me is some Middle Eastern guy. The grenades got him just as he was about to do me. His clothing is shredded, and that harness is on his chest. It and the knife went in my pack.

"Not fifteen minutes later, the M1 shows up, and my platoon comes to get me. Got a Purple Heart and a Bronze Star for that one.

"They sent me stateside to recover. Not long after, my enlistment's up and I'm figuring that harness thing out. When you're wearing it, people can't see you. I figured—why work for the man when I can do better?"

Karl's voice was back to normal: "Thank you for the background. That answers many questions. But how did you find out about Danielle?"

"FBI agent told me. A lunch regular at *The Pink Pole*. Kept talking up the girls about his awesome job. Like he was James Bond or something. Then one day, he lets it drop about this new chick in the office. Goes on about how hot she is. Then he lets it slip that she's an analyst into money laundering. He even told her name, Danielle Mersen. I figured out the rest."

Karl Lark's face was expressionless when he asked, "This agent's name. Give me the name."

Curly hesitated, looking Karl over before divulging, "Dave something. David Polk, Special Agent David Polk."

Karl looked at Illych, then back to Curly. "How did the rest of this get set up? The cartel?"

Curly did an imitation of shrugging and offered, "The rest was easy. The cartel guys know how to interrogate, and I figured it was safer to get her out of the country. The FBI doesn't like it when you kidnap one of theirs.

"With what she knows, I can double my territory, maybe more. Or, at least I could have."

Karl took a deep breath and exhaled, "Thank you for the clarity, Mr. Haenal. After what has happened over the last few days, it is good to resolve the details."

Karl's head tilted just the tiniest bit. "One more question: How did you know we would come for you?"

"People were disappearing. There was a drop-off house that was almost leveled. Some big-shot lawyer's penthouse suite got messed up. Anybody with sense knew someone was shaking the tree hard. And whoever it was, they weren't the cops or feds. I figured it was only a matter of time. Went to ground at the club to wait it out. When the power went out, I knew and got ready.

"The bathroom was a surprise, though. I almost didn't use the harness. I mean, how could anyone get in there? You guys almost got me then. How did you get in there? What are you guys, ninjas or something?"

Illych smirked, "*Or something.* There are things you never want to know."

Curly looked at Illych, fully taking him in. "Aren't you that Green Beret who smoked an Afghani officer? The dude that was raping boys? I thought you went to Leavenworth for that."

"I was released early for good behavior," Illych replied with a coy smile. "Hey, what about that underwater thing? What's up with that?"

"Water messes up the invisibility thing. Not always, though. So, I set up that escape deal. Got the idea from a spy movie. If someone came at me and it was like the invisibility thing, that was my getaway."

Illych shook his head.

Karl stepped away, deep in thought.

Illych joined him and whispered, "So, what are we doing with him?"

Karl replied, "He is no threat. We release him."

Moving back by their captive, Karl asked, "Where would you like to be dropped at?"

A surprised Curly answered, "Like, anywhere?"

"Correct. My colleague here will taser you, and when you wake up, wherever you request, within reason, is your destination. Perhaps someplace in Chicago?"

Curly shook his head. "Nope, losing the invisibility thing ends Chicago for me. Drop me in Las Vegas. I know people there."

Karl replied, "As you wish."

"One last thing, just because you guys have me won't stop the cartel guys getting the info from the FBI chick."

Karl's voice returned to a sharp whisper: "Danielle and the cartel are no longer your concern."

Karl nodded to Illych. Seconds later, Curly lost consciousness under the influence of 80,000 volts.

Illych cut the zip ties. "You're really sending this guy to Las Vegas? Seems awfully altruistic of you. You know, compared to what happened."

Karl repled, "There's nothing altruistic about it. Mr. Haenal is who he is. None of this would have happened if Agent David Polk had not broken faith with his coworkers and the FBI.

"And I have not had time to analyze the invisibility artifact. In the unlikely event I have questions, a living Mr. Haenal will be useful. Additionally, if the artifact was causing some sort of malevolent long-term influence, it will be interesting to observe if he exhibits any changes."

Karl concentrated his focused on the *oculus*, "I also stand by my original statement. Without his invisibility crutch, he is not likely all that dangerous."

Illych asked, "What are you doing?"

"Determining coordinates for a point in Las Vegas. I am using the *ouiblet* to cast the fast *oculus* close to the city. It takes a snapshot and returns. The results show up here. It is an iterative process, perhaps similar to the six-degrees-of-separation concept. After a few tries, I should be able to locate a private drop-off point."

Karl worked the *ouiblet* and *oculus* controls, "And there it is."

Illych interrupted the process to interject, "Wait a minute, Mr. Lark. He knows things about us. Like the fact that we have his artifact. You're sure he should walk?"

"We have actions to take and may need to ask him more questions. There is no reasonable way for us to maintain him as a prisoner. This is not an ideal solution, but it is acceptable for now."

Illych watched Karl's arcane activities, followed by Curly's unconscious form disappearing. "And now what?"

"Time to arrange Danielle's escape."

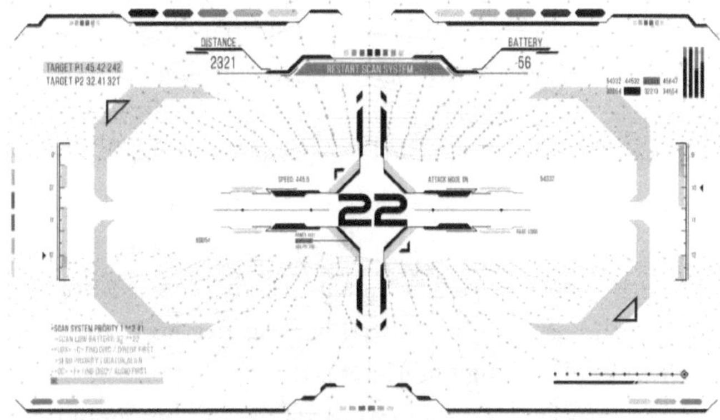

CHAPTER TWENTY TWO

The drugs had started to lose their effect on the plane. Danielle couldn't tell how long they'd kept her under. Her memory of the last couple days—*Was it days? Maybe it was hours?*— was fuzzy and full of gaps.

They left her sitting on a cot. Once the door closed, the sickness she felt rolled over her. Whatever they used to keep her unconscious left an awful hangover. Lying down, she curled up into a fetal position and shivered despite the heat.

Two days—that was more likely. Her hair was in knots, and her clothes were disgusting. And that smell.

Who are these people, and what do they want with me?

After drifting in and out of consciousness, she abruptly awakened. The drugs' effects were almost gone. Other than a headache and mild nausea, she was feeling better.

Sitting up, she took in her surroundings. A single flickering yellowed-with-age fluorescent tube illuminated her predicament: concrete floor and walls, and a very solid-looking steel door. The ribbed steel roof cover looked flimsy enough. Escape would be easy if it were not for the rebar rising up from the concrete walls and then crisscrossing back and forth above her. The quality of the construction left much to be desired, but everything was overbuilt and solid. She was not breaking out of here.

Her eyes landed on a cardboard box with bottles of water and a box of crackers. Pouncing on those, she drank and ate and immediately felt better.

The clearing of her mind brought a singular realization: *They're keeping me alive.*

Some of the seams in the roof were not tight. The bright sunlight outside filtered through, and the room was hot; summertime hot. Danielle realized she was not in Chicago. Probably far from it.

For the first time in a day—*Two days?*—she could think. Her thoughts shifted to when it all started. Whoever had taken her captive in Chicago had done so without warning. She'd been getting out of her car and then…darkness.

Yeah, well, it's time for round two.

Standing, she stretched and did a few deep breathing exercises. Looking about, it was apparent there was not much to work with in the cell: a cardboard box, a now-empty water bottle, cracker wrappers, and a cot. In one corner was a bucket with a lid.

That's nasty.

The cot was a metal frame with canvas stretched across. That was it. Those were all the assets she had to work with.

Wiping the sweat from her brow, she understood she was trapped in a concrete hot box.

She walked over to the door. Metal plate, no window, no doorknob. Running her fingers along the door edges, she pushed and pulled. Nothing except for a cut on her hand from a sharp metal edge.

And no cameras. Nobody was watching her.

Danielle smiled and grabbed the cot. Rubbing the canvas wrapped around the metal frame against the sharp edge on the cell door quickly cut it free. The legs, now removed from the canvas, collapsed into a serviceable club.

It's a start.

Taking up the canvas, she went to work on the next step in her escape plan.

●　　●　　●　　●　　●

Karl announced, "Now that Mr. Haenal is no longer an issue, it's time to arrange for Danielle's release. We need to relocate closer to the compound where Danielle is being held. And I think this will work." He held up the *oculus* so Illych could see a junkyard of abandoned vehicles inside the compound perimeter. One of them was an empty van.

Looking up at Illych, Karl said, "You will want to crouch down."

●　　●　　●　　●　　●

The heat reminded them they were now in a metal box baking in the mid-afternoon desert sun.

Illych whispered, "We're not going to be able to hold this position long before heat stroking out."

"This is a very temporary situation while I send a text." Karl produced a flip phone from a pocket and began his message.

An incredulous Illych asked, "A text? Where did you get the phone?"

"From Curly. I just texted Mr. Hemway this location and the fact that Danielle is here."

Illych frowned, "The FBI will take hours to mount a rescue. This ain't exactly suburban Chicago."

Karl placed the still-powered-up phone under some trash on the van's floor. "If our actions are successful, Danielle will have freed herself to greet them by then."

A bird's-eye view appeared on the *oculus* display. "I can map out safe paths inside the compound on the *oculus*. We can then begin reducing the obstacles she must overcome to escape."

Illych's sweating face turned to Karl as he huffed, "By *reduce*, you mean kill people, right?"

Karl nodded. "Other than the locked door on the room she is currently being held in, people are the only obstacles to her freedom. This will require stealth to begin with."

Illych smirked. "That's what this is for." He removed the recently acquired long-barreled handgun from his pack.

"Bolt-action, sub-sonic ammo, best suppressor available. Completely quiet. Even the action has these rubber pads to prevent the click-clack sound when the next round is cycled in. Not accurate over range, though. I need to be close."

Karl, only half-listening to Illych's gun-fetish ramble, was looking at the nearest building through the *oculus*. Three men were inside, moving things around. "This nearest building is a warehouse, I believe. We can start there. Then work our way around the perimeter."

Illych asked, "What about security cameras?"

Karl shrugged and replied, "Conveniently, there are none. Apparently, there is little concern of anyone attempting to break into a drug cartel compound."

Illych cleared his throat: "Are we ready, Karl? Because I'm sweating my balls off."

Karl nodded. "Open the van back door, walk straight ahead to the building, and stay close to it. Then we go to our left, to an unlocked door. That is how we will enter."

The van door opened with more metallic squeal than Illych was comfortable with. Without hesitation, he stalked straight to the windowless building and paused to look around. Karl was right behind with the *oculus* in his left hand and *ouiblet* control in his right.

Karl pointed to the left in the direction of a door at the far corner of the warehouse. The pair moved there and Illych looked at the doorknob and then to Karl.

Karl shook his head and whispered, "Not locked. One of them is close by. The other two are further away." He held up the *oculus* for Illych to see.

Illych took a moment to work out his next actions. "I've got this. Give me space and watch my back."

He opened the door in a lightning-quick movement and was inside. Three great strides later, the first man went down with a bullet between the eyes and a shocked look on his face.

Illych turned to face Karl, who was holding up the *oculus* so he could see where the next two were.

The remaining two men were working: moving and stacking boxes. A radio was playing Spanish-speaking music that easily covered up what little noise was being made. Cycling the weapon in his hand to eject a spent casing and chamber the next round, Illych stalked to his next target with a silent gait.

The second man saw Illych at the last second before he too was silenced.

From the corner of his eye, the last man in the warehouse saw the body hit the ground and lunged for a rifle with a huge banana magazine. Illych kept moving straight towards his next target, cycling the pistol as he closed in. The man's hands gripped the rifle and began lifting it to a firing position as Illych pulled the trigger. Number three slumped to the floor while the rifle clattered loudly on the concrete.

"Nicely done," Karl said. "Are they dead?"

"Head shots with brass jacketed hollow points. Yes, they're dead. What's next?"

Karl was looking at a pickup truck parked in the warehouse. "They were almost done loading this."

Karl held up the *oculus*.

Illych looked and asked, "What are you doing?"

"Checking on Danielle. It appears she has been industrious the last two hours." Karl angled the *oculus* so Illych could have a look.

Illych smiled when he realized what he was seeing, "That's diabolical. Is she single?"

Karl glared back at him. "We must work faster to make her efforts successful. I have an idea how."

•   •   •   •   •

Danielle held up the sharpened frame piece—her club could now double as a spear. The door had a clearance gap at the bottom. More than enough to open over something flat on the floor without rolling it up. Now, half of the cot canvas was lying flat on the floor, just inside the door.

The rest of the bed frame—not made into a club—was tied up to the rebar overhead and suspended by canvas strips. When she pulled the release, it would swing straight into the open doorway. It was not heavy enough to put someone down, but it should break their concentration and cause them to move. Which was all she would need.

Reaching up above the doorway, she removed the fluorescent tube. Moving back to the middle of the cell, she sat to wait. Spear club in one hand and the fluorescent tube in the other.

•   •   •   •   •

Karl scrolled the *oculus* display. Each building in turn showed its contents and the people within.

Illych said, "Wait, is that what I think it is?"

Karl nodded. "Perhaps it is a drug lab on the other side of the compound. I suspect the workers laboring there are not hard-core cartel. Regardless, the *oculus* shows numerous flammable chemicals are present. If a small cross section of this equipment support is removed from *here*..." Karl zoomed in on a metal rod that was part of a stand holding up a metal bottle. "It will topple *there*..." More scrolling and zooming, "...starting a fire. It will be difficult to extinguish, and the workers will likely be evacuated. The ensuing chaos will be to our advantage as we make a path for Danielle."

Illych smirked, "By *make a path*, you mean kill more people?"

"I see no other way to support her escape."

Illych raised his gleaming black pistol. "Well, I'm ready if you are."

Karl worked the *ouiblet* while watching the thermal image of the lab. The cooler blue of the glass bottle was clearly visible as it fell over. The screen lit up in reds and oranges. Karl zoomed out, showing the workers reacting by streaming for the exits.

Something in the lab ignited, and the screen now had flashes of white.

Illych exhaled, "Wow, it's like the Fourth of July in there."

Karl's face was highlighted by the bright colors on the *oculus* screen. "That is unexpected. There was apparently phosphorous being stored. I missed that. Not a lot, but enough to make this more interesting."

The warehouse door next to the overhead garage door opened, and a man with a rifle charged in, yelling, "Ricardo!" A few paces in, he stopped and stared at the body on the floor. As the situation began to register and play out on the man's expression, his eyes raised to see two men standing nearby. One was holding a box with a handle. The other was pointing an oddly large and bulky handgun at him.

Illych pulled the trigger, and the intruder dropped.

Cycling his pistol, he said, "Looks like your plan worked. This place is about to get more exciting."

Karl pointed to the *oculus* and said, "Here, see." The *oculus* showed vehicles being loaded with the workers. Clouds of dust kicked up as the vehicles hastily exited the compound."

For the briefest instant, Illych saw a smile touch Karl's features before the old man said, "That is convenient. The workers are being evacuated. Now everyone in the compound other than Danielle can be considered hostile."

●　　●　　●　　●　　●

Danielle could hear muffled sounds of vehicles starting and driving away. That and yelling in Spanish came through the sheet metal roof.

The heat and Spanish-speaking coalesced in her mind. Not only was she not in Chicago, she realized she may not even be in the United States.

●　　●　　●　　●　　●

Karl and Illych were standing in the warehouse, looking at the bird's-eye view of the compound. As the workers were driven away, groups of men formed and then broke apart into small, two- or three-man teams. They began executing a search pattern of the compound.

Karl pointed to the screen with his free hand and observed, "They are organized. This will work to our advantage. We can deal with the small teams one by one.

"See this building? They just cleared it and left two men inside. We can start there."

"How are we doing this?" Illych asked.

Karl grabbed the *ouiblet* from a pocket and started working the controls. "The oxygen removal approach we used back in Chicago. After it takes effect, we will translate in."

"Won't the sound of the building collapsing be kind of loud?"

"Not as loud as giving them a chance to shoot back. Ready."

Illych hefted his pistol and nodded. "Ready."

The middle of the building where they translated into was a communal space: comfortable furniture, a television, even a foosball table. Arriving just seconds after all the air had been instantaneously removed, the place was a mess. The damage and debris gave the appearance the building itself had just attacked the two men now writhing on the floor.

Karl had removed only the air in the communal space. The rooms around the perimeter were not vacuumed, so to speak. The result was the surrounding rooms, without an equalized pressure from the air in the middle of the building, exploding under several tons of air pressure. Drywall had been blasted from the walls inward. As the perimeter room's air forcefully equalized, external windows shattered, spraying glass all the way to the core of the building.

Dust and debris were still settling as Illych put the two men out of their misery. "You know, that's like setting off a bomb. Maybe just not as loud."

Karl was inspecting his handiwork. "Agreed. In many ways, it is an inverse thermobaric weapon. Instead of creating an overpressure outside the target, it creates a vacuum at the target and allows the surrounding structures to deliver physical trauma."

Illych replied, "Uh-huh. We're done here. What's next?"

Karl lifted the *oculus* up so they could both observe.

Illych pointed and suggested, "Here, these three standing behind this building." Moving his finger, "We translate here, and I use the long gun. Then we wait for this team to come over to check out the gunfire. Then put them down too."

His finger shifted again. "Then we translate out to this location to wait and watch."

Karl nodded. "Agreed."

Illych unslung his rifle. "Ready."

Everything went black.

•   •   •   •   •

The afternoon sun was hot and bright. They translated in behind a pile of dirt and debris left behind from a construction project. Illych moved up against it, fighting the translation nausea, and aligned his optics on the men next to the building. Two were leaning back, obviously relaxing. The third was standing away from the building, smoking a cigarette, his hands moving animatedly as he spoke. All three of their weapons were leaning up against the building.

Illych whispered, "Sloppy."

The first shot dropped Talking Man. The second nailed one of the men leaning on the wall, and he slid down to a sitting position. The third man pushed off the wall and started to turn when Illych's third shot hit. The man kept moving. Illych tracked him while firing in rapid succession until the man dropped. Shifting his sighting back to his first two targets, he put two more shots in each one.

Karl asked, "Why the extra shots?"

"Dead checking—don't need anybody who is just wounded getting up."

"Sounds prudent." Karl said while consulted the *oculus*. "Three more are coming." He pointed the men out to Illych. "Building corner to the right."

Illych shifted and waited. A man jogged around the corner, followed quickly by another, weapons at the ready. The first man saw his comrades' corpses, slowed to a walk for a few paces, and started looking around. The second jogger did the same.

The third—and last—man arrived right after, and Illych dropped him first. The remaining two immediately began firing wildly in Karl and Illych's general direction, but not for long, as precise gunfire silenced both of them.

After several rounds to dead-check the new arrivals, it all went black again.

●　　●　　●　　●　　●

Waiting in the dark for her captors to return, Danielle was frustrated from not knowing the time. Had it been fifteen minutes or six hours? It felt like forever.

The sound of gunfire broke the silence. A series of spaced shots. Not the *pop-pop* of a 9mm or 5.56. This was the thunder of something with more power. She did not take comfort in this. Whoever was shooting, they were not likely to be law enforcement here to rescue her.

●　　●　　●　　●　　●

Karl and Illych's new position was inside a water pump house. A small concrete building, padlocked on the outside and filled with industrial equipment on the inside. A single caged bulb lit the space. The myriad pipes, pumps, and motors cast stark shadows against the wall.

Illych spoke first: "You know, Karl, I'm not sure killing a bunch of cartel guys is the right way to rescue Danielle."

Karl focused the *oculus* on Danielle and retorted, "The goal is not to rescue her. The FBI is likely en route. We needed to get most of the people away from here. The fire did that. At some point in this killing spree, the remaining gunmen will cut and run. They will not leave Danielle. When they go to remove her from that room, the goal is to increase the probability that her escape attempt will be successful.

"If at any point she is in danger, I will translate her out. Otherwise, I prefer she escape for plausible deniability's sake."

Illych replied, "I get it, but that's a high-risk option at this point. They may just send some guys to kill her before they bug out."

"Agreed, we will take a few moments to reassess the situation and make a decision."

Illych pointed out, "Look, we eliminated these twelve men here, here, and here. The buses and trucks with the workers have left, taking the bulk of the men working security. That leaves what I count as a dozen more."

His finger shifted to the entrance to the main road. "They're organizing a convoy of vehicles here. Perhaps they're planning to leave?"

Karl added, "Between the processing building catching on fire and gunfire they know did not come from their guys, and then finding some of our handiwork in the exploded building, they do appear to be getting ready to leave."

Eight men got into three vehicles and drove out. Once outside the compound, they stopped and waited with engines running."

The remaining four men headed towards the building where Danielle's cell was attached.

Karl zoomed in. Two of the men stopped just inside the building. The other two continued on.

Pointing at the screen, he said, "We translate here. We wait for the other two to open the cell door. I'll give you the signal, and you shoot these two with your rifle."

Illych said, "Inside the building? That will be like a cannon going off."

"We have earplugs, and they likely do not. No time to explain why."

Illych asked, "When?"

"Now."

●　　●　　●　　●　　●

The room they translated into was a workshop. Toolboxes, workbenches with disassembled equipment, and power tools hung on the walls. The place smelled of grease and oil. There was no door between this room and the length of the building, and the lights were off.

Illych crept forward until he could see around to the two standing by the door, looking out the window. Lining up the shot, he looked to Karl, and nodded. Karl's eyes were glued to the *oculus* display. The two men were unlocking the cell door. With a shoulder, one of them pushed it open into the cell.

Karl whispered, "Now."

With a minimal shift in position, Illych fired one shot at each. In the enclosed space of the building, it was thunderously loud. Shifting back and forth, he fired several more rounds in each as the men crumpled to the ground.

Karl never looked up from the *oculus*. Instead, he concentrated on the events unfolding in the cell less than a hundred feet away.

●　　●　　●　　●　　●

Danielle waited in the dark. She could hear the first sounds since the distant gunfire. A door opened not far away. Some words in Spanish. Someone was coming.

Club-spear in one hand and the fluorescent tube in the other, she took some deep breaths. The clank and screech of the door lock were loud in the cell. Then the soft thump of a shoulder pushed the door inward.

A backlit figure followed the door opening and stepped into the cell.

Danielle smashed the fluorescent tube across his head. The same hand now reached back and pulled the release of the swinging bed frame. Swaying forward, it struck the swearing man in the face. He fell down, cursing, and rolled to the side. The second man walked in straight towards Danielle, pausing to push the hanging cot frame out of the way.

Startling, loud gunfire from inside the building rolled down the hall. The man standing just inside the doorway jerked with surprise at the gunfire and looked back up the hall.

Danielle bent over, grabbed the canvas, and pulled hard. The second man's footing slid out with the canvas, and he went down. Leading with the club spear, she pounced on the men lying on the floor, covered in broken glass.

The light from the hall showed just enough of her targets. The spear found the second man's neck, and Danielle dropped her body weight on top of it. Her target's scream ended in a gurgle and a spurt of red. Spotting the semiautomatic handgun in his waistband, she grabbed it and pushed herself back up. She started shooting the first man, who was still struggling in the shattered glass to get up.

The strobe and thunder of gunfire in the dark room continued as she made sure the second man was dead.

Her hearing was temporarily gone due to the gunfire. She paused and looked up the hall to find that no one else was coming. Looking back at the two dead men on the floor, she realized they had rifles slung across their backs. Smiling, she retrieved one.

"Try and kidnap me now, you bastards," she said, walking out the door and up the hall.

●　　●　　●　　●　　●

Karl and Illych had been watching the events in Danielle's cell unfold on the *oculus* screen.

Illych was smiling and nodding. "Your niece is a badass woman."

"She handled herself quite well. I am pleased."

"Wait, did you set that up to see what she would do?"

"No, I did not. But in the end, she has proven herself quite worthy."

"You have some interesting ideas of how to treat family, Mr. Lark."

"Danielle has done well regardless. She is coming now, and we need to reposition."

Everything went dark again.

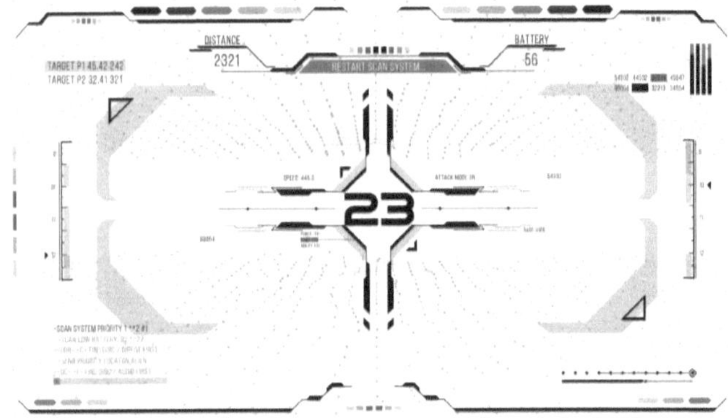

CHAPTER TWENTY THREE

After repositioning back to the pump house, they watched Danielle explore the building she'd been kept in.

The convoy just outside the compound stayed in place, idling for fifteen minutes.

Illych observed and remarked, "They're probably trying to raise their comrades on the radio."

Karl replied, "If they attempt to enter the building Danielle is in, I will be forced to take extreme action."

Illych chuckled, "You know, Karl, after the ten-thousand-foot thing, the car-falling-out-of-the-sky thing, and the building implosion trick, I hope they just drive away. For all of our sakes."

Eventually, they did. Apparently cutting their losses, the convoy drove away, leaving only three living humans in the compound.

Danielle found a cell phone on one of the men Illych had shot and started making calls. Karl and Illych watched this on the *oculus*. Whatever was said, she began stacking toolboxes and equipment against the door, fortifying her position. She found a comfortable place to sit far back from the door and waited.

Illych watched all of this unfold. "My guess is they told her to go to ground and wait. Cavalry is on the way."

Karl nodded. "Agreed."

● ● ● ● ●

Hours passed before the *whump whump whump* sound of helicopters reverberated throughout the compound. Three Blackhawk choppers landed close by while an Apache gunship circled overhead.

Armed men streamed out of the choppers, a haggard looking Danielle was escorted to one of the Blackhawks, climbed in, and immediately took off. The other figures on the display were now going house-to-house. Of course, they found only empty buildings and corpses.

"Time for us to go. We may be visible on their infrared sensors."

Next, there was an empty pump house.

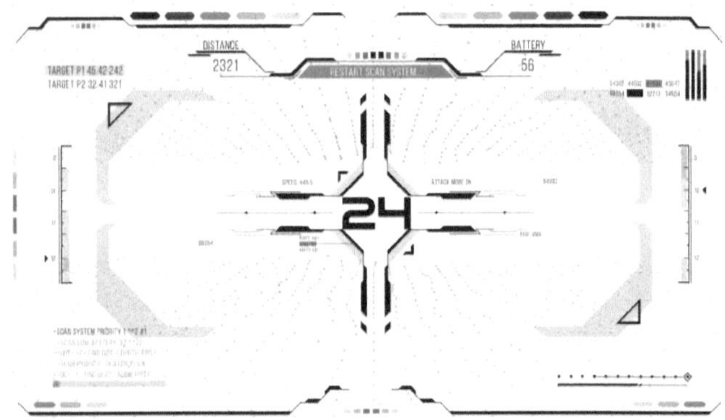

CHAPTER TWENTY FOUR

The pair arrived on the frozen slope up from the cabin. The starry night above illuminated the forest around them in a ghostly, pale light.

Illych took a deep breath and looked at the cloud created when he exhaled.

Karl broke the silence: "There is a final loose end to deal with."

Illych wondered out loud, "How so? Your niece is headed home safe and sound, and the people who engineered the situation are all dead or scattered."

Karl shook his head. "No, there is one person who, had he kept his mouth shut, none of this would have happened."

Illych thought for a minute and then said, "That Dave guy Curly told us about? The one who visits the strip club? What about him?"

Karl's face was devoid of expression, "Dave is going to be given the opportunity to consider the error of his ways."

Based on Karl's demeanor, Illych was not optimistic about that Dave guy's future. *Should be an interesting outing.*

Karl announced, "I shall return shortly with our next destination."

Illych, now alone, shrugged his shoulders, filled his lungs with crisp, cold night air, and started towards the cabin.

●　　●　　●　　●　　●

Illych had time enough to make a fire and dinner before the expected knock on the door. Karl entered, and the two understood what came next without any words needing to be said.

They arrived on another Chicago rooftop, and Illych leaned against a wall to weather the nausea.

Without pause, Karl worked the *oculus*, zooming in on their intended target's apartment.

Watching the *oculus* display as Karl worked his magic, Illych witnessed Dave enter his place, drop his keys on a countertop, and walk over to the TV to turn it on.

Illych asked, "Are we going to wait until he goes to sleep?"

Karl shook his head. "No, we are going to translate straight in, and you are going to point your gun at him."

"Won't he see us just appear out of thin air?"

"He might."

"Doesn't that mess with the secrecy thing?

"Secrecy with Dave will not be a concern for long."

A circular flotation life preserver appeared nearby and fell a short distance to land on the snow.

Karl instructed, "Please prepare your handgun, and carry the life preserver with the other."

Illych was starting to see where this was going. *Yeah, Dave was not likely to be a security risk very soon.*

Karl looked at Illych and nodded. Illych nodded back.

The world transitioned black, and then they were standing in Dave's apartment, looking at a very surprised man halfway into the process of removing his pants.

He fell down and began crab-walking on his backside away from the two men who had just materialized in front of him. "Gah, *what the*—?"

Karl was smiling now. "Mr. Polk, you have been the cause of a great deal of chaos. People are dead, and you have wasted so many days of my time."

Dave backed up into a wall and gave up trying to get away.

Karl continued, "All of that could be forgiven, but you put Danielle in danger. That I cannot forgive."

"D-D-Danielle? B-But she's back safe."

"You spoke about her in your visits to *The Pink Pole*. That is how others learned of her and what she knows. This all happened because you could not keep your mouth shut."

"I didn't know. It was just talk. Impressing the girls . . ."

Karl paused and then asked, "Have you ever heard of Point Nemo?"

Dave's face shifted to confusion. "What?"

Karl continued, "Point Nemo is a point in the ocean that is the furthest from land in all directions. I believe you should be given an opportunity to meditate on your poor choices."

"Illych, hand him the life preserver."

Illych gave the donut a short toss.

Confusion and terror played out on Dave's face as he caught it.

"Goodbye, Mr. Polk."

The man on the floor disappeared.

Illych took a breath and exhaled, "So, you're going to let him float around for a while and then bring him back?"

Karl was already setting up the next translation. "I have no intention of retrieving Mr. Polk. The water temperature at Point Nemo averages forty-four degrees Fahrenheit. He will be dead within the hour."

Illych commented, "I get it, but that's pretty cold."

Karl replied with a darker tone, "The punishment fits the crime."

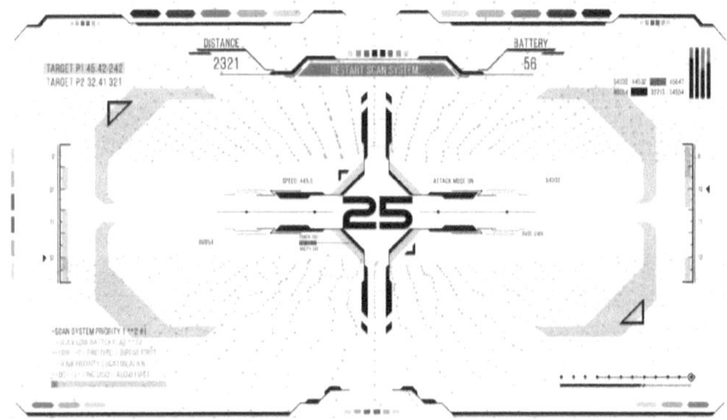

CHAPTER TWENTY FIVE

Jack Hemway was a man recovering from a rough week. His newest employee had been kidnapped. He had been kidnapped. And then he had almost froze to death. The good news was that it had all ended well – she'd eventually escaped, in good health, and would be returning to the job. However, the stress from the experience had left him emotionally and physically drained.

During that same week, there had been an increased number of violent deaths of organized crime members. Notable even by Chicago standards. Most of the deaths had been of an extraordinarily suspicious nature. In some cases, they'd been virtually inexplicable. People died in strange ways. Then there were the disappearances—including an agent from his office who still had not been located. And the killings stopped as soon as Danielle Mersen had escaped from her captors. This struck him as awfully coincidental.

Then there was his own kidnapping by two men he had started referring to as the Odd Couple. One of the two was an old man, perhaps mid-sixties, and eccentric as all hell. The other was a prison escapee. From Ft. Leavenworth, no less, and a Green Beret. The kidnapping had been more annoying than frightening, and the most hazardous part of it had been them dumping his unconscious body, still soaking from a sprinkler main break, into his backyard on frozen ground in the dead of the Chicago winter. If he had stayed unconscious for even five more minutes, he might not have made it.

The old man, Danielle, and the explosion of criminals who'd been murdered or disappeared were linked. He was sure of that. But the evidence at the crime scenes was confounding. All the craziness of a Halloween night, day and night for a week straight, and then just evaporating into thin air, leaving confusion and wonder.

As soon as the paperwork had been completed, Jack put in for some days off. It had surprised his wife, who considered it a welcome distraction from the long hours of their respective chosen professions.

Two weeks at a Caribbean resort. Sun, sand, and sleeping in.

Jack thought about these events while reclining on a beach chair, soaking up the sun and watching an all-female volleyball team give the game their all. His wife would be salty with him if she knew. But her mud bath and massage would take two hours or more. Plenty of time for drinks and volleyball-watching.

So young, so athletic . . .

A shadow blotted out the mid-afternoon sun. Jack looked up at the figure disturbing his concentration.

A sunglass-wearing Illych looked down and grinned, "Hello there."

Jack's eyes went wide. A cold knot formed in his chest in spite of the sun and heat.

Awareness of another person standing to the other side prompted his head to turn.

Karl, also smiling, "Greetings, Agent Hemway. My apologies for disturbing your vacation, but I was hoping to have a few words."

Jack blurted out, "You two? Here now?"

Illych sat in the reclining beach chair next to Jack and assumed a relaxed position.

Karl took a more rigid sitting position on the edge of a similar chair.

"This will not take long."

Jack sighed: "What do you want?"

"As a concerned third party, I just wanted to confirm Danielle is back at work. And none the worse for wear?"

Jack replied, "For the most part. An experience like that has a psychological impact. But I did talk to her, and she's in a good place. Physically, she checked out. No issues there."

"Excellent. If possible, in the future, should there be any unusual situations regarding Ms. Mersen, please contact Steve Mersen more quickly. Also, I would also consider it a personal favor if you never discuss having met us with either Danielle or her father."

"Personal favor? I almost froze to death! I don't owe you anything."

"Let us not be petty, Jack. It is important to be considerate of Danielle's safety."

Something in the old man's tone made Jack's insides go cold.

Karl stood, and Illych did the same.

"Good day, Mr. Hemway. It is pleasant meeting here under less troubling circumstances."

Jack watched as the two walked away. Neither was dressed for the sun or the heat, and they looked distinctly out of place. The two men eventually turned and disappeared between vendor shacks further down the beach.

Jack considered reporting the meeting in. He shrugged with the feeling that actually catching those two on the island was slim. And his wife would be unhappy if he was making work calls.

Resuming watching the game, he concluded they were somebody else's problem now.

A man walked up and sat where the taller of his two visitors had just been. Jack noted his tan and nodded to the man. Halfway into a seated position, the newcomer shuffled forward and extended a hand.

"Alexander Haskins."

Jack stayed reclined and shook his hand. "Jack Hemway. With that tan, you must live here."

"Nope, I'm a regular, though."

"You look familiar. Have you been on television?"

"I'm an attorney in Chicago. Some of my cases have been on the news."

"That's where I've seen you. Go figure, we both call Chicago home."

"Small world."

The two men mused on the coincidence and sat back to enjoy the game.

• • • • •

Illych grabbed a coffee and took up position at one of the small tables in the corner. Karl entered the coffee shop minutes later. He walked straight to Steve Mersen. Steve rose, and the men shook hands.

"Karl, it's good to see you under better circumstances. Like I said on the phone, Danielle is okay. She escaped."

Karl replied, "Thank you for the update. This is the best possible news. She's technically my only living relative. How is she?"

"Tired. The doctors say she's physically okay. Her captors kept her confined but didn't do anything else to her. Actually, the whole thing is kind of strange. The FBI isn't sure of the motive for the kidnapping. Or at least they're not telling. Neither is Danielle."

Karl nodded. "We may never know. The news said the kidnappers all perished."

Steve replied, "The FBI raided the building she was being held in just as Danielle was escaping. None of the kidnappers survived."

Karl smiled. "All is well that ends well. My next appointment requires that I leave now." He stood to leave. The two men shook hands.

Looking at Illych, Steve asked, "What's with the bodyguard?"

"Work colleague. My new job has me paired with a younger co-worker."

"Uh-huh."

"Good-bye, Steve."

"Yes, good-bye, Karl."

Steve watched Karl leave and wondered . . .

•　　•　　•　　•　　•

Illych piled wood on the fire while Karl looked on. For the first time in a week, no urgent situation was demanding their attention.

Illych sat, and the two watched the fire grow. "That was a busy week. I'm beat—looking forward to a few days of R and R."

"Agreed. The tempo of activity has been quite frenetic. All in all, the situation fortunately arrived at an acceptable outcome."

The two men quietly watched the fire for several minutes.

Karl broke the silence: "I am concerned about having my grandniece as a potential target. A point of leverage someone unethical could exploit to get to me."

"Mr. Lark, by the time Danielle freed herself, she was climbing over the pile of corpses we left behind. Anyone who looks at her as your vulnerability will also be looking at the body count from this kidnapping. Even the most jaded types will likely be motivated to consider another path."

"Thank you, Illych, for your reassuring words. The last week's activities had me worrying."

Both men enjoyed the heat radiating from the roaring fire. The flicker of dancing flames and the crackle of the burning wood filled the room. Lounging in comfortable chairs, they enjoyed a rest well-earned after recent events.

"You know, Mr. Lark, this experience opened my eyes to how much money there is to be made breaking the law. Crime really does pay. We got a close look at that money laundering thing. That could be something you could look into."

"Agreed, we live in a world where money can positively influence outcomes. This leads to the conclusion that more is better. And there appear to be lucrative opportunities in less-than-legal business pursuits. Something I will consider for the future."

Illych stood up and added two more logs to the fire and returned to his chair.

"Did you ever get back to the Townshend guy about what we saw with that goblin in that park?"

"I attempted to, but unfortunately, Mr. Townshend passed shortly after our visit."

Illych asked, "What about that momentum thing? And the car falling in the wrong place? Did you get those issues under control?"

"Unfortunately, I have learned that the *ouiblet* operates under restrictions I was not previously aware of. In the interest of safety, it is important that the origination and destination be defined points in the Earth's gravitational field. Objects in motion relative to the field are problematic, and there can be unexpected outcomes."

Illych quipped, "That's what Mr. Helena would say."

"An unfortunate misunderstanding, but the deployment of new technology has inherent risks. More so in something as radical as the *ouiblet*."

Illych said, "So your saying that we've been lucky while you were figuring it all out?"

"In a manner of speaking, yes. The good news is that the information gained from this last week's activities has given me insight into an approach that makes the translation almost absolutely safe."

Illych turned his head to look at Karl, a questioning look on his face.

Mr. Lark acknowledges the unspoken question, "If one of the points of translation is properly anchored, the probability of error becomes virtually zero."

"*Virtually* zero? Not *actually* zero?"

"Precisely. The possibility of the *ouiblet* killing you is infinitesimally small, but never zero."

Illych shrugged. "What about that artifact? The one that Curly guy was using to make himself invisible? There have to be uses for that."

"I will be studying it. The existence of such an artifact builds on my own research that resulted in the *oculus*. Human optical interpretation of the world around them can be influenced or even bypassed."

Illych closed his eyes, exhaled and inhaled. "What did you just say?"

"In layman's terms, it's invisibility. Mr. Haenal stumbled into something, and it eventually consumed him. But his misfortune is my gain. I speculate that the mythology around the Greek Medusa represents the interpretation of a similar artifact. To look upon it directly results in petrification. But viewing the reflection in a mirror has a different outcome. Which then leads to the legends of vampiric aversion to mirrors. In turn, the subject of reflecting pools must also be considered as a way to monitor public places for attempts at invisibility.

"The existence of this artifact and the mythological invisibility record beg the question: Are there more of these ancient treasures out there?"

Illych closed his eyes and relaxed back into his chair. "You should look into that."

Karl Lark's eyes reflected the firelight as he replied. "Indeed, I shall.